THE STORM

THE
STORM

A Novel

Arif Anwar

ATRIA BOOKS

New York • London • Toronto • Sydney • New Delhi

ATRIA
BOOKS

An Imprint of Simon & Schuster, Inc.
1230 Avenue of the Americas
New York, NY 10020

First Atria Books hardcover edition May 2018

Originally published in Canada in 2018 by HarperCollins Publishers Ltd

ATRIA BOOKS and colophon are trademarks of Simon & Schuster, Inc.

For information about special discounts for bulk purchases, please contact Simon & Schuster Special Sales at 1-866-506-1949 or business@simonandschuster.com.

The Simon & Schuster Speakers Bureau can bring authors to your live event. For more information or to book an event, contact the Simon & Schuster Speakers Bureau at 1-866-248-3049 or visit our website at www.simonspeakers.com.

Interior design by Dana Sloan

Manufactured in the United States of America

10 9 8 7 6 5 4 3 2 1

Library of Congress Cataloging-in-Publication Data is available.

ISBN 978-1-5011-7450-6
ISBN 978-1-5011-7452-0 (ebook)

To my father, for all the books you bought me

Once more the storm is howling, and half hid

Under this cradle-hood and coverlid

My child sleeps on.

I have walked and prayed for this young child an hour,

And heard the sea-wind scream upon the tower,

Imagining in excited reverie

That the future years had come

Dancing to a frenzied drum

Out of the murderous innocence of the sea.

—*William Butler Yeats, "A Prayer for my Daughter"*

CONTENTS

BOOK I

Gathering

HONUFA

Chittagong, East Pakistan (Bangladesh)
November 1970

In his dreams her eyes are always green. The green of grasshoppers, leaves and emeralds. Green shot with a darkness that reminds him of shattered jade.

He knows now that Honufa's eyes were gray. The gray of cats and sunless mornings. The gray of the writhing sea.

つ〜つ

THE SOUND AND LIGHT conspire to open her gray eyes late this morning, in a hut whose dirt floor is tattooed with the light of a November dawn, rumbling from the surf.

Honufa sits up. On her windowsill is a house crow. Its black wings are flared, rising from a charcoal body. The curving bill half-open, as though it intends to call out. The onyx eyes focused solely on her.

It does not move as she surreptitiously leaves her bed—never taking her eyes off it—and approaches in slow measured steps.

Only when she reaches out—her hand only inches from its head—does the crow fly away, its parting caws shatteringly loud in the confines of her hut.

As if she were still a child, Honufa spits on her chest to calm her racing heart. A foreboding pads toward her like a hungry and silent predator.

3

The hardwood cot they sleep on was built by her father, bequeathed to her as a parting concession upon her marriage to Jamir, so many years before. Her three-year-old son sleeps on it right now. Warm and full of dreams. The side where Jamir would lie is empty. This is the first time her husband has left for the sea without saying good-bye. Gone for how long to the heart of the bay.

She splashes water on her face from a clay jar and begins her chores—first laundering a stack of clothes that has never reached more than a hand high in their married life, she then tosses the fish bones left from the previous day's meals to the sleepy-eyed cat that often visits their hearth, and steps out to pick firewood from the branches littering the grounds of a nearby woods. From the edges of a pond whose black upward stare reminds her of the eyes of the crow that visited her, she rips dandelion leaves for the midday meal.

She does all this before the dawn can grow to morning, and the pale blue glow that floods the world can give way to violet, orange and finally the nothing color of pure sunshine.

Her son stirs in bed.

Her morning's wares tied with a jute rope and perched on her head, Honufa walks back to her hut.

Three decades of hard living have whittled away feminine softness from her face, deep-etched the lines around her eyes, thinned her lips to less than ideal for a woman of Bengal, given her jaw a square and mannish cast; Honufa is not beautiful, but she is strong, and at five and a half feet, taller than any other woman in the seaside village she calls home. Her shoulders are wide, her hands calloused from the miles of ropes and nets that have passed through them over the years, from the hills of coconuts she has husked.

The length of tree shadows and the height of the sun reckon the hour for her, tell her that it is time to visit the communal well to draw water, an act she is resigned to complete in solitude. In the first years, she held hope that the weight of others' scrutiny, the sting of their judgment, would become easier to bear. But it never did.

On her way, she stops. At an hour in which the beach should be barren, it instead boils with activity. The entire village is gathered here—the gray sand churned to peaks and troughs by more than a hundred feet. Men and women, sinewy—dark from the sun—pull in boats and tie them with sturdy knots to the trees, drag back and fold nets. Children carry back fish caught in cylindrical traps. Through it all, contributions are made as needed, the bright lines of sex, age and size erased for the occasion.

A storm is coming.

She swivels her head from east to west to south, the cardinal directions from which a storm might approach, but there is nothing: the strands of thatch that hang from the hut roofs are still, the sun bright and unoccluded above, yet the village scrambles.

Honufa scans the groups heaving with effort for a friendly face, even one that does not look away.

She finds Rina among a larger group of women folding nets, rolling up one end of an especially long one with the mindless efficiency that comes from years of practice. Honufa takes up the other end and mimics the older woman's actions until the two meet in the middle.

"A storm?"

Rina nods. Diminutive and wiry next to Honufa, she is like a strip of meat left in the sun.

"How do they know?"

"They saw the Boatman this morning."

The net drops from Honufa's hands.

SHE RUSHES HOME. THIS will not be the first storm she has had to prepare for—such is life on the bay. While her son (now awake) is focused on the pursuit and innocent harassment of chickens in the courtyard, Honufa tightens the loose edges of her sari around herself and gets to work.

Their list of possessions is small, their whereabouts ascertained in minutes. On one of the two large kantha cloth bedsheets that she spreads on their floor, she places their cooking utensils—a boti (its blade wrapped) for cutting, a nora for crushing, pots and pans that have boiled rice, lentils, fish and spinach in their lifetimes. Above the second kantha, she gathers their bedding, their clothing, still damp from their morning wash. A rough burlap sack inherits their dry foods.

She steps outside. The chickens, one black with white speckles, the other a deep burnt-orange, possess a beauty that borders on the spectacular. But they are dutiful also, daily producing eggs in some corner of their home, a treasure hunt for her son that ends with him holding a prize—the shell still soft and warm from the hen's body—in his hands.

She looks at the birds now and sighs. Her son's love for them will make difficult what must come next.

She picks up a knife and begins to shine it against a stone.

～∽～

RINA ARRIVES TO FIND her digging in the courtyard, the hole half-a-man deep already. The older woman retrieves a second shovel from the cow pen and begins to dig alongside, falling into the wordless rhythm of work. Between the two, the hole grows at a fast clip.

The two women stand side by side for a moment, sweating, breathing hard, admiring the work done.

"You really think a storm is coming?"

"The Boatman has not been wrong so far."

Across a quarter century, thrice has a lone boatman been seen sailing under black sails on the bay, always headed south, his back facing those standing on the beach or on the craggy green hills beyond.

Each time he has appeared, a great storm has followed.

"Who do you think he is?"

Rina looks at her meaningfully. "We have our guesses. But all I know is that it is no man that stands below those black sails."

Honufa shivers from the uncanny romance of the image.

"Where is your son?" Rina asks.

"Inside. He threw a tantrum. He didn't take well to what had to be done."

"Then he is well on the way to becoming a man."

Honufa smiles. In her young son she sees more of her husband's quiet strength and soft heart than her fire, her fierce will. Perhaps that is a good thing.

Her son has a grand name, chosen from a book that the village zamindar read to her when she herself was a child, a book of stories within stories nested like mirrors facing one another, going on until you lost yourself utterly.

The women drop the sacks into the hole (including the chicken, slaughtered, plucked and packed into clay pots) and replace the dirt after setting a long stick in the center to mark the place. They pound down the earth with the flats of the shovels.

She invites Rina into her now empty home. Her son sits on the naked cot, his dusty face streaked with tears. He runs to Rina, who lifts him up into her open arms and swings him onto the hollow of her hip.

She tickles him. "What are these tears I see?"

He points an accusatory finger at his mother. "She killed the chickens."

"Were they friends of yours?"

"Yes."

"If she hadn't, then the storm would have snatched them up and you'd never see them again anyway."

While Rina is occupied with her child, Honufa approaches the far wall of her hut, cursing herself for not remembering such a critical detail sooner. She reaches up, standing on tiptoes, her blind hand hunting for the spot where she knows a letter rests, but finds nothing. Her heart racing, she now scrabbles and grasps at the dust and dirt, pushes her bed up against the wall and stands on it to look. The letter she deposited on top of that wall with such care and secrecy more than two months ago, one whose existence she would verify with an obsessive zeal whenever her husband was away, is gone.

She climbs down and finds Rina staring at her.

"Whatever is the matter with you?"

Her face ashen, her voice small, her throat nonetheless manages to birth a lie. "A set of gold earrings. A gift from Jamir's mother. They're gone."

"Oh, that is too bad, child."

She can only nod, her mind thrown into turmoil. She thinks of Jamir, floating like a speck on the vast ocean. He has told her so many tales of the sea, of the marvelous things he would catch, of the fights and drunkenness of sailors, the unending stretches of water housing only waves flecked with sunlight, tales that made her wish she were born a man, freed from the baggage of domesticity.

Now is one such moment.

Once, he rowed her to a key by the bay to buy pretty jewelry made of seashells and stones. The wind was fearful that day but the boat was steady, weighed down by them and sacks of sand. *This is ballast,* Jamir said with a smile as the wind whipped his hair. *The weight keeps you safe.*

Her husband and son similarly settle her in life. With them on board, nothing can capsize her boat.

She sits next to Rina. "I worry for him."

"Why? He has been out there so many times already. He's on a trawler, those are giants. They don't sink like our piddly boats. They have a radio on board. He likely had news of the storm before us and is on his way home even as we speak."

Honufa shakes her head. Rina does not know. How could she? The danger posed by the letter Jamir carries surpasses that of any storm.

"Never mind my foolish chatter. How much time do we have?"

"A few hours, from the looks of things. The zamindar is letting people take shelter in his house. That Rahim is a good man."

"He is," Honufa says, and does not elaborate, recalling those afternoons she spent in his mansion as a child, poring over the letters of the alphabet, one by one, as his wife served them sweet biscuits and tea. It was not long before letters would grow to words, words to sentences and soon her eyes would gallop across pages, chapters and entire books. She was—the zamindar would one day claim—a faster study than he ever thought possible for a child to be.

Rina grimaces. "I forget sometimes that the two of you are on poor terms."

"He's a rich landowner. We're a family of poor fishermen. Whatever friendship blossomed between us now feels like a dream. And we all must wake up someday."

Rina scoffs, then, surveying the hut, furrows her brows. "Are you done preparing then, Honufa? Nothing else needs your attention before the storm?"

"Just our nanny goat still grazing on the hills. I was waiting for you to get here so you could watch my boy."

"Very well. But you don't have much time, child. What if you're delayed?"

"If I am, would you take my son there yourself?"

Rina considers the implications of her words. "And what of you?"

"I'll find you, take shelter there with the others. We have to set bitterness aside when a storm comes."

"Rahim is a kindly man. It has been years, Honufa. Why not patch things with him? It will be less difficult than you think."

"It's too late for that." Honufa shakes her head, thinks of the letter that is no longer in her possession. She was the one who pushed the boat off so many years before, and by now, the currents of time and circumstance have carried her and the zamindar, Rahim, too far apart.

Her friend's eyes cloud with disappointment. "I suppose you know best, but your family needs more friends than just me in this village."

Honufa nods, goes to a corner of the hut to retrieve the only thing she has not yet buried. "If you do end up going to the zamindar's house without me, I want you to take this too."

The older woman lifts the cloth bag to assess its heft. "What is it?"

Honufa hesitates, then opens it to let Rina view the two objects inside, two things that are unlike anything Rina has ever seen. Her eyes widen; she looks to Honufa, who sighs.

"I'll explain when I see you again."

MINUTES LATER, SHE IS climbing a hill that is a riot of jam, jarul, and toon trees, girded with dense undergrowth and dotted with brakes of bamboo. A fickle breeze stirs and lifts the dank air of the forest floor to her nose. There is the rustling of creatures around her, the cries of kites whirling above, the steady clop of her feet as she follows a narrow path that to her looks like the part of a Hindu woman's hair, the red earth like the vermillion that proclaims one married. Under the sun of a different fate, it is the way her hair might have looked.

She reaches the summit in an hour. The goat is where she left it the day before, roped and tied with a stake driven deep. It favors her with a slot-eyed regard before returning to chewing its cud.

She extracts the stake from the ground with a grunt of effort, unties the goat and slaps its rump so that the creature waddles away, bleating. Knowing the way home, its hooved grasp of the hills surer than hers, it will descend with speed.

About to follow, she stops to assess the heavens. The sky is clear but for a few scrapes of cirrus shaped like the stalks of kans grass. In the distance, more clouds drift past, white and unhurried.

Could this be the one time the Boatman is wrong?

She heads for a nearby ring of pines. In the center is a small grave, oblong and unmarked, fenced by bamboo strips that have moldered in the rich sea air.

But for the hiss of the branches slicing the wind above the grave, the silence is complete. She stands still. As always, overcome. An intruder, she drinks in the beauty of her surroundings.

Eighteen years. You would have been a man full-grown by now, child.

Rain lilies have grown on the grave since her last visit. They shimmer in the wind. She takes three as gently as she can and whispers a good-bye.

Close to the unmarked grave is an abandoned temple. Bodhi saplings sit atop it like wooden horns, their roots gripping the crumbling stone.

With the flower offerings in her hand, Honufa stands before the entrance. The darkness inside swirls and beckons. There is the sound of fleet feet, the chatter of vermin. But she knows who really waits inside.

She stands at the door of the temple to gather her courage. Aware that she is about to betray her faith, she closes her eyes and puts a steadying hand on the temple's cool mortar before walking in.

Immediately, it is as though she has dived into a lake of darkness and silence, a place unmoored from time. She stands and waits for her pupils to adjust as the chill of the stone floor penetrates her calloused soles.

The interior is ten paces on each side. At the far end, dimly lit by the hole-ridden roof, is a fiercely beautiful woman. Tall, with midnight skin, she wears a garland of severed heads, a skirt of limbs. Her lolling tongue reaches beyond her chin to point to the vanquished demon she tramples underfoot.

Honufa kneels before Kali—the Black One. The One Beyond Time. The One Who Destroys.

She places before the dark goddess the offering of flowers she has brought. She prays to her, ignoring the voice inside that reminds her that her new God is a jealous one, that this act is *shirk*, one of the most unforgivable that a Muslim can commit—that of placing another on equal status with God Most High. But as a child burning with fever seeks her mother, Honufa cannot help herself.

When she was little, her father told her the story of the goddess's origins as revealed to him by a Brahmin priest. Enthralled, excited, she would forever pester him afterward to retell the legend, and even so many years after her family separated themselves from her, still remembers it word for word:

There was a time when all three hundred and thirty million gods and goddesses trembled before an invading demon army led by General Raktabij—Bloodseed—whose blood once spilled to the ground would birth a thousand more like him. To battle the demon army, the gods called on Durga, who felled many demons. But when she faced their general, with each spray of blood her spear brought forth, innumerable clones of the demon would sprout, leaving the battleground swarming with even more enemies than when Durga joined the fray. In her fury, the goddess scowled until a swirling cosmic cauldron grew between her brows, and from it a new being sprang forth.

Kali.

The demon army withered before Kali's fury, decimated before her four sword-wielding arms that were blurs of blood and steel, leaving her to face Raktabij, whose blood the Dark Goddess's lolling tongue lapped up before it could hit the ground, and her mighty blows pushed him back foot by foot, until he finally weakened enough so that she could bring the demon general to her great fanged mouth and drink him dry.

Blood-drunk, her victory complete, Kali let loose a roar that made the heavens shudder, began a dance of destruction that shook the foundation of the universe, until the gods and goddesses again grew fearful and called on Shiva, her consort, to intervene. He did, throwing himself down before his raging lover, whose frenzy finally subsided at the sight of her husband at her feet.

Honufa closes her eyes and prays, not for herself, but for her husband, Jamir, her sons, both living and dead. She prays until the world fades.

Although she opens her eyes not knowing how much time has passed, when she steps outside she knows something is gravely wrong, the world without nearly as dark now as the one within the temple. The cooing birds silent. The breeze replaced by a sullen hush.

The horizon makes her gasp. Iron-gray clouds are moving toward the shore on legs of lightning—purple-white—trotting on the sea.

Cursing her foolishness for delaying at the temple, desperate to return to her son and Rina, she rushes down the hill, an eye aimed at the sky where towering clouds the color of dreams and ashes gather.

As she streaks across a now violet world, a wind that bears flecks of rain begins to blow, no longer desultory, but keening with intent, carrying memories of the bitter cold of unnamed lands.

She reaches the valley, marked by cuts and scrapes from the branches that block her way, her feet battered and bloody from the rocks. She is close to home, at the meeting point of the hill's earth and the shore's sand. She wraps her sari tight around her waist and breaks into a full sprint toward a sea churning with foam.

A badger-hole catches her foot. She falls. The ground rushes up to meet her face. Her head strikes a rock as a vicious bolt of pain passes through her ankle.

For moments that span eternity, she dreams
Remembers
She is a child again
Out in the rice fields
In her hand is a pail to fetch water
She is seven

A faint sound that is at first a buzz then a hum then a drone so
loud it fills not just her ears but nose eyes and mouth she screams for
her father mother brother but the sound eats everything eats her
words. A metal bird is overhead its silver belly flashing as though it
has swallowed a star on its flank a red sun set against a white field.

She opens her mouth to scream just as the sky explodes with
colors
Butterflies
That fall
And fall and fall
On her face
And she sees that they are but paper

THE SPLASH OF RAIN on her brow returns her to a world black as
night, where the wind screams, having gained the deadly sharpness
of lifted sand. She extracts her foot from the hole, touches her forehead to find a painful knot. She struggles not to cry out when she
puts weight on her fast-swelling ankle. She looks around in desperation. There are no branches from which to fashion a walking stick.

Honufa assesses the dilemma her injury has forced on her. She
asked Rina to take her son to the zamindar's house should she not
arrive in time. Has Rina made it to safety, or is she still waiting for
her at the hut? She has neither the time nor strength to make both
journeys. The zamindar's home sits in the opposite direction from
hers. Should she first go to her hut and Rina has already departed

with her son, that will seal her fate. Go the other way while Rina and her son are waiting, and that will seal theirs.

Storm clouds hammer lightning down into the beach like silver nails, blinding her. The sea rears and lands like a mad horse. The rain falls so hard and fast it threatens to bruise her skin.

The Earth releases a primeval moan as the storm erases God from the world.

She screams her son's name again and again.

And when no one answers, decides.

Shahryar & Anna

Washington, DC
August 2004

They were on I-66, headed to McLean, toward Anna's house. Until just fifteen minutes ago, the cars and trucks had been a solid shimmering mass in the late-day heat. But now when he looks back, the schemes of the sky are apparent, its dark plot revealed by the array of gathering clouds.

Shar feels a strange thrill when the storm arrives like a rushing train freighted with water, its ferocity reminding him of home, the first drops splattering fat and heavy on the windshield, drumming the car with an insistent, percussive beat. The wipers whip side to side to keep a billion-strong army at bay. The brake lights of the cars ahead bloom into pastel blobs. The world is melting.

Anna is in the back seat of the car he rented that morning to drive her to a fair in Gaithersburg, focused on her Game Boy.

"This is some storm, huh, Anna?"

He repeats himself when she does not answer.

"Yeah, I guess. Does it rain like this in Bangladesh?"

"For days sometimes. We even have a season known for storms. Kal Baisakhi—the Dark Spring."

He thinks of his childhood, the parts of it he remembers: watching television, reciting the national anthem under his breath when it was broadcast before the Bangla newscast at eight and then the English at ten. The picture on the screen would wink into oblivion without warning. The darkness tumbling onto them whenever load-shedding happened. Rahim, Zahira and Rina would stumble around in the darkness calling out to each other until someone located the long, thin candles in a drawer in the kitchen and lit them using the gas stove. They then headed outside to a world lit by moon and starlight.

He recalls the two big floods in Dhaka, when boats plied the streets and the water reached halfway up the wall of their house. It was the same grand house where he would wake up to the harsh cries of crows that he misses so in America, as he does the smell of parathas frying in the morning, tea and sweet biscuits rolled in on trolleys to bedrooms while slow winter fog wet the iron of their windows. There were flying roaches. Fat moths flapping against hurricane lanterns. As a child he would run out to the brusque summer tempests—thick hard rain that scored the earth and hurt the skin, left behind giant toadstools.

He has told Anna of these things in fragments, struck every time by how that vital force of occurrence was missing in the retelling, the beauty expunged through translation. It made him question their value.

More wet lurches along the highway before she speaks again. "Are we going to get home okay, Baba?" she asks, using the Bangla word for *father*, one of the few words in the language she knows.

"We might be a little late, but yes."

"How much longer do you have?"

The randomness of the question startles him, as does the unintended morbidity. "What do you mean?"

"Mom said you only have three months to stay here."

"Just about, yes."

"What're you going to do?"

"Hopefully I'll find a job here by then and we won't have to worry about it."

"You can't just tell them that you're my dad and you have to stay?"

"I wish it were that simple, sweetheart." Everything seems like a surprise now when none of it should be. He came back here on a student visa six years ago, when Anna was just three. He has always known that he would get a one-year work permit upon completion of his PhD but that there would be no permanent solution for him to remain. And yet now it is as though he is on a boat rushing toward the end of a waterfall, blithely watching its approach for long, yet only now beginning to panic.

The rain thins by the time they take the exit, the sky a bruised purple. Gusts of wind give their car playful shoves as they leave the highway, a bully reminding them he will see them in the playground later.

Gravel crunches as they pull into the spruce-lined driveway of Anna's house, the Chevy Malibu looking as incongruous against the facade of the large French Colonial as Shar feels. He waits, takes a deep breath and steps out.

Val meets them at the door, casual in a loose off-shoulder sweater and yoga pants, her red locks tamed by a scrunchie.

She musses Anna's hair. "Hey, kiddo. You have a good time with your dad?"

"We had candy corn." Anna gives her mother a hug.

"How was it?"

"Kinda gross, actually."

Val laughs. The peck she lands on Shar has only the most impersonal warmth. "What about you?"

He smiles. "I brought her back in one piece."

Anna is pushing past them. "Where's Jeremy?"

The hallway reverberates with a baritone. "In here, sprout."

Anna runs in with an enthusiasm Shar finds deflating.

"You have a minute to chat?" he asks Val.

They move out to the driveway. "Did you happen to tell Anna about my visa situation?"

Val settles her glance somewhere over his shoulder, the crow's-feet around her eyes the only evidence of the decade he has known her, and even then, only revealed when she smiles.

"I had to tell her something. She's been asking about Christmas plans. The fact that you might not be here seemed important."

"I'd have preferred to tell her myself. Or you could have at least given me a warning that you were going to discuss it."

"And when would that have been?"

He sighs. "I don't know."

"Have you made any progress on the job front?"

He shakes his head again. "No, but I'll find something."

"Well. Time is running out."

⁓

LATER, HE WAITS WITH Anna upstairs as she prepares for bed, counts the seconds as his daughter brushes her teeth (stopping when he reaches 120), supervises her flossing, stands beside her door as she changes into her pajamas and tells him that he may enter.

Her room is a converted attic. Woody and warm. The bed sits under an eave that descends at an amiable angle. The single lozenge-shaped window looks out to a weeping world; the rain has returned as promised. Branches of the front-yard oak sway against the glass. Thunder rumbles soft and low.

"I have something for you," he tells her as she burrows under her covers.

He reaches into the backpack he has carried all day, his fingers hunting past the Ziploc bags of apple slices, cheddar goldfish, bottles of water and other evidence of their day together. The book he retrieves has a fabric cover the color of a wolf's pelt, tattered at the corners. The title is embossed in bright, socialist red. In Bangla, it says: রুশ দেশের উপকথা—*Fairy Tales from Russia.*

"This was my favorite book when I was your age. A book of Russian fairy tales translated into Bangla."

When her enthusiasm does not match his own, he feels that old stumbling inside, the sense that everything he does as a father is wrong.

"You don't want to give it a try, sweetie?"

"I don't read Bangla."

"I know. That's on me. But I can translate."

Deciding that it is easier to ask for forgiveness than permission, he begins to read about Russian heroes (inevitably named Ivan), gallant sentient horses, eagle-lords who can speak like men, Baba Yaga—the wicked witch who lives in a house that stands on the legs of a chicken. He trudges on for a half hour before putting the book down.

"You don't like the stories?"

Her curls sway from side to side as she shakes her head.

"Why not?"

She does not answer, looks up with her large gray eyes, the one thing she inherited from neither him nor Val. "Can I tell you something, Baba?"

"Of course."

"Jeremy wants me to call him 'Dad.'"

It takes all his strength to keep his tone light. "Oh, really?"

"Yeah. At least I think he does."

"And how's that?"

"When he tucks me into bed and kisses me goodnight, I can sort of tell he wants me to."

"And, do you want to?"

"Will you be mad?"

"No," he says. "He's a great dad to you. It's totally okay for you to call him that, if you want."

"Really?" she asks, the hunger for permission, for approval, plain on her face.

"Really." He embraces her, still reeling from the possessiveness that this piece of news has sparked in him. He should not be surprised, he thinks. He owes Anna, not the reverse. In a life upended by revelations, this is simply one more thing to which he must adjust.

JAMIR

Chittagong, East Pakistan (Bangladesh)
November 1970

Jamir rises before dawn. In the moonlight slanting through the window, his body is wiry, dark, the same as a hundred other fishermen in the village.

He has risen an hour earlier than he normally does for work, knowing that Honufa will not be awake. He stands by the door and lights a biri he plucks from the knot of the lungi tied around his waist. He leans against the mud and rattan wall of their home and takes deep, long drags. The sky is painted with clouds stark and strangely bright against the dawn. Other than the soft sounds of the surf, there is only the constant *reeee* of cicadas, the chuckle of geckoes.

By the time he finishes the biri, there is the taste of smoke on his tongue, salt from the sea breeze, cool against his skin. He enters the hut again. Taking his gear—a rolled-up rexine cloth wrapped around both his shirts and a spare lungi—he edges to the wall, and, watching the still forms of his family on the bed, reaches up to the top, where it meets the thatch roof. He shudders when his fingers again find what he discovered a few days before. A long, flat rectangular form.

A letter.

He walks out with it in silence.

⌒

BEFORE HE CAN HEAD west along the shore, to the far side of the harbor where his trawler is moored to a rickety pier, he must first pass his old life—a huddled mass of sea boats on the beach. Without the sun, the vessels can only be identified by their shapes—flat-stemmed sampans with two horns, long slender balams, the smaller bhelas.

Shadows flit between the boats. Other fishermen. They glance at him but say nothing.

The trawler's blocky silhouette emerges in the gloom before long. It is called *Sonamoti*—the Golden Girl—the name painted in wide green letters on the hull. It is the only double-rig at the port, the grandest at sixty-five feet.

He crosses the gangplank, the thin wood grunting in protest under his weight, and heads to the bilges, where he must face water shining with rainbow patches of oil that takes him the better part of an hour to bail out. A rude sun emerges as he works.

The ship's captain, Abbas, arrives with the remainder of the crew: Gauranga is a grizzled Hindu deckhand, who only stops talking to spit jets of red juice from the betel leaves he constantly chews. Humayun is his taciturn Muslim counterpart. Both are experienced fishermen who coach Jamir on how to grade and sort sea fish, the rudiments of inspecting seine lines, and engine maintenance.

Abbas's son, Manik, is of an age with Jamir and a frequent antagonist he best tries to avoid.

The men toss him quick greetings and disperse to their respective stations: Abbas to the wheelhouse, the rest below decks. Soon the trawler begins to separate from the jetty, and the curious emptiness Jamir always feels at the moment of departure returns. He has spent two months as a sea fisherman—after an entirely unex-

pected invitation from Abbas to join his crew. Despite this time, he has not developed a knack for this type of fishing. Not an even fight between men and waters as when he was a rowboat fisherman, the trawler tilts the balance firmly toward the former, its great nets dipping ever deeper into the water.

His most pressing work complete, Jamir moves to the kitchen and galleys, the location of his makeshift bed of old army blankets and a flat, thin pillow.

As he marks inventory, he hears creaks on the floorboards above, muted conversation, then heavy treads on the stairs. Abbas descends. He is middle-aged and wears a pressed white shirt that strains against his large belly. Jamir offers a salaam to him as he unloads the contents of the bag he carries on the galley table, covering its surface with long fragrant limes, green guavas, massive spiky jackfruit, wood apples, bunches of spinach and red chard. Protein from the fish they catch will complete their meals.

The last item Abbas places on the table is a copy of the *Daily Ittefaq* that features above the fold the picture of a mustached man wearing a black waistcoat over white shirtsleeves, addressing a great gathering.

"What do you think of this Mujib fellow?" he inquires.

Unsure of where his captain's political sympathies lie, Jamir does not rush to answer. He makes a show of consideration, then eventually says, "He seems to be a good man. The villagers say that they will vote for the Awami League in the coming election."

"And you?"

"Come election day, I will be on the boat, with you."

Abbas guffaws. "You don't care for his Six Point Demands? So that our nation can sort its own affairs, free of the meddling and looting of the West Pakistanis?"

Jamir shakes his head, embarrassed. "Babu, don't ask such grand questions of a man who cannot even read. Politics is the con-

cern of rich men, the likes of landholders such as the zamindar, Rahim."

Abbas's mouth curls in distaste at the mention of that name. "I wouldn't put so much stock in that man. He knows less of the world than you'd think."

Years ago, before Rahim—the current zamindar—moved from the great bustling metropolis of Calcutta to the village and assumed ownership of vast tracts of sharecropped lands and fishing boats, Abbas was in charge of the fleet of vessels belonging to Rahim's predecessor. After Rahim's arrival, however, Abbas was removed from the role with shocking swiftness and lack of ceremony. Over the years, rumors have spread as to the cause of the falling-out.

"I can understand that," Jamir says. "We've had our own difficulties with him."

Abbas nods. "Of course. We all remember how he abandoned you and Honufa when the two of you most needed him."

Jamir shrugs. "If anything, he was closer to my wife. Ever since she was a child, she saw him as a father. But it has been years now, and we are fine without his help. As for me, all I need is a boat to stand on and the use of all my limbs so I can provide for my family."

Abbas puts a warm, heavy hand on his shoulder. "So long as I am alive, you will always have a boat to stand on."

JAMIR RETURNS TO THE deck to inspect the nets for rips. Nearly a mile long, it is wrapped around a great iron winch. By the time he finishes, a fat sun is dipping its toes into waters that have turned a sparkling peacock blue. They are far from shore.

He stretches, ready to stop, when he is startled by the sound of a splash. A school of flying fish leap up beside the boat, their mouths agape, the fin-wings glowing pink against the setting sun, a prolonged silver streak as they skim across the water. Jamir is

reminded of the first time he encountered these incredible creatures, the first time he realized how alien he was to the ocean, to
this depthless world of wonders. The flying fish's brief forays into
the air are like his own journeys into the heart of the sea—a fleet-
ing excursion into a dazzling otherworld.

"Incredible, isn't it?" Jamir starts when a voice speaks next to
him. It is Gauranga, wearing a lungi wrapped like pantaloons
around his legs and a thin white shirt. He wears a patch over his left
eye that—combined with his craggy, unshaven face and windblown
hair—makes him look the part of a sailor.

"Fish jumping out of the sea, birds diving into the water. What
a wonderful world God has created for us."

"It is," Jamir says, at ease in Gauranga's company.

"I saw you speaking to the captain. Is something the matter?
Are you in trouble? Are we?"

"None of you are in trouble. As for me, I don't know."

"I'm not so sure about that," Gauranga says. "You see those
lush clouds? Dark as a woman's hair? Those bleeding red lines
like the vermillion in her part? It means a storm is coming, a big
one."

Jamir follows Gauranga's finger. Clouds have indeed massed in
the west, bunched as though shoved into place by an angry cosmic
hand.

"Have you told the captain?"

"No, because I suspect that he isn't blind. In any case, the storm
looks as though it's headed to shore. We should be able to skirt it,
given that we're headed east, toward Burma."

The shore then, where Honufa and his son will face the storm
alone.

Gauranga guesses at his thoughts. "I wouldn't worry too much
about your family. Unlike the sea, on land there is always somewhere to run to."

"Provided they have warning," Jamir says, his gaze caught by the pendant around the older man's neck. Gauranga smiles when he notices, removes and hands it to Jamir. It is unlike anything he has seen before. Long as his hand, serrated and sharp. It resembles a spear tip made of bone.

"The tail of a stingray," Gauranga explains.

Jamir nearly drops it. Stingrays are rare in the bay, but he has seen a few in his lifetime. Their mystic glide, their great wingspan combining to make them one of the sea creatures he fears.

He makes to return the pendant to Gauranga, who shakes his head. "Wear it. See how you feel. It helps to find something physical through which to channel your worries. I've always calmed myself by touching this pendant at times of stress."

"I can't possibly keep it."

"You can, and you will. Keep it until your mind quietens. Then you can return it to me if you wish."

Jamir dons the string, tucking the odd pendant under his shirt. It digs into his skin, the dimensions and hardness unsettling against his chest.

"You'll get used to it soon enough," Gauranga says. "My father said that it's good to always be a little uncomfortable. It keeps you honest."

"Then I must be very honest indeed," Jamir says. "Thank you for this."

"Happy to help." Gauranga leans closer and drops his voice an octave. "No doubt you've worked hard all day. When you have a moment to yourself this evening, join me and Humayun in the engine room for a drink." He points to the stinger. "Maybe I'll tell you where I got that."

～〰～

AFTER GAURANGA DEPARTS, JAMIR works a half hour further before heading down to the galley for a quick catnap. But when he walks down the stairs and arrives at his bedroll, he finds someone rifling through it.

He crosses the distance between him and the figure in three strides, but Manik holds up the letter so high that he cannot reach it.

"What's this I've found?"

"Give it back. Who said you could go through my things?"

"Easy." Manik pulls the letter out of the envelope. He frowns, fixes exaggerated puzzlement on his sweating, pockmarked face. He shakes his head as though the act will better finesse the meaning of the words into it.

"What's this? A love letter from your wife? I didn't know you could read. What are you doing on a boat? You should be at university."

"Manik." Abbas stands at the door, his countenance grim. "Put it down."

The captain pushes his bulk into the galley. Sweat trickles down Jamir's back from the heat of three bodies in such a small space.

Stared down by his father, Manik drops the letter on the bedroll and departs sullenly.

"It's never easy to see your children grow up, behave badly," Abbas says. "I'm sorry for my son. He is my youngest, and because of that, escaped the allotment of beatings that I should have administered. Perhaps he would have turned out differently if I did."

"I work for you. It is I who should apologize," Jamir says. More words escape his mouth in a confessional tumble before he can stop them. "The letter your son was holding. I found it in my hut. I think my wife was hiding it from me."

"I see. Do you wish for me to read it to you?"

"Yes."

"We can also just throw it away, forget of its existence or that you ever found it."

Jamir shakes his head. "No. I must know what it says. I humbly request that you read it to me."

"So long as you are sure." Abbas holds out a meaty hand. The boat sways, as does the light bulb hanging from the ceiling, drifting Abbas's face in and out of shadow. Jamir hands him the letter and steps back as though a malevolent spirit might escape from it. In what is the longest minute of Jamir's life, Abbas scans the letter silently, front to back. Upon finishing, he turns and looks out the porthole window.

"What does it say?"

"Horrid things. Shameful things," Abbas says.

"Tell me what exactly. Who is it from? What does it say?"

"No name is given. It is better that you not hear the illicit things that are written there."

Jamir falls to his knees. "Read it to me. I beg of you."

The captain raises him to his feet. "I won't poison the air by uttering the words on this page. What more do you need to know? I'm sorry, my son. I'm your neighbor, your friend; I've known both you and your wife for so long. Even that time a few months ago when she worked as my housekeeper, my wife had nothing but praise for her. Her betrayal only brings me sadness."

"I don't believe you." Jamir shakes his head. "I don't believe you. You're lying."

"Is it really so hard to believe?" Abbas holds his gaze.

The allusion to Honufa's past makes Jamir rage. "How dare you bring that up? She was barely more than a child. I've forgiven her, even if others haven't."

Abbas holds the letter to him. "If she is innocent, would you not simply ask her?"

He takes it, manages to walk away. The captain says something more, but the words register as noise to his ears. The boat has hit a patch of calm waters. *Sonamoti* is steady and for that he is grateful, for he thinks his legs may fail him. He somehow ascends the stairs and comes onto the deck, where blue-black shadows have pooled.

The scuppers need to be cleaned.

He weaves his way to the grates. Falling to his hands and knees, he works on them until his fingers bleed.

Shahryar & Anna

Washington, DC
August 2004

Shar reads to Anna until she falls asleep, kisses her cheek and steps out of her bedroom.

He goes downstairs. On his way to the foyer, his eyes catch hold of the long credenza against the wall, lined with photos. He stops to study them. A set shows Anna, Val and Jeremy attending a show at Wolf Trap, another, them at the Mall on a summer day, his daughter perched on Jeremy's broad shoulders. The pictures proceed chronologically along the length of the table. In the earliest ones, Anna is small, swinging a tennis racket at a ball not yet in the frame, walking hand in hand with Val as she looks back at the camera, sitting on fresh snow, legs splayed, face peeking up from the hood of her jacket. At the other end, among pictures of a younger Jeremy, are ones of Val. In one, she is blowing out candles on a birthday cake, one hand pushing an errant lock of hair away from her face. In another, she lazes on a chair by the fireplace, heavily pregnant. Here she is, surrounded by friends, raising a glass of something or the other toward the camera, and then alone, her profile contemplative as she looks out a window to distant hills.

He is in none of the photos.

꙰

SHAR RETURNS HIS RENTAL car and takes the subway home, reaches his apartment in Southwest DC well after ten. He eats cold rotisserie chicken and coleslaw in front of his television.

The coming presidential election dominates the news. He watches with mild interest as the junior senator from Maryland, Pablo Aguilar, speaks at the ongoing Republican National Convention. With his height, glossy brown hair and bright teeth, Aguilar comes across well on the screen. He speaks with passion and apparent sincerity, his voice booming as he expounds on the importance of seeing through the war in Iraq, then wavering with emotion as he recounts his background as a son of Mexican immigrants. His father drove a truck, he says. His mother cleaned hotel rooms— jobs they were vastly overqualified for, but that they accepted to provide a better life for their son, who would go on to attend Yale and become a Rhodes scholar. What helped them succeed, Aguilar concludes, was their indomitable belief that hard work was rewarded in America, and that where one comes from is never as important as where one is going.

The typical Horatio Alger fantasy that conservatives like to cling to in the face of a mountain of contrary evidence. Shar scoffs and turns off the television.

꙰

HE SITS ON HIS bed later, processing the day.

Time is running out, Val had said to him earlier, and he had tried to reassure her that he has something of a plan, that he will find a job.

It is not as though he is unemployed. For the past year, he has worked as a research analyst at the Institute for Policy Dialogue, a federally funded think tank focused on public policy such as health, immigration and consumer protection, among others. The job was facilitated by a member of his thesis committee who referred him to the director, Albert Volcker, who previously worked for UNICEF, in Dhaka, Bangladesh, for several years following the War of Liberation in 1971.

The job offer was precipitated by a coffee meeting one morning between him and Volcker that stretched to lunch as the two men connected on the role of civil society in urban development, the eternal battles between two entrenched dynastic parties that dominate Bangladeshi politics and the merits of chicken biryani compared to mutton. The following day, an email from Volcker appeared in his inbox, offering him a position with the institute, which—he would soon discover—is best described as a glorified internship: For twenty hours a week he helps draft policy papers and coordinate speaking events for the director. The salary is adequate for covering rent, but little beyond. Despite all this, he asked Volcker about the possibility of an extension of his contract, receiving in response a gloomy shake of the director's head. They do not have the money or resources to sponsor a foreign student. When Shar's work visa expires, so will his job.

He exhales and rises to perform the final component of his nightly rituals. From the upper shelf of his closet he retrieves a cloth bag, a bag as old as he is, the two objects within older still. He takes them out and stares at them a long time before he can fall asleep.

RAHIM

Calcutta, India
August 1946

On a morning a year before India is to be cleaved in two, Rahim Choudhury is being driven to work in his '34 Morris Wolseley. With a copy of the day's *Statesman* on his lap, a thermos full of tea, his briefcase by his side and his driver, Motaleb, at the wheel of the car, this morning is a typical one for him.

Rahim reads the paper with growing dismay. There is little news on the front page that does not concern tomorrow's strike, called for by the Muslim League.

India has fumed and seethed this year, its foundations trembling in anticipation of strife between Hindus and Muslims that independence would inevitably trigger. The secular, Hindu-dominated Congress party opposes a subcontinent divided along religious and ethnic lines, which they believe is nothing but a ploy of the departing British to leave weaker the country they have ruled for two hundred years but now must abandon. The Muslim League, on the other hand, supports separation, having long argued that without the patronage of the British, Muslims would suffer as minorities in an undivided India. And to press their claim for an independent homeland of their own, they have called for a citywide strike—a Direct Action Day.

Rahim is a lukewarm supporter of the Muslim League; he does not approve of its leaders, who in recent months have traveled the nation, delivering incendiary speeches to crowds already combustible as kindling. Nor can he fully disavow them, aware that as a wealthy and successful Muslim in Calcutta, he is by far the exception.

He is still absorbed in the paper when his vehicle reaches a block in the road. The flow of cars, rickshaws and red double-deckers is stymied by something up ahead. Rahim makes the mistake of rolling down his window, for along with the noise of the street, smog and dust billow in.

"There's been an accident," reveals a rickshawallah, standing up on his pedals to catch a better view. "A boy, hurt badly by a car. There's blood everywhere. The crowds are threatening the driver."

Rahim begins to step out and approach the scene. But Motaleb stops him.

"Careful, sahib. The people are already angered, the sight of another rich car owner may be oil on the fire."

He sits back down, feeling powerless. The Morris Wolseley extricates itself from the street and squeezes into a narrower one that connects Park Street to Hungerford Road. Here, along the crumbling multi-storied tenements built in the past century, colorful tin billboards advertise everything from fancy tailoring to Ayurvedic cures for venereal diseases. Saris, petticoats and dhotis hang from railings. Rickshaws and pushcarts trundle past, respectively pulled and pushed by bare-chested, single-minded men, who leave dark drops of sweat on the ground. The scent of bodies, sewage and old wood mingle with dough, cumin and potatoes frying in oil.

As the car makes stately progress, some pedestrians pause to mutter and point to the cap that identifies Rahim as a Muslim.

They reach the main road before long, having bypassed the jam. Soon, he can spy in the distance four central steeples that come together to hold aloft an observation deck; the building that houses Britannia Biscuits was an observatory before it was converted for business use.

A thickly sweet smell wafts in from the nearby factory. In his first months, when he would go home redolent of baking dough, his wife, Zahira, would playfully complain that she did not know whether to embrace him or dip him in tea. Now she barely notices.

The guards at the gate offer him smart salutes as his car glides past them and stops at the main door. Rahim springs out, taking the steps two at a time and evading an orderly scrambling to carry his briefcase for him. He likes to arrive early for important meetings, and the morning's detour has cost him precious minutes.

He runs up the central stairs to the second floor before taking a right at the landing into a long porticoed hallway.

Breathing hard, he stops at a door that says *Theodore Drake—Managing Director.* He looks at his watch. He has a minute to catch his breath.

At the exact moment the second hand on his watch flicks onto twelve, he knocks on the door.

"Come in."

Theodore Drake sits behind a sea of Burmese teak. His smile is warm and friendly.

"Choudhury. Great to see you. Have a seat."

Rahim produces a folder from his briefcase. "I've prepared what you asked for, sir."

"Excellent."

As Drake studies his work, Rahim's eyes are drawn to the framed map of Rangoon that dominates the wall behind. Before Britannia, Drake was a colonel in the British Army. He served with General Wingate in Imphal when the Japanese invaded Burma, and was a crucial part of Mountbatten's offensives to retake the country. After the war, he left the military to join private service in India, an unusual choice for an officer.

Drake looks up. "This is quite good. I hope it wasn't too much trouble to put it together at such short notice."

"No," Rahim says, even though compiling the folder required a great deal of work. In it are articles of incorporation, bylaws, minute books and organizational charts, the details of accounts receivable and payable, inventory, general ledger and a list of physical assets and intellectual property applications. It is as thorough an overview of the enterprise as could be produced in the two weeks he was given.

"If I may speak freely, sir—this package seems like something a potential purchaser might request as part of their due diligence efforts."

Drake nods, impassive. He is not yet thirty-five, with the first shards of gray peeking through the brown at his temples.

"It could also be part of an annual audit requested by the board."

"Which I'd be informed of. And an audit can always be requested by an external buyer."

This time Drake laughs. "Will we continue sparring or is there a question in there somewhere?"

"How long do we have?"

"There's no need to sound so fatalistic about it. This is simply a precautionary measure that the board has requested that I take."

"Is there an interested buyer?"

"We've had approaches. The strongest interest is from a group of local investors, which—given what's on the horizon—is entirely expected. British companies all over India are divesting, fleeing back to England. It's just Britannia's turn."

"Not all of them are leaving."

"No, but it's coming. It's the first crack in the cup. The one you know will spread before the whole things breaks. Independence seemed far off when I joined last year—fresh off the war—but it's a matter of months now, not years. I half-believe that's why the board hired me in the first place. To ease the transition."

Rahim absorbs the news, the implications roiling his stomach. It is not news that management in the larger companies across the country is transferring from British to native hands, even if the speed has caught many off-guard. This departure has been prolonged and bittersweet for not just the occupiers, but the occupied as well. In many ways, the British are like the Mughals that they deposed, the glue that holds this country of many languages, cultures and religions together.

"We employ more than a thousand people. What happens to them in case of a sale?"

"I won't make empty promises. You of all people know that it's exceedingly rare that there aren't redundancies after a sale. I'll be the first one, actually." Drake laughs. "But your job should be safe, at least for the time being."

"I don't follow, sir."

"What I mean, Mr. Choudhury, is that I'm done with Asia, with the colonies, with the dust and flyblown romance of the Orient. I'm looking forward to returning to England. In fact, I can't wait."

"I see."

"I mean no offense."

"I took none."

"What about you? If your country is to be divided along the lines of religion—as it seems likely—will you stay here, or move to East Bengal? I understand that that's where the Muslims are expected to transfer should your leaders get their way."

This is a question that Rahim has asked himself nearly every day for the past year. Is he first a Muslim, owing his allegiance to a nation carved out from India for other adherents of his religion, or an Indian, with his heart sworn to a flag rather than a God?

He answers truthfully. "I still don't know, but I'm hoping to have an answer if it becomes a reality. My wife would prefer that we move back to East Bengal, whether it becomes a separate nation or a Muslim-only province. She is from there. For her, it will just be going home."

"If you need an incentive to remain, I'll recommend to the

board that you be promoted to the position of managing director upon my departure." Drake shrugs. "You'll be a young MD, but it's nothing more than you deserve. And the new board is likely to be all Indian, more open to, say"—he hunts for the right words—"seeing a different face at the helm of the company."

Rahim can hardly trust himself to speak. "Thank you, sir."

He has been at Britannia for five years, more than half of that time as chief accountant. When the previous MD, Waddingham, died from a heart attack last year, he thought there would be a reasonable chance of him being named as the replacement. But Drake was named instead.

Do your job, Zahira told him in the wake of his disappointment. *Your time will come. I know it.*

So he did. He worked closely with Drake, guiding the novice MD as the two led a large-scale restructuring of the company's public debts that saved it a considerable amount of money, strategizing together on the company's direction should independence come, developing a detailed plan that laid out risks and contingencies. Over the course of the past year, he has come to respect Drake's incisive intellect, his occasional bursts of dry English humor.

"Is that sufficient incentive?" Drake asks.

Rahim smiles. "You've certainly given me much to think about."

"I should hope so. And I expect an answer soon. Opportunities like this don't come knocking every day, Mr. Choudhury. Don't let it pass you by."

An orderly enters and hands Drake what appears to be a telegram. He reads it quickly, crumples it and throws it in the dustbin.

"It seems your co-religionists are stirring up trouble around the city. I've been advised to go home for the day. I will suggest the same for all other employees as well."

"But this Direct Action Day is supposed to be tomorrow."

"The thing about trouble is that it gives little notice. The word has gotten out that the Moslems will be mobilizing around the city tomorrow, so now the militant Hindoos are preparing to do the same. Force will meet force."

He rises from his chair and holds out a hand for Rahim to shake, which he does. "I do hope you will give this serious thought. But I think that whatever country ends up gaining you will be the true winner. Go home and have a chat with your wife."

"But what if I'm not able to persuade her to remain?"

"Then you make her happy. Be a good husband, Mr. Choudhury. Fight for your family. Unfortunately, they don't give out medals for that."

‿‿

RAHIM'S DRIVER IS READY for him at the main door. At the gates, a stream of employees make their way out, their faces stamped with worry.

"We're going back to the house, Motaleb," Rahim says as he climbs into the back of the vehicle. "Take the same shortcut through the alley. I think the main roads might be jammed with people trying to get home."

"Yes, sir." Motaleb hunches close to the wheel, as has been his style since he first began to drive for the family, back when Edward VII sat on the throne. In his years of driving stately tourers, first for Rahim's father and now for him, Motaleb has accrued the gravitas of a sea captain, helming the steering wheel with confidence.

Rahim sits back, wondering how he can broach this new development with his wife. For the past few months, he has vacillated over what to do should the country be divided, and only in the last year has Zahira persuaded him to consider a move should it come to pass.

Unbeknownst to her, and with a fair amount of misgivings, he has taken preliminary steps to making this a reality; at the prospect of geopolitical schism, Hindus who wish to move out of what will become East Bengal, and Muslims who plan to move there have agreed to house swaps, easing the emigration process considerably for both sides, even if in most cases the scarcity of willing partners means that one side often ends up with far superior accommodations, as well as the reverse.

He has been in contact with a rich Hindu landholder in the south of East Bengal willing to swap his seaside mansion for Rahim's. For months, the two men have exchanged letters describing their respective homes and amenities, developing the details of an agreement. All that remains is for Rahim to send a check to complete the deal.

But he has been reconsidering of late, calling two months ago for a halt in negotiations to think things through, not entirely cured of his doubts about the prospect of leaving Calcutta. Creating nations by excising them out of larger ones never made sense to him, much like severing a leg and expecting it to grow into a person. And now with Drake's offer the pendulum has swung even more toward staying.

He solicits his driver for advice. "What do you think, Motaleb? Can Hindus and Muslims live together once the English leave?"

The driver's rheumy eyes meet his in the rear-view mirror. "We've been living together for a thousand years already, sir. Hindus and Muslims are like my wife and me. We've been fighting for so long that we'd miss it if we stopped."

Rahim laughs. "I marvel, Motaleb, that two people so different can share a land, live together and die. We Muslims believe in the One God, unseen and unquestionable—whose appearance we're not even permitted to imagine, much less draw; the Hindus believe in millions, all shapes and sizes and colors. We can't go a day without meat, while their Brahmins won't touch even onions and garlic. Our God gives us dominion over all life on Earth, while they hold cows and monkeys as sacred."

They turn into the same alley they traversed earlier in the

morning. Motaleb slows the car to match the speed of traffic. "If you'll indulge an old man, sir, I wish to tell you a story."

"Please do."

The chauffeur clears his throat.

"Thank you, sir. When I was little, my father, having failed at being an apprentice cobbler, an apprentice goldsmith, and an apprentice sweet-maker, decided to try his hand at carpentry.

"We were six brothers and sisters, of whom I was the youngest, so one day, when my mother fell sick, my father took me with him to the place of his work—to the home of the master carpenter.

"His home was a simple one of earth and thatch, but the courtyard was spacious, broom-swept clean and polished with cow dung until sparkling. *Sit there and do not move,* Father said, pointing to the hog plum tree in the corner, handing me a carafe of water, bread and jaggery. I was five, and out of fear I sat in the spot, ate and drank, and did as told.

"Eventually, curiosity got the better of me and I wandered into the kitchen, where the embers of the morning's fire still glowed. I then visited the smaller room adjacent to it.

"Standing at the threshold, it took a while to make out what stood at the far end.

"I walked in, hesitating—feeling perhaps this was not a place I was meant to be. But the object at the other end of the room drew me on strongly—a clay statue, standing no taller than my knee. It was of a boy, the handsomest one I'd ever seen. Intricately carved, so detailed and lifelike that if a breeze blew in, his clothes could flutter in response. Bare-chested and blue-skinned, he wore a saffron stole around his neck, his arms raising a flute to ruby-red lips on which a small smile played, as though the child was amused by some secret that only he knew.

"The room smelled of earth and wood. The eyes were locked on mine. We stood staring at each other like this for a while.

"I reached out toward his cheek.

"It was a piercing shriek that stopped me, and to this day I'm unsure whether I made contact or not.

"'What are you doing?' The carpenter's wife rushed in with a sweep of sari and the scent of coconut hair oil. She grabbed my hand in a vice-like grip and dragged me out to the sunshine as one does an insect from beneath a rock.

"'Are you there? Oh, are you there, husband?' The old woman wailed until the man in question emerged from the workshop behind the house. He was tall, bearded and bare-chested. My father followed.

"'What has happened, wife?'

"'Right in front of the thakur, this brat was about to . . . to . . .'

"Overcome by the heinousness of my crime, the carpenter's wife broke down before she could finish her report.

"The carpenter looked at me, sternly, but not angrily. 'Where else have you been, child? Tell me quick.'

"Bawling, I pointed to the hearth.

"The old carpenter calmly and methodically began to take all wares—save the statue—out of the rooms I'd visited, smashing the clay pots and pans against the ground until it was littered with shards.

"'Please understand,' he explained to my father, who led me away with gritted teeth. 'This must be done if a non-Hindu visits our kitchen or place of worship. It is not a question of whether I believe in these things, but I am bound to them, as I am to the happiness of my wife.'

"Thus ended my father's brief foray into carpentry. But as silent as he was on the way back home, he never hit, rebuked, or even blamed me for what had happened, accepting the incident as fate. But the boy-god's radiant blue beauty would stay with me. His name, I would later learn, was Krishna. And to this day, even though I take out my prayer mat five times a day and bow toward Mecca as a good Muslim should, I still have a picture of him in my room."

ENTRANCED BY THE STORY, Rahim is about to speak when the car comes to a shuddering halt. He looks up. Their way is blocked by three young men who wear dhotis and hold thick bamboo staffs in their hands. On their foreheads are three white slashes centered by a red dot of vermillion.

Motaleb and Rahim exchange worried looks. The driver whispers, "The symbol of Shiva—the god of Destruction."

"But also Creation and Preservation," Rahim says, and Motaleb looks surprised. "Let's hope that these gentlemen agree."

When the man at the center of the group, tall and lean, gestures for Motaleb to exit the car, he looks to his employer with fear. Rahim puts a restraining hand on his chauffeur's shoulder and rolls down the window.

"Is anything the matter?"

"Get out of the car," the tall man says. He caresses the bonnet with his staff. The other two young men observe with arms crossed over their chests.

Rahim climbs out of the car and stands ramrod straight. He towers over most people, but he can see that the tall man tops him by a few inches.

A crowd gathers to watch the spectacle.

Rahim addresses the tall man. "What is the matter, bhai?" he asks, the Muslim term for *brother* in Bangla slipping from his mouth by mistake.

"I'm not your brother."

"Forgive me. What is your name, dada?"

The malevolence emanating from the three infects the crowd; men and women mutter obscenities and egg them on.

One of the toughs comes up to Rahim, his breath a sour waft. "You don't need his name. This is a Hindu neighborhood. What are you doing here?"

"No need to be rude," the tall man admonishes. "I'm sure he was about to explain himself."

He walks over and faces Rahim. He is no more than twenty-five. A knife scar marks his right cheek. "Who are you? Speak truly and quickly. We don't take well to Muslim League goons here. We know of the riots you all are planning."

Aware that an ill-chosen word can spell his end, Rahim's hand on the roof of his car is nonetheless rock steady, as is his voice. "We're just passing through. I don't want trouble with you or anyone else. I'm not political. I've nothing to do with the League. But in any case, they're not planning violence against anyone. They're just speaking out so that the British treat the Muslims fairly when our country—our Hindustan—is liberated of their rule."

Rahim knows that this is not the entire truth; spoiling for a fight, the League has been agitating Muslims into a frenzy for months now. But these facts are inconvenient with one's life at stake.

Sour Breath circles Rahim's car and orates to the crowd. "Are you listening? *Our Hindustan!* He's talking about our Hindustan while his League thugs plan to go out tomorrow to try and take our lands and create their own nation, where we won't be allowed."

The crowd responds with an ugly cheer, shouting *kill him*, and *fucking nera*. Sour Breath turns to face Rahim and says, "Maybe we'll send you to the land of the pure right now."

"Easy." Knife Scar smiles at Rahim. "My apologies. As you can see, my colleagues are very upset by this Direct Action Day. Emotion appeals to them. Not reason. So trying to have a political debate with them while at the center of a mob is not advisable, janab?"

Rahim does not offer his name despite the invitation. Names have power and he must retain the little he has in this situation.

Knife Scar leans close and whispers. "Your bravado will prove nothing. I'm all that stands between you and the mob. One word from me and they will be on you."

"And what word is that?"

"One sent home through your driver—if your family wishes to see you again, they'll have to fetch us a very large sum of money."

Shahryar & Anna

Washington, DC
September 2004

He stands outside Anna's school, where tanned, attractive mothers wait to pick up their children. There are a handful of men as well. They wear sunglasses, shorts, sport bellies grown either through indolence or unemployment, he is unsure.

Thurgood Marshall Elementary is brick and white limestone, wearing on its face the late afternoon shadows of the trees on its front lawn. Shar stands under a paper birch off to the side. Other than an occasional smile or nod to appear non-threatening, he does not engage the other parents, who give him curious looks.

Anna is among the stream of children that spills out of the doors at 2:55. She offers a somber wave when she sees him, whispers a quick good-bye to her friends and trots over. He wonders if she is embarrassed by his presence, if she was secretly hoping to see Jeremy.

"Hey, shona," he says to her and gives her an embrace that he hopes is permissible in the presence of her friends. A woman approaches them. A petite brunette. Young and pretty in an anodyne way. A large diamond ring glitters on her left hand.

"Hi, is everything okay?" She looks to Anna.

He smiles. "I'm her dad."

"Oh, uh. I don't think I've ever . . ."

"That's alright, Mrs. Stein," Anna says. "He's my dad. He usually doesn't pick me up."

She appears embarrassed. "Of course. I didn't . . ." She extends a hand. "Hi, I'm Lisa. I was her third-grade teacher."

He shakes it and tells her his name.

Her eyes swing from Anna's face to his. "I should have known. Anna looks just like you. Except for her eyes."

"Yes," he says. "Except for her eyes."

༄

THEY WALK IN SILENCE toward the main road afterward, leaving behind the school buses, the Audis and Infinitis in repose by the sidewalk.

"What're we doing today?"

"It's Friday. You know what that means."

She groans. "Not Bangla school again?"

"It's only been a month. Is it really that bad?"

Anna's body slopes in a hangdog manner. "Those Bangla letters are so hard to draw. I'm still stuck on *talibo shaw*."

"That's the prettiest letter in the Bangla alphabet. Two loops and a straight line at the end."

"Can't you teach me instead?"

"I'm not as good a teacher as your grandfather, but I can help you practice. Besides, don't you like the songs and dances you get to do at Bangla school?"

"They're okay," Anna looks up. "I like the food, though."

"Spoken with the true honesty of a child. Let's hurry up and get on the bus then. I think they're supposed to have chicken biryani today."

"Yay!"

༄

THE DC BANGLA SCHOOL operates out of a community center on Glebe Road in Arlington. It takes them an hour and two buses before they get there. They are a few minutes late for the first class—watercolors—so he takes Anna's backpack as she runs and joins one of the groups circling large chart papers laid out on the floor. He sits near the entrance, selects a copy of *Desh* magazine from a stack on the table and begins to read, hoping no one will ask questions about which child is his. About her mother.

The other parents are in an amiable clump near the back, the women in saris, some with hijabs covering their hair, as is the new fashion. They lay out long aluminum trays of steaming food, the silver bodies bending from the weight of biryani, chicken curry, cucumber salad or fish dopiaza, the paper lids spotted with grease.

"You look new here," says the man one seat over from him, in Bangla. He is thin, with a thatch of straight hair that would be salt and pepper if not hennaed red. The suit he wears is tailored with care, silver-gray with a slight sheen.

"Which one is your daughter?"

Shar curses silently. "The girl in the green shirt, over there."

"Oh, she's a lovely child. Such fair skin and pretty eyes. Pardon me for asking, but is her mother . . ."

"Yes, she's American," Shar says, trying not to be curt. It is a dance, the Bengali conversation, with broad parameters that allow it to whirl blithely into the personal, yet retaining a delicate balance that even a touch of rudeness could upend.

"Sorry. I don't mean to get personal. My first wife was American as well. My daughter from that marriage is named Rebecca. She has blue eyes. I know all about looks and strange questions when you're walking with your half-American daughter."

"First wife. So you're . . ."

"Divorced. Food, language, upbringing, culture. These differences add up to a lot. No matter how in love you are. They live in California now. My daughter is a junior at UCLA. I've remarried since. A Bengali woman the second time. I've had two more children."

He points to a teenage boy playing table tennis at the far end. "My son, Sumon. I drive him here after school so he can play with his chums."

"How often do you see her? Your daughter from your first marriage, I mean."

The man's smile is melancholy. "Not often enough. She'll visit during Christmas. Or I will. She's met her step-siblings. The years we can't meet, I FedEx a gift. She calls every now and then. Sometimes it feels like she's ticking off a box."

Shar struggles for a response, finding the man's revelations to be more burdens than gifts. He wonders how deep into his own history he must dive to reciprocate.

"I'm sorry to hear that."

"No, listen. I'm the one who should be sorry. We just met and I unloaded half my life on you. You can take the Bengali out of Bengal but not the reverse, eh?"

He extends a hand and Shar shakes it. It is warm and dry. "I'm Faisal Ahmed."

"Shar Choudhury."

"What do you do, Shar?"

"I just finished my doctorate last year. Now I'm doing policy research for the federal government."

"How wonderful."

"And you?"

The man hands him a business card in response, and when Shar reads it, Faisal Ahmed—Faisal Ahmed *Esquire*—suddenly gains a full hold of his attention.

"I think we need to talk," Shar says.

ZAHIRA

Calcutta, India
August 1946

In a grand house in Calcutta called Choudhury Manzil, Rahim and Zahira Choudhury sit and have breakfast.

On the table before them are plates of jam and toast, butter and fruit, but also grander things that fill the spaces between conversations. The moment for deciding is drawing near. The British, their exchequer drained through war, resented by Indians who will no longer tolerate their rule, are close to announcing their departure from the subcontinent, leaving their empire behind to return to their small, gloomy island to lick their wounds. But it will not be the clean break that they desire. In light of their departure, Hindus and Muslims have already begun squabbling over the future of the nation. Once unthinkable, a fracture of India along the lines of religion now seems inevitable.

"Have you given it more thought?" Zahira asks.

Rahim lowers his copy of the *Statesman*. Even this early in the day, his face gleams with sweat.

"Wipe your face, then answer," she says.

He does as he is told. She knows that he likely hides a smile underneath the handkerchief, finding her assertiveness endearing. Not until the day of their marriage, three years before, had they met or spoken to each other. At eighteen, she was at that age when her marriage was a topic of active and urgent discussion in her family. One day, after classes at college, she came home to find a group of expectant people gathered in their drawing room. Seeing the flash of her sari through the door, her mother rushed to pull her aside before she could stumble into the guests, who were unprepared to see her unprepared.

"Let's go upstairs," she whispered. "A very good family has come from Calcutta to look at you for their son."

A month later, Rahim rode a piebald horse into the wedding festivities, wearing a turban with a screen of flowers. Zahira knew little about the man she was about to marry; Rahim's father had forged a friendship with Zahira's at Hare School, the two promising upon parting to join their families through marriage should circumstance allow it one day. So when Rahim was twenty-three, his father informed him that he was to marry the daughter of his childhood friend Abu Bakar, who lived on the other side of the river Padma, in East Bengal.

In response, Rahim had uttered the only words permissible— *Yes, Father.*

On her wedding night, she sat with her henna-branded arms folded on her lap, her face hidden behind the cowl of her sari, a face he would not get to glimpse until later, while upon their wedding bed. And when he finally did, she could see him struggle to contain his disappointment.

Her plainness was not news, but she was still surprised by how wretched she felt at that moment, a sense that only deepened when she overheard him speaking to his mother, a legendary force in the family and a reluctant signatory to the marriage, having set her sights on a less educated but more conventionally attractive Calcutta girl for her son. *It is better to marry a plain woman,* she told him, the words of comfort a slap to Zahira. *Other men won't covet her, and her devotion to you will be greater.*

Rahim was tall and handsome, polite, quick to kindness toward others and seemingly immune to the arrogance that his lavish upbringing would breed in others. So, despite his misgivings about her appearance, she fell quickly for her husband. She vowed to mitigate the handicap of her looks, leaning on her quick wit, her abilities as a conversationalist, her singing, her knowledge of Chaucer, Blake, Keats, Yeats, Dante and Russell.

That first year of pursuing his affections was a prolonged dawn, the light of their love growing stronger until she could see the reward for her dogged efforts—when the face Rahim had once thought plain became one to which he was increasingly drawn. But what she had not expected was that three years into the marriage they would still be eating breakfast alone, their dreams of having children yet to be fulfilled despite many visits to the best physicians Calcutta had to offer—both allopaths and homeopaths. After exhausting their knowledge of this army of medicine men, Rahim and Zahira made their way to the soldiers bringing up the rear—to a ragged company of Ayurvedic experts, kobirajes, pirs, sadhus and outright hucksters and charlatans who prescribed remedies ranging from eating blessed fruits to bathing in the light of the moon. Eventually the couple acquiesced to their fate, the emptiness of Zahira's womb echoing the cavernous house in which they live.

"Sorry, what were you saying?"

"You heard me."

He sips water to buy time. "Please don't tell me it's about leaving Calcutta again."

"I thought we'd agreed on this?"

"We said that we'd consider it. Even if the country is to be divided it's at least a year away."

"And you want to wait until that moment of madness to make decisions? We'll be caught short, without a home and without options if we decide too late that we do want to move out of West Bengal."

He counters with questions that have been an effective line of defense against this issue. "Where would I work? What would I do in East Bengal?"

"Dhaka. The biggest city. You could work there. Maybe you won't get a comparable position, at least not in the beginning, but that will be temporary uncertainty we can live with."

He grimaces. "Maybe you can live with it. Dhaka's such a backwater. It's barely a city compared to Calcutta. If we have to go to East Bengal, I'd rather just live in the country."

"All of it is a backwater, Rahim. And will be for some time. At least at first. That's why they need people like you. You think there's much hope for East Bengal if the best and brightest Muslims stay back here?"

He raises the newspaper to his face. "We don't even know if it'll happen," he says, and she knows what he is referring to immediately.

"Sure, maybe Nehru, Jinnah and Gandhi will wake up one morning and magically decide to get along with each other. But the British are leaving, sooner or later. All I'm asking is that we have a plan in place if we do. Do you want to stay or go? Just give me a clear answer."

He lowers the paper again, sighs. "All I know is that I'd rather risk the unknowns here than in a place I've never been."

"That's fine. But I'm from there, and I tell you if we go you will fall in love with the East."

Zahira's arguments have established beachheads on his psyche and now, as they advance, he reaches for a weapon of desperation. "What about my mother and father?"

Rahim is one of three children, with an elder brother and sister. The latter is settled in Bombay with her physician husband; the former manages a prosperous steel mill in Lucknow. A few years back, with Calcutta's heat no longer tolerable for them, his parents moved to live with his brother. Since then, Rahim and Zahira take the train twice a year during the Eid holidays to see them, visits during which they make clear to him that the weather in Lucknow agrees with them, and that they have no intention of returning to Choudhury Manzil, or Calcutta.

"If you really wanted to be close to them, we'd have already moved to Lucknow."

He rises and brushes crumbs from his jacket, looks around to see if any of the servants are near, and circles around to Zahira's side of the table to lay a quick peck on her head. "We will decide soon. I promise you. You crossed a border for me, maybe it's my turn. I have to run now. I'm late for my meeting with Drake."

FOLLOWING HIS DEPARTURE, SHE goes up to her bedroom on the second floor, walks out to the expansive balcony that looks out on a Calcutta about to enter its noontime somnolence. Leaning on the sun-warmed railing with one hand, she lets the other caress her belly. Taut and strong like the skin of a drum, and like it, just as empty. Maybe that will change if they move back east. Maybe the air and water here conspire to keep her barren, rip off life before it can take root. She laughs. Desperate women will convince themselves of anything. And then convince their husbands.

Something catches her eye.

A bird sits on the railing. At the far end. Massive and fearless. Black feathers. Claws and eyes. It studies her with an immortal patience, the sunlight dappling its plumage dark violet. This is no timid gray-hooded crow but a great dar kaak. Carrion crow. Raven. As a child, the stolidity of these creatures, their inscrutable gaze, frightened her, a phobia she now discovers time has not diminished. *Jah, jah.* She yells to dissuade the bird from its perch, stomps her feet as accompaniments. Seemingly bemused, the raven lets out a mocking *gronk* as it flies away, a single feather spiraling down in its wake.

Shaken by her wildlife encounter, she retreats to the cooler environs of her bedroom, lies down on the bed with the intent of calming her racing heart, which it does, but only at the expense of a great lethargy that overtakes her. She begins nodding off as though drugged, and before long a darkness that looks to her like raven's wings spreads before her vision. It threatens rather than lulls her into black dreamless sleep.

SHE IS WOKEN BY the sound of a throat clearing. One of her maids stands at the doorway.

She scrabbles up on the bed, feeling as though she has been dipped in treacle. "Nargis, oh my goodness. How long have I been asleep?"

"A few hours, begum sahiba. It's noon."

"Why didn't you wake me?" Noticing the fearful look on her face, she adds, "What's the matter?"

"I . . . I don't know, begum sahiba. Please come down."

She rushes down the stairs, to the solarium. Motaleb stands in the middle, encircled by household staff speaking in low concerned tones. Their faces are grave; a few of the women cover their mouths in distress.

"Motaleb, what's happened?"

The old man bursts into tears.

"What are you all waiting for? Get him a chair."

The seated Motaleb is handed a glass of water. Trembling like a leaf, he recounts the events of the afternoon, ending with, "They told us we have until the end of tomorrow to get them the money."

She speaks in a daze. "Or what will happen?"

He does not answer. Some members of the staff—both men and women—start softly weeping.

She whirls on them. "Stop with your childish tears! How will that help the master?"

The edge in her voice and its volume have an electric effect, ending the murmurs and incipient wails as though a radio has been switched off. She puts a hand on the wall to steady herself. Fear and weakness can spread like a plague if unchecked.

She looks to Motaleb. "Who are they and how much do they want?"

"I don't know who they are, begum sahiba, but they had a mark on their foreheads. Some manner of Hindu gang. They want one lakh."

Taking a piece of quicklime, then dipping his finger in powdered cayenne for the dot, Motaleb recreates on the floor the symbol he saw on the foreheads of the men.

Zahira stares at it as her world spins anew. One hundred thousand taka is an astronomical sum, even for a family as affluent as Rahim's. She does quick mental accounting and estimates that in the safe upstairs there is at most a third that. She must find a way to make up the rest.

"Have you gone to the police?"

"They said they would hurt sahib if we did. I was told to come home with the message right away."

She subjects the elderly man to a withering gaze, not feeling the least bit of pity for his state. "You have failed your master, Motaleb. You have failed me. If your loyalty to this family meant anything, you would not have let him fall into the hands of those thugs, but since you did, you should have stayed behind."

He does not meet her eyes.

She rushes back upstairs, locks the bedroom door behind her and opens the safe to do a hurried count of the notes within, punctured and bound together with thick red and white bank threads. Forty-three thousand two hundred takas. A bit more than she thought they had.

Recessed in the far wall of the first safe is a second one; she opens this and sweeps out its contents with her palm into a velvet bag. There is the glint of gemstones, the clink of metal as the objects fall in. Most of the jewelry belonged to her mother-in-law, and a small portion to her own mother, brought over when she married Rahim. Looking at the velvet bag, she reconsiders and swaps it for a plainer cotton one. The stacks of money she wraps in brown paper and places in the bag along with the jewelry. Combined with the cash, she should have enough to meet the ransom.

Her next stop is Rahim's study, where she opens his address book, thumbs to "D." She picks up the receiver of their phone. They have had it for less than a year, one of the few households in Calcutta with their own line.

"How can I place your call?" Asks the woman's voice at the other end, in English.

Zahira recites the four-digit number.

"Just a moment. I'm connecting you."

The line is answered on the second ring. "Theodore Drake."

She freezes. She has studied English literature, read hundreds of books in the language and has even practiced speaking to her father in English, but now she must converse with an Englishman in his native tongue.

She composes the sentences in her head first. "Mr. Drake, my name is Zahira Choudhury. I am the wife of Rahim Choudhury," she says finally, the words stumbling over each other.

Drake is silent long enough to make her wonder if she made a mistake in calling, but then he says, "Mrs. Choudhury. This is a most pleasant surprise. I don't believe we've spoken before. Is anything the matter?"

"Yes, Mr. Drake," she says. "I am afraid that my husband has been abducted."

～

DRAKE, AS IT HAPPENS, is a good friend of D. R. Hardwick's, the police commissioner; a car arrives in a half hour, bearing an inspector and two constables. She sits the men in the drawing room.

Vivek Nandi is the inspector assigned to the case. He is tall and heavy-set. A thick, jet-black mustache covers his upper lip. Seeing the circles of sweat in the armpits of his khaki uniform, Zahira asks the servants to turn the ceiling fan on. Along with the telephone, electricity is another newcomer to Choudhury Manzil.

"Have you already paid the ransom?"

"No. But I have the money ready."

"That's fine. We'll handle all matters. It's best that you don't get involved in the dirty stuff with these thugs." Nandi takes a loud slurp from the cup of tea poured for him, followed by a bite of samosa that leaves crumbs speared in his mustache. "Can you tell me more about the symbol your driver drew?"

She describes it and he nods immediately. "*Tripundra*. The mark of the Shaivites. The three lines represent will, knowledge and action, or Brahma, Vishnu and Shiva, as you will. The red circle is the third eye. They tend to be a bit aggressive, but it's still odd for them to behave the way your driver describes."

"What happens now?"

He points to the constables taking notes. "We've entered a general diary of the incident. We are now going to look into the local gangs around the neighborhood. There certainly are enough of them—nominal followers of various sadhu babas and other religious ascetics. They claim to be soldiers of faith but are actually thugs recently out of jail. Toss a few hundred takas their way and you can easily put them up to mischief. Thankfully, the mark will help us narrow it down, unless it's meant to throw us off, of course. We'll knock a few heads and slap a few faces until we get answers. In the meanwhile, I'd like some time alone with that driver of yours."

"Why? He's been working for the family for thirty years."

Nandi stands, covers his mouth and imparts a polite belch. "More reason to speak to him, madam. Any fruit goes bad if you leave it out long enough."

"How long is all this going to take, Inspector? Why can't we go there right now? Every moment we delay increases the danger for my husband. What will the kidnappers do if they don't get their money on time?"

"Who is the policeman here, madam? You or I? Please let me do my job. I know what I am doing. We'll begin with that driver of yours to get some answers, and then ascertain our next moves."

"Fine. But please hurry. As for Motaleb, I ask that you treat him gently. I hope I do not have to explain further."

"Understood." Nandi instructs his constables to fetch Mota-leb. When they leave the room, he addresses her in a lowered tone. "Madam, there really was no need to consult a gora for this matter. You could have called us directly and we would have come right away."

"I doubt that."

"We would, madam. Perhaps not quite as fast—this order came down from the commissioner after all—but quickly enough. There is talk of riots that might take place tomorrow, when the Muslim League marches. Many of our men are tied up bolstering areas in the city where we think there may be trouble."

He leans forward. "We both know, madam, that the English are on their way out, sooner or later. Hindus and Muslims may as well get in the habit of approaching each other about our problems, and not running to the white man as soon as we scrape a knee."

Zahira is indignant. "Nandi Babu, I've just learned that my husband has been kidnapped. What is this nonsense you're spouting about going to the English? About scraped knees? Would any other housewife in my position have done things differently? Why shouldn't I do everything in my power to save my husband? Are we truly going to stand here and pretend that there is no animus toward Muslims these days in light of coming independence? Calling Drake ensured that you'd get here in a hurry. I'd make that choice a hundred more times if I had to."

"Any other housewife would not have been able to pick up a phone and call the police."

"What do you mean?"

"What I mean is that you're privileged. There are no more than a thousand private phone lines in this city, and your home is one of them. Your husband is from a respected family. You're connected, rich and well established. Your religion matters little—if at all—in this case. Are the police biased? Do we favor some over others? Certainly. But it's not about Hindu or Muslim. Our biases are boring. If the man calling us is rich and powerful, it matters little to us whether he heads to a mandir, mosque or church at the end of the day."

Having taken the measure of the man, Zahira nods. "If wealth and power is what you respect, Inspector Nandi, then it's even more apparent that I made the right decision in calling Mr. Drake."

"Perhaps, madam. But this country has outgrown the need for the English. We Hindus and Muslims best learn to work together to trace a future without them. You and your husband plan to leave India, no doubt, should the country shatter?"

The question surprises Zahira, if only for a second. "What business is it of yours?"

"None, Mrs. Choudhury. That's the tragedy and comedy of it."

ᓚᘏᗢ

SHE RETREATS TO HER bedroom, furious. Nandi's plan is to interrogate Motaleb and others of the household staff, and then to leave behind a constable for her protection while he investigates the area where Rahim was kidnapped.

She considers calling Drake again. This time to complain, alarmed by Nandi's insolence. His nonchalance. His unsolicited political hectoring. Her faith in the police, an ankle-deep puddle at the best of times, is fast evaporating. She weighs the bag of gold and cash in her hand. What other options does she have? She hates being a woman at that moment. A bit actor in every scene on the world's stage.

She goes out to the balcony, the ceremonial throne of so many housewives. Whatever investigation Nandi has conducted so far, it cannot be accused of being lengthy, as she soon spies him lumbering toward the police jeep, along with one of the constables. He senses her regard and looks up. She fashions a cowl from her scarf and pulls it over her head, takes a step back.

"Remember what we discussed, madam," Nandi says, his tone conversational, the words vague by design. "We have the situation well in hand. We will telephone you once we know more. It may be difficult, but I suggest you get some rest. These matters require a cool head."

SHE IS PACING HER room when there is a knock at the door. Nargis again. She composes herself. It will not do to let the servants see her distressed.

"What is it?"

"It's Motaleb, begum sahiba. He's asking to see you."

He is waiting for her at the bottom of the stairs, his chauffeur's hat literally in his hands and being wrung like wet cloth. She does not descend the stairs completely, rather stands near the foot to retain higher ground. Motaleb's eyes are red, his uniform askew and ill-fitting on his bony frame. On his best days, he looks old; today he looks ancient.

"I will ask you just one question, Motaleb, and on your honor and service to this family, I want the truth. Did you have anything to do with this?"

"I'd lay down my life before I let any harm come to sahib." Motaleb's voice is choked. "You must believe me in this."

She stands for a full minute in silence, observing him. He shrinks further under her gaze.

"Wait here," she says.

She visits the lavatory and declares to Allah her niyat, the intention to cleanse herself ritually and why. Then she quickly performs a wudhu—washes her face, feet, mouth, ears and arms. In order. She ends with a quick prayer bearing witness to God and his prophet, her right index finger pointed to the sky.

Ritually and spiritually transformed by her ablutions, she visits the library, a long room whose shelf-lined walls hold well over five thousand books in Bangla, English, Farsi, Hindi, Urdu and Arabic—collected across several generations of the Choudhury dynasty. On ordinary days it is her favorite room, and this evening, warmed by a day's worth of sunlight that has poured in through the large windows that face south, it is redolent with the scent of old pages, leather and mahogany. She stands on a chair to reach one of the higher shelves, which holds but a solitary tome—the family Koran, more than a hundred years old and wrapped in protective red cloth. On its first pages, inscribed in the careful hands of Choudhury patriarchs, are the birthdates and names of every child born to the family.

Motaleb is waiting where she left him. She thrusts the book before him. "Put your hand on this."

His eyes flare with recognition.

"Put your hand on this and swear that you speak the truth."

He reaches for the book tentatively and flinches just before touching it, as though scalded. "I'm not cleansed. I haven't performed the Maghrib prayers yet."

"Then do so. I can wait. Don't bother going to the servant's lavatories. Use the one here."

He does. She puts the book on a side table. Motaleb takes a long time to finish, and when he emerges, his rolled-up trouser legs attesting to the thoroughness of his efforts, he approaches the Koran as one would a wild, dangerous animal.

"Place your hand on it and swear to me that all you say is true," she says when he wavers. "Why do you hesitate?"

"It's not because I don't speak the truth, begum sahiba," he says, impatience entering his voice for the first time. "It's just that this book belongs to the family. I've seen it ever since I began working here."

"The Koran is the Koran whether in a mansion or a hovel."

"As you say." Murmuring a quick prayer, he places his right hand—the palm cupped so that only his fingers and wrist touch the surface—on the holy book.

"I swear on Allah that what I said to you was true—I'd lay down my life before letting any harm come to Rahim Sahib."

"Very well," she says. "I believe you."

"Thank you, begum sahiba." He looks relieved, then as though he might again cry.

"If I may ask, what did the police say that they're going to do?"

She sits on a chair by the wall. "They'll pursue their investigations, but we can't approach the thugs with the ransom."

"And what do you make of their advice?"

"I have little faith in the inspector, Nandi," she says, her exhaustion making her candid.

"Neither do I, begum sahiba."

"Then what are we to do?"

He looks around to see if they are alone, and once satisfied that they are, lowers his voice. "If you will permit me, I might have a suggestion. Let us go and meet them. We can't leave sahib's fate in the hands of this bumbling inspector. These kidnappers seemed a dangerous sort to me. Who knows what they will do if they get wind of the fact that we've spoken to the police."

She sits back. It had occurred to her to defy the police and meet the abductors with the ransom directly. A risky approach, but was it not superior to sitting and waiting?

"But Nandi Babu advises us to wait."

Forgetting himself, Motaleb leans forward, his voice coaxing, determined. "What policeman wouldn't, begum sahiba? They're busy with the Direct Action Day coming up tomorrow, not even thinking about Rahim Sahib's abduction. Every minute we wait puts him in greater danger."

"Would the police not be watching the place?"

"Perhaps, but even if they did, they don't know what to look for. I will give them half the ransom, and promise to reveal the location of the other half should they deposit Rahim Sahib safely in my hands."

She makes a show of long and thoughtful consideration. Her desperation has not blinded her; she needs to determine if the gleam in Motaleb's eyes is stoked by the old man's eagerness to act or by motives more sinister.

"This is not a half-bad plan, Motaleb," she finally says.

The chauffeur beams with delight. "Then you agree?"

"Yes, but for one thing. You cannot go by yourself."

"Should I take one of our guards with me, begum sahiba?"

She shakes her head slowly. "No. I have someone else in mind."

Shahryar & Anna

Washington, DC
September 2004

Faisal Ahmed's chambers are located at the corner of Vermont and K, in a building the same ubiquitous gray-brown granite of downtown DC. Walking up to it from the McPherson Square subway, Shar counts ten stories.

He takes the elevator to the seventh floor. Ahmed's suite is behind a white door with a gold decal that informs visitors that they have discovered Law Offices, the suite number below on a slightly more impressive brass plaque.

He awoke this morning hopeful, buoyed by the encouraging conversation he had with Ahmed the previous week at the Bangla School, when the lawyer mused that he might be able to help him find a way to remain in America. Ahmed was cautious in the promises he made, but in the intervening days those words of comfort had metastasized into unwarranted hope and optimism. So he came expecting an office behind a glass facade, a head-setted receptionist on the other side. In reality, he confronts rickety wooden dividers that demarcate desks, chairs, tall stacks of files; dingy blue carpeting in a room smelling of stale tobacco smoke.

Along the wall is a row of chairs where other clients wait. He offers a quick nod of greeting and sits down next to a burly Hispanic man in paint-splattered clothing, a hard hat on his lap. There are

66

others, including a young African couple who Shar guesses to be Somalian by the woman's manner of dress. They are occupied with a child of about a year old. The remaining handful of men and women appear to be South Asian like him.

He sits and picks up a magazine. He reads it for ten minutes before the door opens and a young woman comes and stands before him. She is tall, blond and unsmiling.

"Are you Mr. Choudhury?"

"Yes." He stands.

There is a Slavic drawl to her words. "Please come with me.Mr. Ahmed is waiting for you."

"Wait a minute," the male half of the Somalian couple interrupts. "Excuse me, please. But we come before him."

"That's fine," Shar says to the woman. "They're right. They can go first."

"Just come with me, please." She turns to the irate man. "I'm sorry, Mr. Magid. This is urgent. It won't take long. You're next in line."

The man retreats, clearly unhappy with the turn of events. The woman ushers Shar to a door at the far end of the suite and knocks.

"Come in!"

Faisal Ahmed is sandwiched between a window that looks out to Vermont Avenue and a desk. He stands and greets Shar in English. "Was just reading your CV!" He waves it around before shaking Shar's proffered hand.

"I hope you don't mind if Katerina joins us. She's my legal clerk."

"Not at all." Shar takes a seat and Katerina sits next to him, a notebook and pen in hand. She has a sharp profile and bright blue eyes.

"I'll make you repeat some of the things you told me at the community center. Katerina wasn't there and she needs this information for your file. Remind me of your status in America?"

"I came as a doctoral student on scholarship at GW six years ago. I finished my degree last year and am currently working here on an Optional Practical Training visa. That's only good for three more months. If my current employer doesn't sponsor me for a green card—and they've told me that they won't—then I have to leave. That's unless I find another employer willing to hire me."

"Right," Ahmed masticates the end of a Bic Cristal. "And who do you work for right now?"

"The Institute for Policy Dialogue. It's a federally funded—"

"I know it. Your director's Albert Volcker, right?"

"Um, yes," Shar says, both surprised and impressed. The briefest of glances is exchanged between Ahmed and Katerina.

"How did you know?"

Ahmed laughs in a disarming manner. His teeth are small and even. "I'm a lawyer in DC. It's a professional requirement to know people, Shar. By the way, your name. It's short for something, I'm guessing? Is it Sharif?"

It is his turn to laugh. "Sharif would be pretty easy. No, it's short for Shahryar."

Ahmed's half-grimace is meant to convey empathy, he surmises. *The concessions we must make to live in this country, eh?* it says.

"Hey, you should have heard all the variations on my name *I* heard when I first came here twenty-five years ago. I took to calling myself 'Faz.'"

"Mr. Ahmed told me you have a daughter here, Mr. Choudhury," Katerina interjects. "What is her citizenship?"

"American. So is her mother."

"And the two of you are not married?"

"No."

"Were you ever married?"

". . . No."

Katerina looks to Ahmed. "I'm asking because we have to consider the obvious."

"Good point, Katerina," Ahmed says. "Shar, I have to ask you, and sorry if it's too personal—is there any chance you could reconcile with the mother of your child? Marry? That would make our job a hell of a lot easier."

He shakes his head. "She has a boyfriend. They've been living together for several years now."

"That's a shame." Ahmed inflates his cheeks with air and releases it slowly, taps the pen against his desk. "I must say, Shar, and maybe you know this already, but I don't see a lot of options here."

"I see . . ."

His dejection must have been apparent because the lawyer hurries to reassure. "Now, now, I don't want you to think that this is hopeless. We've closed one avenue. We can consider others."

He scrutinizes Shar's CV. "Do you have computer skills? Can you program?"

"Just Microsoft Word, Excel. Things like that."

"What about engineering?"

"No. If you look at my CV . . ."

"Your PhD. What was the field?"

"Social Anthropology. My dissertation was on the fishermen of the Bangladeshi coast. On their social economy."

Ahmed looks up, his curiosity aroused. "That's an interesting choice. Why that particular topic?"

"My roots are there," Shar says, and does not elaborate.

"Okay, I think we'll have to be more creative than usual with your case. Why don't we call it a day for now, Shar? Katerina will be your primary contact point from now on. She'll be in touch with next steps."

"Thank you. We haven't discussed your fees."

Ahmed interrupts him with a raised hand. "Let's not worry about that right this moment. I have a sliding scale. My fees won't be anything you can't afford."

Katerina escorts him to the entrance, past the row of waiting clients, whose numbers have now been reinforced with several newcomers.

At the door, he turns to her. "You really think he can help?"

Her handshake is firm. "If anyone can, it's him."

CLAIRE

Rangoon, Burma
March 1942

Dr. Claire Drake awakens in stifling heat, her back stiff from lying on the cot that dominates the doctor's rest room. The radium-lined hands of her Omega Seamaster—a gift from Teddie on their first anniversary—tell her that it is a quarter to five in the afternoon. Before this brief respite, she was awake for twenty consecutive hours.

Head throbbing, she nonetheless stumbles to her feet. Of the eighteen medical officers in Rangoon General, she is the only woman, so it is not enough for her to simply meet the quality of work and industriousness of her male colleagues, but to exceed them significantly. Only then can she be seen as *keeping up with the lads*. As a woman doctor, she must run to stand still.

She lurches into the hallway. There is no shortage of wounded soldiers; a fresh batch of casualties has arrived from Singapore, which fell just weeks before to the Japanese.

Weaving slightly, she does her rounds in a fog until Nurse Pershing, an ornery Scot who has seen war assignments at both ends of the Empire—Singapore and Tangiers—nearly pushes her out the doors. "Heavens, Doc. You have to go home before you kill some poor lad from Sheffield who picked the wrong day to be shelled by the Japs."

She heeds the advice, and once outside, rejects the car allotted to her as an officer in favor of fresh air. Her white coat unfastened and flapping over her dress, she walks out to a main road devoid of people and cars other than for the occasional army lorries that zoom by. Rangoon has steadily emptied over the last few weeks as the threat of Japanese invasion has grown. Teddie speculates that it may only be days away now.

Unused to walking home, she orients herself using the golden peak of the Shwedagon Pagoda, the twin spires of St. Mary's, walks until the gloomy teak expanse of the Pegu Club arises in the distance.

She is on Budd's Road, which is lined with street stalls that display large pots of oily curries and noodles mere feet from open sewers. Her stomach growls with hunger at the sight, and she finds herself veering close to a stall boasting mounds of translucent noodles garnished with leaves that she cannot identify. The stall owner jumps up, her face alternating between alarm and elation at the potential of a customer of Claire's stature. The Burmese diners sitting on low wooden stools are more wary. Some scoot out of her way, but none rise or leave.

The stall owner lifts the lids of the pots one by one and sweeps a hand over each with a magician's flair, revealing in turn braised greens, tea leaf salad, lamb, chicken, and what Claire strongly suspects is curried frog.

"Thank you. That's alright," she says, losing her nerve at the last moment. She and Teddie were adventurous with the local cuisine when they first arrived. But they fell ill after a street-side lunch on their second week. Since then, his meals have always been taken at either home or the Pegu Club. But Claire has retained a weakness for Burmese food, particularly for mohinkhar, a unique concoction of rice noodles, fish broth, fried chickpeas and hot peppers. Her ayah, Myint, prepares it daily for her breakfast unless told otherwise.

Today, it is she who meets Claire at the gates of her house. Not yet twenty, Myint's slim, small-breasted profile is elegant in a green blouse and clinging yellow longyi. Her face, wide and smooth, breaks into a pool of sweetness whenever she smiles.

But her expression today is stern as she ushers Claire inside.

"What are you doing, thakinma? It is dangerous to walk home. Looters everywhere. Robbers. What happened to car?"

Amused, Claire gives her a quick embrace. "Pardon my sweaty clothes, Myint, but it's lovely to see you as well. I just couldn't sit in a blasted car after the day I've been through. I needed to clear my head."

"You want clear head? Stay home and clean house like me. I go to hospital and be doctor like you."

Claire throws her head back and laughs, feeling some of her exhaustion fall away. "I accept! How soon can you begin?"

Despite her amusement, she does not think the offer entirely devoid of merit. Recently, Claire has become convinced that the young woman is wasting her potential as a housekeeper, and has resolved to discuss with the matron at Rangoon General the possibility of enlisting Myint as a junior nurse.

Myint's father was their gardener before he passed from a heart attack two years before. He was under Claire's care at Rangoon General on his last day, and he extracted from her a promise to provide employment for his young daughter living in Kalay, who would be orphaned upon his passing, her mother having died at childbirth. Claire kept her word, and with Teddie's consent, sent for Myint to come work as an ayah. The girl proved a quick study in English, reaching fluency in a year; in addition to keeping their large house spotless, she has become a savant of both Continental and Burmese cooking.

"Were you able to get the pork chops?" Claire asks.

"Difficult. But I get it."

Claire appreciates the trouble Myint must have gone through. With the run on supplies in Rangoon only intensifying as the Japanese approach the city, meat was a rare find in the markets.

Myint offers to cook the meal, but Claire politely insists on a collaborative effort, the day being Claire and Teddie's fifth wedding anniversary. So the women slather the meat with salt, black pepper, crushed rosemary and the precious final drops of olive oil bought during a visit to Porto. Toss potatoes into a pot of salted boiling water for the mash.

The lights in the kitchen flicker off at one point, and this close to dusk, the darkness seems to plunge down on them. They light candles, set them on the counters, on the windowsill against the blood-cream sky.

Competing with the scent of broiling meat is that of jasmine, bailey, queen of the night and honeysuckle wafting in through the kitchen window. There are sounds too—from magpies returning from a day's foraging that alight on the massive rain tree across the street. As the women cook, a particularly large specimen boldly hops down the length of a branch that comes within touching distance of the kitchen window. It fixes Claire with an amber-eyed regard. She steps back and looks for something disposable to toss at the bird. Settling on a potato, she is about to throw it when a hand gently clamps around her wrist.

Her ayah's face is dark with disapproval. "No, thakinma. They are spirit birds, nats."

"Fine." Claire drops her hand. "But they're such horrid creatures."

"It is gone. Look." Myint gestures to the abandoned branch.

Minutes later, assuaged by the bird's departure and satisfied by the extent of her contributions to the evening's meal, she departs for a bath.

Their house is a fin de siècle originally built for a British major, but the bathroom is newer, with marble floors and modern fittings that Teddie requested prior to their arrival. In it, she turns the crank so that the large casement window yawns out into the dusk. There are flashes in the distance. The rumble of thunder. A storm is coming to break the sun's siege at last. Until then, the cool water already drawn in the claw-foot tub must do.

She sinks in and remains until the liquid turns cloudy. She emerges—wrapped in a bathrobe, her hair in a towel—to a house that smells of rosemary pork. The clock on the wall informs her that it is half past seven. Teddie will be home soon.

In the kitchen, Myint has already taken the chops out and set them on the counter. Claire melts butter for the potato mash, and is instructing Myint on how to prepare the string beans when there is a sharp knock on the front door.

She opens it to two soldiers, who offer her smart salutes. They are men from Teddie's company. Claire clutches the front of her bathrobe, hoping that the heat she feels on her face does not show.

"What's happened? Where's Colonel Drake?"

"We're here at his request, madam," says the taller of the men. He has dark hair and blue eyes. His name, according to the name stitched on his uniform, is Waugh.

"They've given the evacuation order," elaborates the shorter, blonder soldier—Geary. "Colonel Drake is safe. He's asked us to collect you so you can join him at the train station."

"The hospital. I'm done with my rounds today, but I have to be there."

The men step inside. "The hospital staff and patients will be evacuated by ship. You'll be taking the train with the other officers," Waugh says.

"I have a duty to my patients."

"My apologies, madam. I'm only following instructions."

She bites her lip, overwhelmed by what needs doing. They have been hearing about the Japanese for so long, their exploits, their relentless encroachment on the British Empire that it was easy to think of them as myth. No longer.

"I suggest that we hurry, madam." Waugh gestures to the eastern hills through the open door. She follows his finger.

When she first saw them from the bathroom window, the flashes in the sky she assumed to be lightning, the rumbles thunder. She realizes now how gravely she was mistaken. Their nightmares are now in the clouds, fighter planes circling them from above like metal vultures.

She sighs. "I don't suppose we have time for pork chops?"

SHE AND MYINT HAVE kept their most essential things ready to be packed for weeks. Now the two women rush to prepare. After helping Myint gather her modest belongings into a leather bag, she crams a suitcase with clothes and slings over her shoulder a panic bag that holds her signed first edition Graham Greenes, photographs and jewelry. Waugh and Geary assist, promise that the RAF will do their best to deliver the rest to her afterward.

They run out. No more than ten minutes have passed since the men arrived, but the rumble and flash of the raid is much closer. Sirens shatter the air as bright blooms burst like mustard flowers against the sky.

They pile into the Lanchester parked in the driveway. The men sit in the front. Geary takes the wheel. They hurtle out of the gate and roar down Halpin Road. Turn sharply right at the intersection onto Godwin, the car's rear wheels screeching and wreathing in smoke. They pass the parade grounds from which panicked crowds stream out pointing at the sky. A heavily pregnant woman slips and falls, vanishes under the stampede in seconds. Claire looks away.

Geary is melded to the steering wheel, untouched by the chaos around him. The Lanchester's carriage strains and groans as he swerves to avoid hitting the pedestrians who stray into their path. One man is a moment late to move and the car strikes him with a sickening crunch. He spins in the air for what seems an eternity before landing on the footpath, where he lies prone.

Claire and Myint scream in horror but the car does not stop. Claire seizes Waugh's shoulder and he turns. "We can't just leave him there. We have to do something."

Waugh looks her in the eyes, unmoved. "We *are* doing something, madam. We are taking you to safety."

They reach the rail station gates, which are locked and barred. British soldiers stand in formation in front, brandishing rifles at the crowds exhorting them to be let in.

The men part to let their car pass. Geary stops the vehicle and displays his identification to a soldier who approaches them.

"Who're you transporting?" he asks, following a cursory glance at the card.

"Captain Claire Drake, RAMC," Claire replies.

"She's a doctor?" The man is incredulous, addressing the question to Geary, then hastily saluting her. "Why isn't she at the wharves for the medevac?"

"You can speak to me directly, Corporal. I'm neither deaf nor a child. We're here to join my husband, Colonel Drake."

The corporal reassesses, then shrugs. "You can go in, but not your girl," he says, pointing at Myint.

"She's with me," Claire speaks with authority. She takes Myint's hand in hers and finds that it is trembling.

"I can see that, madam. But this isn't up to you or me to decide." The man disengages when he sees a commotion up ahead— civilians scuffling with soldiers.

"You blokes make her understand, please," are his parting words as he rushes toward the crowd.

"She's not going back," Claire warns, but when she looks to Waugh for support, he does not meet her eyes. Geary stares straight ahead, fiddling with his identification with one hand, the other on the wheel. The car's engine still runs, but the gate remains barred.

"We must apologize, madam," Waugh says, "Geary and I discussed this before arriving at your residence. We decided not to tell you because we thought it might delay us. Time was of the essence."

"What're you saying?" she asks even though she knows the answer, has known it all along. She looks back to the crowds. Some are screaming at the soldiers to let them into the station, others are fleeing for shelter.

Some lie on the ground. Unmoving.

Not a single face among them is white.

⸎

THEY HEAD TO THE officers' cabins at the front of the train. In contrast to the chaos outside, the platform is a showcase of organization and efficiency: soldiers load luggage while officers supervise, their families guided to the cars by solicitous conductors. The wives and children appear frightened but composed, the officers and soldiers tense.

She spots her husband, who wears an army greatcoat despite the heat. She also recognizes the officer next to him. Selwyn. A bachelor, he has visited their house once or twice for supper, but his crass sense of humor and endless thirst for scotch left her unimpressed.

Teddie is tall and handsome, with deep-set gray eyes. He nods to Waugh and Geary, who have carried Claire's trunk forward.

"What's the matter?" he asks Claire, seeing her expression.

"You need to tell the soldiers at the gate that Myint will be joining us. She's waiting there now."

He moves in close and puts his hands on her shoulders. "Claire, the trains are for His Majesty's subjects only. This comes down from McLeod himself."

"We can't leave her behind, in . . . in this."

He holds her gaze for a moment, then says. "No. No, of course we won't."

He takes Waugh and Geary aside and has a furtive discussion that catches Selwyn's eye; he drifts close. The group parts to accommodate him.

He soon explodes. "Are you joking, Drake? Just who do you think you are?"

As Teddie struggles to contain him, Selwyn confronts Claire. "Are you behind this nonsense? You think the rest of us like leaving our staff behind? This train would be full of bloody Burmese if we had a choice."

She does not respond, holds his gaze until he is forced to look away.

Teddie, his face grim, puts a hand on his shoulder. "That's enough, Selwyn. You will not speak to my wife that way."

Selwyn shrugs and steps back. "Sorry. Sorry. Just a bit stressed from all this. My apologies to Claire, of course."

"I've had a chat with Waugh and Geary," Teddie tells her as Selwyn wanders away, lighting a cigarette. "We can't take Myint with us, but there are separate evacs for soldiers and staff. Waugh and Geary will make sure that she gets on the latter."

"Are those trains also?"

"Trains for the soldiers. Lorries, cars and whatever else we can spare for the staff."

"What assurance do we have that she'll make it to her village?"

"There are no assurances for any of us."

"I'm not leaving unless I know she'll be safe."

"The best way to guarantee her safety is for her to leave this station as soon as possible."

"What do you mean?"

"Come with me."

The platform is now emptying. A group of soldiers sweeps from end to end to ensure that the last of the luggage has been loaded. He leads her to the head of the train, past the engine car so she can witness what lies on the other side—army sappers scurrying with sticks of dynamite, depositing them in strategic corners—along the tracks, by the walls. Once they leave, nothing will be left behind for the Japanese to use.

There is a sound like firecrackers near the gates. Rifle shots, she registers dully. Nausea floods her senses.

Teddie takes her hand. "We need to go, darling."

DINNER IS SERVED IN the dining car a half hour after the train begins to move—cabbage soup and pot roast, followed by pink jelly. One officer rescued several bottles of claret from his personal cellar before leaving. They are opened and shared. Claire, who has little appetite, finds herself asking for a second glass, a rare occurrence.

Normally, the men would retreat to the smoking car after dinner while the women stayed behind, but tonight the gravity of the situation binds the sexes together. They remain sitting long after the tables are cleared, the women sucking on boiled sweets, the men, cigars.

Selwyn joins them at their table without asking and acts as though nothing happened on the platform. Teddie tries to catch Claire's eyes, but she stares straight ahead. She has not spoken a word since they left the station.

Selwyn lights a cigar. Teddie opens the window an inch and the smoke drifts outside. The smudged outlines of Burmese flora rush by against the night sky.

A long journey awaits them. The train will cross Mandalay,

the ancient royal capital replete with stupas and palaces, before it reaches Myitkyina, the city where the English summer. From there they will fly to Imphal, only to take yet another train to Chittagong.

"We'll never hold our heads up in this country again," Selwyn mutters. He is gaunt but athletic. With his thin trim mustache, he would be considered handsome if not for the mouth below, which is always on the edge of a sneer.

"Who is the CO in Chittagong?" asks Teddie in an apparent attempt to change the subject.

"Some odious little Irishman. We served together in Kirkuk."

"Explain."

"Oh, you know, typical state school specimen. You'll know him when you see him. He's scrubbed his accent, but can't do much about the red hair and freckles."

"Right," Teddie says awkwardly. But for the current CO being Irish, Selwyn may well have described Claire, whose look of contempt he misses.

He taps ashes out of the window, grinning. "The only thing I'm looking forward to in that backwater is his reaction when he finds out that he's to be under my command. He'll have kittens!"

"About that," Teddie says. "I'll be in Imphal the first few months, under Slim. I do hope you'll keep an eye on Claire in my absence."

Selwyn smiles. "After our little incident on the platform, I might keep two."

Claire rises. "Excuse me."

She walks to the back of the train, goes through the end-door and out into the veranda, where the brakeman and a brace of waiters stand, smoking, all Burmese. Her sudden appearance puts them into wide-eyed shock that further deepens when she asks for a cigarette. The brakeman lights it for her and steps inside with the others. A few minutes later, she hears the door open. Teddie leans on the railing beside her.

Minutes pass in which they say nothing, only observe the darkened Burmese plains fall away from them.

"How'd you know I'd be here?" she asks eventually.

"It's a train, Claire. There are but two ways to go. Unless you'd jumped out the window and were running back to Rangoon."

"How could you say that to Selwyn? Asking that rude twit to keep an eye on me as though I'm some child who needs minding?"

Teddie sighs. "Like it or not, he's to be CO while we're there. It's best to have him as an ally. Besides, every time he's said something daft in the past you've hit him for a six. I don't imagine that tradition changing."

She weighs her response. Teddie means well, and in him she rarely detects the disdain with which other officers speak of the colonies and their native inhabitants. But when he accepted his assignment in Burma, she noted the eagerness with which he wore his new mantle of authority. It did not change him, but brought to the fore an easy arrogance that had not been apparent in the first years of their marriage.

Perhaps that should not have surprised her. The blood in his veins ran from purple to blue if one went back a few generations. The portrait gallery in his family home in Hampshire is an endless array of admirals, sea lords, marquises and earls, until arriving at their roots in the morganatic branches of the House of Hesse-Darmstadt.

She is of humbler stock, her father the owner of a construction company that profited off the wave of demolitions that befell the manor homes in England at the turn of the century. A man who, even after becoming quietly wealthy, insisted on preserving the memories of his childhood by passing them on to his four daughters, of whom Claire is the third. They never bought a car, nor moved out of the small Yorkshire farmhouse where Claire was born. Following her entrance to King's College, she was told to survive on four shillings a week and to utilize luxuries such as cabs for *only the direst emergencies.*

It was one such emergency that facilitated her first meeting with Teddie. Having taken a hackney cab to St. Pancras to catch her train home for Easter Holiday, Claire realized with horror that she had left her wallet at home. With the train about to leave in minutes, Teddie, alighting from a nearby cab, approached to pay on her behalf, and afterward lent a hand with her luggage. He refused her offer to repay him when she returned, and countered with the request for a *stroll along the Thames and a coffee.* She was reluctant to take things further once she learned of his social status, but his easy charm and persistence made her lower her guard. When they announced their betrothal a few months later, neither family was thrilled, but each acquiesced to the enthusiasm of the couple. Her father, of sufficient means given his thriving business, and unwilling to be shown up by his toff in-laws-to-be, was willing to spare no expense. However, the wedding was a restrained one at Claire's request; she felt mortified by the attention the young and eligible Theodore's marriage was generating from a bored press.

As she stares at him, Teddie takes her hand. "This day hasn't caught us at our best. But I know that better days will come."

He retrieves an object from his jacket pocket that gleams silver in the starlight. "I'd hoped to give you this under more pleasant circumstances. I didn't forget, you know."

"It's lovely. Thank you." She turns the flask over in her hands. It is small, concave on one side. Even in the dark, she can appreciate the exquisite craftsmanship.

"Turn it over," he says, and she does. In the dim light, she can discern engraved letters—her initials surrounded by a wreath of leaves. She traces them with a finger.

"Happy anniversary, Claire Louise Drake."

"Happy anniversary."

"Is this as good as it gets, Theodore?" she asks after they kiss and embrace. Teddie's back is to the railing, and over his shoulders she can no longer see the flash and fire of bombs, a faint carpet of lights dwindling in the distance the only evidence of the city she has called home for the last three years.

"What do you mean?"

"Is this as good as we can be here in the colonies? Taking the best of it and then running when things get hard? What was it that Forster said about us? That we're cold and odd, moving like ice-streams through these lands? I'm beginning to think he was right."

"If there were anything I could do to get Myint on this train, I'd have done it, but we did the next best thing. Waugh and Geary are two of my best men. They'll make sure she's part of that evac. Myint will make it north to safety. I'm sure of it."

A CABLE FROM WAUGH and Geary awaits them in Chittagong, confirming that they did put Myint on the staff evac, but despite urgent telegrams to their remaining contacts in Burma, no further news about the men and women on that convoy arrives as the Japanese sweep into the country and erect a wall of silence across the border.

Claire and Teddie are put up in a bungalow called The Hermitage at the city's western edge. It overlooks the Bay of Bengal and is set atop a hill at the end of a gravel path. The house is staffed with a bearer, two maids, a dorji for clothes she might wish tailored, a chaprasi to ferry messages from Teddie's office to home, a khidmatgar to wait tables at dinner, and a chef who can cook both Western and Indian dishes. A gleaming '37 Hispano-Suiza is provided for transportation, along with a driver.

But over the course of the first week, she arranges for alternative employment for most of their staff, retaining only the services of the bearer and the maid. Teddie protests, but only mildly. He will be lit-

tle impacted by these decisions, stationed as he is in Imphal, coordi-
nating the Burma Theatre as generals Slim and Wingate plot how to
recapture the country. He would work in Chittagong no more than
two weeks out of every twelve. In his absence, she explains to him,
she does not wish to live in a house full of strangers. But they both
know the truth, that the fewer people she is surrounded by at her
house, the less the chance that she will become close to one as she
did with Myint, the less chance that she will leave someone behind
should they once again be forced to flee.

She reports for duty the same week. Unlike Rangoon, the garrison hospital in Chittagong is small—a casualty clearing station
that provides post-operative care to patients already treated at
the field dressing stations and advanced surgical units. Including
Claire, there are four duty doctors, a staff of twelve nurses and a
handful of orderlies who assist them day to day.

The war continues in the east. Day after day, soldiers wounded
or dead, and refugees arrive after epic treks through the Arakan
jungles, emaciated and swaying with hunger, their eyes yellow
from typhoid and cholera. Once they recover, she gently inquires
of them if they have been in Kalay recently, if they know of the
convoys that made it out of Rangoon on the eve of the invasion.
She describes Myint, hoping that someone has seen her, heard of
something, anything.

Teddie leaves, and while he is away, the officers' club offers
her some respite from the war. But other than the occasional pink
gin by the bar, she takes little advantage of the club's facilities: she
misses the film nights, declines invitations to the all-ranks dances
with officers and sergeants from Chittagong and those furloughed
from Burma with injuries that vanish during conga sessions by the
bar, the men dancing until they strip off their uniforms to reveal
undershirts dark with sweat, the women until their finger-waved
hair wilts and hangs on their cheeks, the war forgotten. Later,

under the blue haze of cigar smoke and above the detritus of broken glass, they slump against each other, swaying to "A Nightingale Sang in Berkeley Square," forging rambling off-key choruses to "The White Cliffs of Dover."

She restricts her friendships to women she meets at the club, and over her first month in Chittagong a group emerges with her at the nucleus. All officers' wives like her, but unlike her, none officers themselves. She forges the closest bond with Rachel, a pale, sad-eyed beauty from Cumbria whose husband, Harold, is also stationed in Imphal.

The women, all of whom live close to each other, play rummy, bridge and carom at each other's homes, the last leaving talc on Claire's drawing room floor each time she dusts the board. They venture out as a group. For a picnic to the beach, Claire packs a basket full of bully beef, cottage loaf from a local bakery run by a Welsh woman, and cabbage salad. They bring swimsuits but never quite gather up the nerve to wear them and splash on the surf; under the watchful, disapproving eyes of the locals, they feel too exposed.

Instead, they drink gin from their flasks as tiny crabs dance nearby, just feet from the line of the surf. Rachel bursts into tears at one point and admits that she and her husband Harold are having troubles. They console her the best they can, even as she suddenly throws her sandwich into the water and screams "Sod it all!" and laughs.

The flock of local children watching them crowd in. Claire offers one corned beef on bread, but the child's mother pulls him away, offended, assuming the meat is pork.

♁

DECIDING TO VISIT RACHEL the next day, she crosses the narrow tree-lined road between their homes. But when she knocks on the door there is no response. She walks in to find her friend in bed, awake, staring at the ceiling.

"Hullo, dear," Claire says, concerned.

Rachel does not speak. The clock says it is half past ten. Seconds pass before Rachel trains her eyes down to Claire and offers a wan smile. In a low husky voice, she says, "You're a pleasant surprise."

Claire takes a seat by her bed. "When did you wake up?"

"At seven."

"And you've been in bed the whole time?"

"Yes."

"Oh." As she has gotten to better know Rachel, Claire has discovered that despite her breezy manner and endearing quirks, her friend has a dark cellar in her, full of broken things. Fearful of encroaching too deep, she has probed Rachel on this only gingerly.

But this day she does not need to, for Rachel says, "I don't know what's wrong with me, Claire. I feel so black sometimes, like some whirlpool is always pulling me down."

Claire takes her hand. "There are doctors who specialize in these things now. I can have a psychiatrist talk to you if you like."

Rachel snatches her hand away. "Why? You think I'm a lunatic?"

"Of course not. We all go through hard times when we're not at our mental best."

"Did you?"

"At times."

"And did you talk to a psychiatrist?"

"No. My work was busy enough to take my mind off things."

"Fine then. All I need is something to do."

Claire bites her lower lip, assessing. "Alright. Maybe there's something we can do about that as well."

꧁꧂

SHE IS COMPLETING HER morning rounds two weeks later, on a Sunday, when she hears a whisper from behind. "Psst, you there, pretty lass."

Rachel looks demure in her white-and-blue Red Cross uniform and hat. Her friend has excelled as a Voluntary Aid Detachment nurse so far. Amongst the other privileged wives and daughters of the well-to-do and powerful, she has stood out, performing less pleasant duties such as cleaning bedpans without complaint, quickly learning to administer injections (she admitted to having practiced on limes beforehand). In the process she has become someone Claire has begun to rely upon.

"I thought I made it clear that I'm to be addressed as Captain Drake on hospital grounds," Claire says with mock sternness.

Rachel covers her mouth with her fingers and feigns distress. "Beggin' your pardon, ma'am!"

She draws closer. "Is your evening sorted out? I was thinking of getting a few drinks at the club tonight."

Claire looks out the window. The sun is shining bright, the leaves of the rain trees on the front grounds laved with the subtlest of winds.

"I've a better idea," she says. "When did you last catch a sunset on the beach?"

❧

WHEN SHE WALKS OUT to the lawn at the end of the day, Rachel is already waiting, looking smart with coiffed hair and red lips.

"What's all this?"

"Don't flatter yourself, darling. It's not for you."

"That's a relief. Harold's back from Imphal, is he?"

Rachel does not answer.

As a captain, Claire is permitted the use of a hospital gharry— an open-top jeep—and a driver, a fellow Yorkie lad named Joe. The three drive to the beach, no more than ten minutes passing before the car's tires are cutting deep grooves into the sand and the salt air is lapping their faces.

They head east along the sea, which is calm this day—a deep gray and blue. Rachel stands up so that the tail of her yellow-and-black scarf streaks in the air and lets out a cry of joy. Claire bursts out laughing.

The jeep begins to slow, stopping beside a fishing boat made of light-colored wood. Twenty paces long, its prow—painted a fading red—surges up in a dramatic angle.

Joe twists around in his seat to face them. "I know the fellow who owns the boat, Captain. On Sundays, he's happy to take people out for rides on it. Ever been out on one of these?"

THEY ARE SOON DRIFTING along the glassy shores of the bay, their faces held out to the beat of a kinder sun. Rachel—who managed to produce a flask filled with particularly fine scotch—is asleep at the stern, snoring softly. Claire is in the middle of the boat, looking out to the shore, where Joe and the jeep are tiny scale versions of themselves. Hashim, the boatman standing at the prow, has not spoken a word since they came on board, focusing his energies on rowing. He is stocky and wide, his hair shot with premature gray and brushing his shoulders. A boy of six or seven sits by his feet and looks to Claire and Rachel with wonder in his eyes, his mouth slightly agape.

Claire smiles at him, attempts a mixture of English and Bangla. "Hullo. Tomar ki nam?"

The boy gives a shy smile and squirms closer to his father. He is bare-chested, his face thin, hair long and bleached reddish from the sun.

"His name is Jamir," says Hashim.

"Oh. Jolly good to meet you, Jamir." She searches her purse. The Hershey bar is a bit melted in the heat, some of the chocolate leaking through the corners of the silver foil. She holds it out to him.

Jamir looks from her to his father, who nods and says something to him in Bangla.

Jamir reaches out for the sweet, takes it and turns it over in his hands.

"You should eat it now, or put it under the prow. Or it'll melt."

Hashim translates for his son, and he chooses the latter option.

"Where did you learn to speak English?" she asks the man.

"When not fish, take sahibs and memsahibs for boat ride."

"Oh," she flails around for a follow-up. "Your son. Does he go to school?"

"Yes, memsahib. Class One," Hashim says with quiet pride.

"Claire!"

They all start at Rachel's shrill tone. "Stop interrogating those poor dears. Let the man get back to rowing."

She looks to the sky, and then addresses Hashim in loud, over-enunciated English. "It's getting late. Can you take us back, please?"

"Yes, memsahib." Hashim begins to turn the boat. Claire gives him an apologetic smile and returns to the stern.

"What were you three yammering about?" Rachel asks.

"Just chatting to pass the time."

Rachel laughs, incredulous. "And what fascinating insights did they have to offer on current events?"

"I wasn't asking about current events. I was asking about the man and his son."

"Whatever for?"

"Never mind." She shakes her head, wondering why they were friends.

‿‿‿

THEY RETURN TO SHORE, where Rachel shoves a wad of rupees in the boatman's hand and heads for the jeep. The sun is setting in a great conflagration across the bay, giving the water a rainbow shimmer. In another part of the sky, lush dark clouds are massing.

Claire takes the boatman's rough, calloused hand in both of hers and holds it for a beat. "Thank you, Hashim. That was quite lovely. I do hope to ride in your boat again one day."

For the briefest moment, the boatman's impassive mask slips to show surprise. "Bye, memsahib."

She pinches the cheek of Jamir, who still holds the Hershey bar—uneaten—in his hands and is looking at her with fascinated awe. "And you. Keep up with your studies, young man."

They drive for no more than five minutes before there is a bang and a hiss. Joe parks by a stand of firs and inspects the damage. It is the left front tire. They have driven over the jagged lip of a rock that protrudes from the sand.

"What are the chances?" He removes a toolbox from the back of the car. "It doesn't normally take long, but I need something to brace the jack on."

Rachel sighs with exasperation. "Fine. But do try and hurry, Joe."

They descend and sit on a log embedded on the beach as Joe begins his work. Claire removes her shoes and sinks her toes into the sand, where the day's warmth lingers.

She gestures to Rachel's made-up visage. "So, when did Harold get back?"

Her friend looks away.

Claire is mortified. "For goodness' sake, Rachel."

"What do you mean?"

"Don't tell me you're having an affair."

Rachel is sullen. "You of all people should know what it's like to not have a happy marriage."

"I certainly do not! What are you implying?"

"Come on, Claire. You're here. He's in Imphal. You hardly ever talk about him. And when you do, I don't hear in your voice that you miss him. And how hard is it for him to request a transfer if he wants to be here with you?"

Claire sputters, Rachel's words a cold slap. In the first year of their marriage, she and Teddie could hardly be kept apart, writing lengthy missives to each other in the period when he was assigned to Cairo and she was still completing her medical training in London, exchanging parcels, his maddeningly creative—alluring Arabian perfumes contained in bottles shaped like daggers, boxes of dates packed in straw, and once (what would become her most cherished gift) a tiny vial of sand that he claimed to have scraped off the stones of the Great Pyramid. Her parcels—containing everything from writing paper, spats, shirts from Hawes & Curtis, a barograph and shoes with soles of vulcanized rubber—were less exotic in comparison, predictions of his needs rather than divinations of his wants. So she compensated for her lack of imagination with affection; when he returned to London they would rush to each other, their meetings collisions of physical and emotional need.

It is true that she has not much thought about her husband while he has been in Imphal. And she is unsure which is worse—the fact that they have not written each other since he left or that she is only noticing this now.

She mounts a weak defense. "He's a colonel. The Japs already have Burma and are about to invade Bengal, for heaven's sake. Wingate needs him in Imphal. And we have a million sick patients and just four doctors here."

Rachel opens her mouth as though to answer, but closes it with a snap. She frowns. "Do you hear that?"

Claire focuses and is about to say no, when she hears it too. A faint whine growing stronger by the second. An air-raid siren begins keening, its plaintive wail swallowed by the ocean's hungry maw. They rush toward the trees, the women hand in hand, their row forgotten; Joe brings up the rear. They huddle under the stand of pines as the buzz builds to a roar. Rachel points to the darkening eastern sky and shouts.

She sees it then. A bomber, gliding down in a straight line toward the beach, a trail of smoke from its tail fluttering like a pennant of defeat. On its body is the flag of Japan—the red sun on a white backdrop stark against the veil of the fast-falling dusk.

Shahryar & Anna

Washington, DC
September 2004

Shar receives a phone call at home on Saturday. He does not recognize the number, but the voice on the other end is unmistakable.

"Hey, Niten," he says. "New number?"

"I'm calling from the office. Yes, on a Saturday. Such is life."

"You have to put in the crazy hours to make the crazy money," Shar says with a laugh. He met Niten when they were in Georgetown, years before. His friend is close to making junior partner at a K Street law firm.

"How's the battle to stay in this beautiful country of mine?"

Shar briefs him on his encounter with Ahmed and the subsequent meeting.

"Is he the only person you've met with?" Niten asks when he finishes.

"I've talked to others. But he's the most positive of the bunch."

"Hold on," Niten says. There is the noise of him opening a drawer. "Tell me the guy's name again."

Shar does, spells it for good measure. "Why, though?"

"Just want to look him up. I don't want to speak ill of my kind, but I trust immigration lawyers about as far as I can throw them. Let me run him through my network and see what the verdict is. How much is he asking for a retainer?"

"He doesn't want anything now. Said he has a sliding scale and that his fee is affordable."

"Can I ask you something?"

"Of course."

After a pause, Niten asks, "Why did you leave all this stuff until so late, Shar?"

When Shar says nothing, Niten adds, "Look man, I'm sorry. It wasn't my place to ask."

"No. No. It is. I've been asking myself the same question."

"Have you told Anna why you weren't here for those first three years?"

"No. Neither has Val. Every time I think about telling her, I convince myself that she's not old enough."

"That's true," Niten says. "But maybe you never are."

∽

SHAR CALLS KATERINA ON Monday, after work. Apart from him, his office—a three-story brownstone on Wisconsin Avenue—is deserted.

"I was calling to see if there were any developments," he tells her when she answers the phone. "I have barely two months left on my work visa now."

"There are some things that Mr. Ahmed is working on. But as he said, this is an unusual case, Mr. Choudhury. We're doing the best we can, but a lot of it will depend on you."

"If it's an issue of payment, I can certainly—"

"I have some clients waiting," Katerina interrupts. "Why don't we talk about this in more detail in person?"

"I can hop in a cab during my lunch hour tomorrow."

"No. I was thinking that we could meet outside of work. Sometime. Just you and me. Maybe this coming Friday. Around seven. Do you know Dragonfly in Dupont Circle?"

"I do."

"Well, I'll see you then."

"See you." He ends the call, more puzzled than ever.

HE HAS ANNA FOR the entire afternoon the next day. He collects her from school and they travel to Chinatown, to her favorite restaurant, where sushi labeled and covered with transparent plastic lids passes by on a conveyor belt.

Anna eats California rolls through deconstruction, nori hanging off her plate like iridescent black tape. She finishes the first and is working on the second when she asks if they eat fish in Bangladesh.

His thoughts flash to Jamir, whose fate was so tied to that of the sea. "Yes. It's a land of rivers. Some people even eat it three times a day."

"Oh."

"I used to eat fish with my hands, just like you," he adds, eager to trap her interest before it evaporates. "But it was cooked, and"—he rubs together an index finger and thumb—"I had to pick out all the bones."

He pays the bill when they finish and realizes that he has few ideas for the remainder of their time together. There are two hours still before he is to return Anna to Val.

They stand in the courtyard between the MCI Center and the Gallery Place. A movie and sports event have concluded simultaneously. People stream out.

He kneels so that they are level. The gesture makes him feel weak. "What do you want to do next?"

He considers suggesting the scavenger hunt at the National Gallery, which was nearby. They discovered it last year. They were in the museum, standing before *Christ Cleansing the Temple*, tucked in a corner of the East Wing. In it, against blocky architecture and a sapphire sky, Jesus was resplendent in a blood-red robe as he whipped a group of usurers, his pose imbued with a dancer's grace. In one corner of the painting, a naked boy reached out for a parent lost in the pandemonium.

He was explaining to her the meaning of the artist's name, El Greco—The Greek—when he noticed a girl and her mother scribbling something on a piece of paper, gesturing to the painting with excitement. Consulting the security guard solved the mystery. It was a scavenger hunt. Children were handed a piece of paper with clues they must find in the paintings and sculptures in the labyrinthine floors of the gallery. Anna loved discovering them the first day, being awarded a Lincoln Memorial pin for successful completion.

But he remembers now how her enthusiasm for the game dropped with subsequent visits.

"I've an idea," he says. "We can go to Air and Space. There's a new exhibit on World War Two bombers from Japan that I really want you to see."

She shakes her head. "I already did that last week."

"With who?" He speaks before realizing that he may not want the answer.

"With Da—with Jeremy."

A part of him—the one not immediately engulfed by irrational jealousy—is grateful to Anna, amazed that she would have such consideration for his feelings at this young an age.

He manages a smile. "You can call him Dad. We agreed on that, remember?"

ICHIRO

Central Burma
March 1942

Lieutenant Ichiro Washi sits at his desk, leaning over a leather-bound journal. He is in a hospital that has been converted into a makeshift garrison for the conquering Japanese. The three other officers in the room are all asleep. Not daring to turn on the bulb that hangs over him, Ichiro uses the light of the moon streaming in through the window to write.

He looks outside for inspiration. The moon hangs a palm's breadth above the horizon, its reflection undulating like a ghostly finger on the Irrawaddy, which traverses the length of the country before emptying out into the Andaman Sea near the port of Rangoon, the capital of Burma and the jewel in the crown of the British Empire, a city whose conquest has consumed the nights of Japanese commanders with fever dreams.

They came in like a pincer, the Japanese, through Tenasserim in the south and Pegu in the north, with plans for the two armies to join hands in Rangoon in a month's time, an event whose prospects brighten by the day.

They never expected their invasion of the country to be this simple, in this land of mountains that create endless mazes of peaks and valleys, where an ambush could hide in any of the jungles that look so majestic from above but in actuality pulsate with tropical disease and parasites. Given the land's natural resistance to invasion, the pathetic fight put up by the British was completely unexpected. Now the mood in Ichiro's division is one of simmering excitement, seasoned with a tinge of disbelief. The suddenness of their success has lent everyone—from the highest-ranked general to the common infantryman—a swagger to their walks.

A breeze blows in through the window. Ichiro breathes in deep the alien air of this land, scented with the must of rich red earth and the sinuous perfumes of cannas, margosas and bougainvillea.

As an infantry pilot, his first view of the country was from the sky. Beholding the rich textures of greenery, the rows of hills and mountains folding into endless patterns, cradling villages in their valleys, their summits tipped with pagodas painted a glinting gold, he thought Burma a young land, wily and wild, an impression quickly disabused once he stood on the ground, feeling miniscule before the enormous reclining Buddha in Win Sein Taw Ya, receiving the curious stares of young women with thanaka-yellow faces, witnessing the somber processions of maroon-robed monks collecting their morning alms.

As he looks out upon the Burmese night, the foreignness of his surroundings makes him gasp for home; a voice in his head bellows so loudly and suddenly that he shivers—*you will die here.*

His mind unshackled by this foreboding thought, he leans over the blank page of his journal to write, his fountain pen skating across the paper's surface in neat cursive English until a cramp settles into his hand, and his back aches from leaning over. The moon rises high up in the sky, its cratered face obscured by a beard of clouds. From the rubber forests, the lonesome calls of foxes and other creatures of the night drift in.

Ichiro returns to his bed, carefully tucks his journal into a pillowcase, and lays his head down onto its hard surface. His heart and mind spent on paper, sleep finds him quickly.

꒰꒱

HE RISES FULL OF purpose the next day, the melancholy that entangled him the previous night burned away by the clear sunshine that streams in through the window. He dresses and heads out.

He seeks out a teashop by the river, takes a seat near the window. The morning is chillier than the night. Vines of mist curl along the water's surface. The occasional steamer passes by, horns blaring.

Before him is a battered thermos full of green tea that is so ubiquitous here, filled hot and ready for any customer to tuck into, but this morning he orders two by-products of British rule in Burma: samosas filled with a savory potato filling and a cup of lahpet-ye, black tea made with milk and sugar. They arrive quickly, the tea making his head buzz after a few sips. He smiles. *A beverage of action rather than contemplation.*

Yet he is the only one smiling in the shop. The other patrons look away when he tries to meet their eyes; the ones that do not, seem unfriendly. This is no surprise, for the Japanese never expected to be greeted as liberators in this fiercely independent country.

He spots his friend picking his way across the street. Tadashi raises a hand in greeting when close and nearly slips on the moss-slick pathway separating the shop from the main road, setting off a roll of snickering among the teashop crowd that falls into a dismayed murmur when he enters. Tadashi is oblivious to the lack of welcome as he marches straight to Ichiro, who holds up a piece of paper triumphantly.

Tadashi inspects the leave form. "Honto? How did you manage this?"

"I saved each can of salmon mother sent my way. Set aside five cigarettes from each box of rations. In short, I've been showering the CO with gifts for months."

He pours tea for them both, feeling satisfied that matters are coming together as he intended. Tadashi appears ambivalent, perhaps feeling dragooned into accompanying him. But Ichiro has an inkling that the destination he has in mind will appeal to his deeply Buddhist friend: Bagan, a valley strewn with Buddhist temples, many nearly a millennium old and of legendary dimensions.

IN THE END, IT takes less effort to convince Tadashi than he imagined, and the two men rise before dawn the next day to pack haversacks with pickled plums, rice, natto and salted cod. They take water bladders, a detailed army map of central Burma, and two infantry Type 38 rifles in case they encounter the unexpected.

At the camp gates they present the leave form to the soldiers on duty, who wave them through when they see the CO's signature. They look out to the road that lies before them. Red. Rock strewn. It winds away south, fading into a valley made deep by the cobalt shadows of dawn.

Their destination is a multi-hour hike along Nyaung-U Road, which runs through to Mandalay like a purple serpent. They set off on the mostly abandoned road. The central Burma heat is stifling even in the morning, and the men soon must strip to their undershirts, tying their fatigues across their waists. The occasional pedestrian or cyclist they encounter gives them wide berths.

Around noon, they stop at a roadside shack to eat their lunch. Afterward, Tadashi consults a map while Ichiro procures from the elderly owner two cups of palm syrup, a light sweet drink refreshingly cool on this hot day. The man trembles visibly as he serves them, and refuses the money—Japanese-branded Burmese currency—offered him. Knowing this cannot be from lack of need, Ichiro leaves the notes under their cups.

For the next hour of their march, hills draped thick with trees and greenery close in, fall away, a cyclical geologic dance that ends when the road nearly bursts out into a wide valley. They stop. Before them is a vast plain. A crucible broiling yellow-brown in the heat. Dense with scrubs and bushy peanut and palm trees, it shimmers and beckons. They take shelter beneath a bodhi tree by the road.

"How much farther?" Tadashi asks, panting from the heat. He has tied a bandana on his head to protect it against the merciless sun. "We've not thought this through. We are halfway through our water. We should have filled up at the shack."

"We're here already, look." Ichiro points to the distance. At the limits of their vision, they can see temples dotting the landscape, too far away to ascertain their states of ruin.

Tadashi squeezes in between gnarled tree roots that form a rough cradle, closes his eyes. "We have time. Can we not rest here until the sun softens a bit? They say that the Buddha gained his enlightenment under the shade of such a tree. Perhaps if I take a nap I'll gain insight into why I let you talk me into this."

Ichiro chuckles. He takes out his journal and a pen from his belt holster, opens to a blank page. "Very well. How long do you think you need?"

Already asleep, Tadashi does not answer.

Ichiro smiles. The landscape is inspiring him to write.

Prior to his division's arrival in Nyaung-U, he was part of a forward detachment, his mission to fly over territory they were advancing on in anticipation of ambush. Of enemy installations, there were none, the British having abandoned the heart of the country to mass defenses at the Assam border. He found instead a valley strewn with innumerable temples. Awestruck, he took the plane down so low he was nearly skimming the tops of the tall palm trees that stood like silent sentinels, his wings close to grazing the great stone monuments—ancient and unearthly.

He had flown over Bagan then, but now he wished to walk

through, to touch the stone with his hands and breathe in the mystic air. But he did not want it to be a solitary experience. He had met Tadashi during university, where they were both students of philosophy before enlisting for the army. Their friendship had only gotten stronger during their brutal training, the worst of which they endured by turning their faces to the heavens for courage and sustenance. He to Jesus, and Tadashi to Buddha.

He knows his friend has a gentle soul, and in his heart, just as questioning of this war that they fight in. Although Tadashi is less quick to utter his doubts, in the moments when Ichiro has felt the most despair, when the still pool of water inside him has been the most turbulent, he has only to look to Tadashi's quiet fortitude to will himself to endure.

One more day. One more day.

Who better than a devout Buddhist by his side as he explores this valley? If this day can be an island of calm in this endless ocean of war they find themselves in, it will be a good one.

HE STOPS WRITING AT three. The sun has rolled to the west, still strong but at a less fierce angle. Shadows have spilled across the bronzed, parched valley. There is the hint of a breeze. The chirrup and buzz of insects. He shakes Tadashi awake.

They leave the road, venture forth into the plains, cross acres of fallow land, descend and ascend dry canals, dust plumes dogging their steps as they pass temples with darkly inviting entrances.

They discover one that is smaller than the others but tall, its three stories terminating in a wide pavilion at the summit. Removing their shoes at the door and bowing, they enter. A large statue of the Buddha sits under a vaulted roof, his eyes closed, his smile serene and knowing. The thumb and index finger of each of his raised hands—one palm pointing out and the other in—connect into circles. Tadashi kneels for a quick prayer, as does Ichiro, out of respect. They finish and ascend the narrow, worn steps that wind up the temple's side.

Accustomed to the darkness of the interior, they emerge blinking at the fierce golden brightness that accosts them at the pavilion. But once their eyes adjust, the men behold what lies before them with silent wonder.

The valley is flooded with the light of the dying sun, cradled by the jagged outlines of the Arakan Yomas and the Irrawaddy's shimmering curves, studded with countless temples both spired and blunt-topped. Some are a weathered white, others as dark as night. Many a blood red that is stark against the yellow-brown of the dale. They number so many it is as though the Earth, in rivalry with the heavens, has birthed its own constellation.

Tadashi falls to his knees while Ichiro lets the unreal wonder of the sight fill him, each fiber of him resonating to the soundless music that emanates from this sacred place.

After some time, Tadashi rises, places a hand on his friend's shoulder. "I'll never forget this sight, Ichiro. Thank you for bringing me here."

They descend and head to the grand temples they spied in the distance. In that moment, Ichiro feels like Solomon Kane, Allan Quatermain—the pulp novel heroes of his childhood—as they traverse a city that appears to be crafted by the gods themselves, following wide, straight avenues that connect towering stupas of corroding mortar.

Occasionally veering into deserted temples, their calls ringing in the barren interiors, they explore the valley until dusk descends. But for them, the only other creatures are made of stone—snarling chinthe that flank entrances, majestic karaweik birds that sit atop spires.

The air cools, and whippoorwills call out, the haunting cries making Ichiro anxious to find shelter for the night.

"Let's camp here," he tells Tadashi as they approach a large temple, the sky behind it the hue of strong Indian tea.

The temple interior is vast and oblong, dominated by a giant reclining Buddha breathtaking in size, painted a shimmering gold. Its head is cradled in one colossal palm, the eyes half-closed from the weight of eternity.

At the foot of the great statue, a lone monk sweeps the floor with a long-handled broom, the first living creature they have encountered in this desolate valley.

The rustle of their uniforms startles the monk from his task. He stands straight, his face obscured in shadow as Ichiro and Tadashi convey with a mix of gestures and pidgin Burmese that they seek shelter. There is a pregnant silence when they finish, after which the monk makes a grunt of assent, seizes a hurricane lantern winking in an alcove and gestures for them to follow.

He takes them around the statue and into a winding low-ceilinged hallway that leads to a small room—bare but featuring a clean floor on which the travelers can lay their bedrolls. They express their appreciation with bows that the monk does not acknowledge. Rather, he leads them to an adjacent washroom, equipped with carved stone stalls and basins filled with clear water. He sets the lantern on the ground and departs, apparently more comfortable in the darkness than they.

The men wash, change and rest. While Tadashi is in a state of serene acceptance of how events have transpired, Ichiro brims with excitement as the scale of their adventure expands.

"It feels like an incredible coincidence," he whispers to Tadashi. "That this monk would be in the very temple where we chose to spend the night."

As though summoned by his words, there is the sound of a throat being cleared at the doorway. The monk has returned bearing three bowls on a tray—Burmese noodles in broth.

The men sit down to sup. The dish is simple. Hot and delicious. They focus their attention on the food until their bowls are empty.

They follow the monk out to the hallway afterward, their marker the blue rectangle of night showing through the doorway. He leads them out to the courtyard, where, perched on the elevated pavilion that surrounds the temple, they can see the moonlight that now floods the valley, drowns out the stars, the temple a ship adrift in an ocean of silver-blue.

The monk retrieves cigarettes from the folds of his robe, lights them. They smoke and take in the night, the scent of unnamed flowers wrapping around them like warm scarves.

Ichiro makes another attempt to engage. He gestures to the temple and utters the Burmese word for *name.*

"It has no name," says the monk in accented but clear English.

He laughs at the shocked silence that follows, raises the lantern to a face that is a tanned pink, the eyes an ice-blue.

"Are you surprised?" he asks. The accent sounds Germanic to Ichiro.

"Yes. We thought you were Burmese," Ichiro replies in English. Not having spoken the language in some time, he finds that he must first consciously arrange the words in his head.

"Are you German?"

"Austrian."

"*Würden Sie es bevorzugen, Deutsch zu sprechen?*" Ichiro asks, knowing that his phrasing is too formal.

It is the monk's turn to be surprised. "*Ja,*" he says and continues in German. "Where did you learn the language?"

"We were selected for the army while in university. We were both students of philosophy. German and English were among the languages we were expected to master to read books by Western philosophers. My name is Washi Ichiro. My friend is Nakagawa Tadashi."

Tadashi addresses the monk for the first time. "May we inquire as to your name, Holy One?"

The monk waves a weary, dismissive hand. "Back when such things mattered, I was called Julian. Julian Krähe. Now I'm just an old man living in a temple."

Where the grass meets the trees beyond the wall, a patch of black moves against the night. It snorts and turns a massive head toward them, eyes glinting in the moonlight. *We are in the land of gods and monsters*, thinks Ichiro.

The beast assesses them for some time, then snuffles and lumbers off into the trees.

"Buffalo," says Julian. "Sometimes they are attracted to the light."

"Are there more dangerous animals here?" asks Ichiro.

"If by that you mean animals with claws and teeth, that eat flesh, then yes, there may be leopards or tigers here still, although I can't say that I've ever encountered one. In any case, fire and light seem sufficient to keep them at bay."

The monk lifts the lantern, giving them another look at his typically European face—long, strong-jawed. With his wrinkles, Ichiro estimates the man's age to be anywhere between forty-five and sixty. "But as for things that are actually dangerous, that already have and will do further harm, there is only you."

"What do you mean?"

The monk extracts another cigarette and lights it in an unhurried manner. "Let me ask you this: Why have you come here now?"

"We heard much about Bagan. Given the many Buddhist temples here, and being from a country where the religion is widely practiced, we were curious to see it."

"That does not answer my question."

"Why not?"

Julian shakes his head. "You are intelligent young men, yet you play dumb. I am not asking you what you're doing here on this very day and at this very moment. When I say *you*, I do not mean you as an individual, I mean you in the collective, the plural, the nation of Japan. When I say *here*, I do not mean this very ground, the temple or these steps. I mean the nation of Burma. And when I say *now*, I do not mean today or this evening, I mean the last six months."

Dark shapes fly overhead, flaps of leathery wings so close that Ichiro can smell the creatures' musk. The bats that roost in the nooks of the temple. At that moment, under the stars, shadow and the limitless night sky, he feels as though they are the only three people on Earth, that its fate rests in their hands. A thousand thoughts clamor in him for release. For months he has never dared put forth his questions about the war anywhere but in his journal. Now the opportunity has arrived to unburden himself.

That is the intention with which he opens his mouth, but what emerges instead surprises and disappoints him.

"We are here to fight for a continent free of colonial aggression from Westerners, one where all of Asia can stand united against exploitative Western powers," he says in a monotone. The shame of his cowardice heats his ears.

"You don't even believe that yourself," says Julian. "So, I ask you again why you're really here."

Tadashi replies before Ichiro can, quietly but with the finality of a mahogany coffin. "We are here to fight because we were asked to by our emperor. We fight for Japan's interests first and foremost. All else is secondary."

Julian is puffing away, the moon above his head now wreathed in smoke. "At least your friend here does not hide behind platitudes."

He directs the next question to Tadashi. "Are you a Buddhist?"

"Yes, Holy One."

"And you believe in bloodshed?"

Tadashi does not answer. The monk looks to Ichiro. "How about you?"

"Are you asking about what religion I practice or whether I believe in bloodshed?"

"Take your pick."

Ichiro tells the monk that although he is a Christian, like many in Japan, he follows Shinto ceremonies for birth and would follow Buddhist ones for death.

"So your life terminates in Buddhist principles. Should not the rest follow?"

A slow simmering indignation reaches a boil in Ichiro. "But are you the right one to lecture us? How long have you been following the Buddhist way? Are there not monks in China who have mastered the sword, spear and bow? Who move to defend their temples at the slightest threat, not hesitating to spill blood? Peace is priceless, Holy One, but it is not free."

"All good points," Julian says. The moon, resembling a pale grapefruit, haloes his head. He takes a final drag of his cigarette and extinguishes the stub against the stone of the banister. "As you say, being an outsider to your religion, I have no standing to lecture you. And indeed I am not. But is it that impertinent of me to ask a few questions?"

Though the monk seems unoffended, there is a pause in the conversation in which Ichiro becomes embarrassed by his outburst.

"How did you find your way to the Buddha?" Tadashi asks eventually.

"It is a long tale, better suited for another venue and occasion. For now it is enough for you to know that it happened while I was a soldier—much like you—in the Great War."

Ichiro does not miss this opportunity to twist the knife. "I find it odd that you are so quick to judge us, given that you too partook in a war no more just than this one."

Julian nods. "For some time. But then I followed a path east. For I met a man who taught me the values of patience, enthusiastic effort, generosity, ethical discipline, focus and wisdom—the six perfections of the Buddha."

"Perhaps," Ichiro says. "But not all of us have the luxury of pursuing a peaceful, godly life. Not yet, at least. Some of us still have an obligation to our nations."

"And what do you think of those who reject those obligations? Are they cowards?"

"I was almost one of them," says Ichiro, recalling the beatings from their superiors, the ritualized humiliations of military training.

"What do you fear?" asks Julian.

"The same thing as others: death. I could hear a thousand tales of heaven, of the afterlife, but deep down the fear of the black void pervades."

"Then why do you choose to fight?"

How could he make the monk understand the fever of the nation when he enlisted? To a Japan dreaming of glory, blinded by it, the air was thick with the germ of war. "I could have chosen not to. By right of primogeniture, firstborn sons are exempt from military service, as are students and teachers. I was both when the army enlistment officers visited our university. But not enlisting was not acceptable. Refusing the call to war was not acceptable. Shaming my family with my cowardice was not acceptable. So, I volunteered. The government accelerated our degrees so that we could graduate early and join the army as soon as possible."

"Is the fear of shaming your parents not cowardice also?"

"Should they suffer because I refuse to do my duty?"

"Should you suffer by obeying? Should others? Is your duty to your God or to your nation?"

"It is to both. I am here because a part of me believes in the mission. Western nations have been sucking the Orient dry for centuries. They have scoured Africa and Asia clean of resources. They stockpile gold, gems, wood and oil, draining it out of earth that belongs to the yellow man, the brown, the black, the red. Whatever small hand I can have in preventing that, and as part of however flawed and cruel a machine, I would take that opportunity, yes. But to answer your question, by being here, I serve God. Your retreat from the world and society is a selfish act. History will swirl around you while you mop your temple floor. Perhaps its tides of violence will break at your door, sweep you away. The difference is that I jumped into the waters while you stood back and waited for it to arrive."

Julian scoffs. "Mighty words. Is it your contention that the Empire of Japan will deliver this salvation? What have you done to differentiate yourself from the British and the French? I have a shortwave radio. Your tales of cruelty and atrocities are fast becoming infamous. You think we haven't heard of what happened in China four years ago?"

The monk's reference to the Nanking Massacre shakes Ichiro. "That was before my time in the army. I have no doubt that many wrongs were committed in China, but it is possible that some reports are being exaggerated."

Tadashi startles Ichiro by speaking, his voice heavy with acceptance. "They're not exaggerations, Ichiro. You and I both know that. Even Matsui admitted to it afterward."

Of course not. How much longer could he pretend that they were? Why should he expect an army that treats the lives of its soldiers with such disdain—throwing them at the fortresses of the enemy like so many bags of meat—to treat those of others any better? Ichiro stares at his friend, who has walked a few steps away and contemplates the moonlit valley with his back to them.

Even as his future dims, the past becomes sharper, until memories glitter with a diamond's edge. Those days of university seem so long ago. He and Tadashi were two of the many first-years who had escaped to a cheap izakaya after their first day of classes. He did not like shochu, but kept drinking that first night after Tadashi told him that all drinks taste the same after the third one. They sang the words to "Dekansho" (for Descartes, Kant, and Schopenhauer) along with the others, bonding over the fact that they were both from Kansai, spoke the same dialect. The remainder of the evening, and the next three years, passed quickly. Too quickly.

He turns to Julian. "Would you have us lay down our arms? Declare that we are no longer willing to fight for this cause? We would be shot for even having this conversation with you."

"I have no doubt," says Julian. "I would not presume to give you advice. Wait here a moment."

He hops off the banister and reenters the temple. He is gone no more than a few minutes before returning with several cups made of fired clay and a large jug that he lifts up so the others can have a whiff of the pungent liquid within.

"Fermented from palm syrup," he explains. "I have a man who passes by every week. Kind enough to supply an old man with drink and batteries, among other things."

They stay awake for hours more. Talking at first, and as the liquor dissolves the sombre mood, laughing and even singing Burmese ditties that Julian teaches them. At one point, Julian expands on the tale of his arrival to the religion of the Buddha, of his origins. The men listen, rapt, to the extraordinary circumstances that defined the monk's youth, that set him on his current course.

When they return to the shadow-inked interior of the temple—hours past midnight—the statue of the Buddha looks even grander than before to Ichiro, as though it has been gorging on the darkness. He lies on his bedroll and wonders why it was so hard to reconcile his private self with his public. Why he was so eager to defend his nation's aggression against this most unexpected of men. He always thought himself immune to the blind tribalism that leads a man to say *my country, right or wrong*, yet it was Tadashi, quiet Tadashi, who rose to the occasion and did not flinch when asked to look at all that Japan has wrought on the world.

༺༻

HE RISES, SORE AND tired, when timid light arrives through the lancet windows set high on the wall, at dawn. Tadashi remains in his bedroll. Julian is nowhere to be found.

He washes his face in the basin and ventures outside.

The valley sparkles under the early light sweeping across the woods. Compared to the heat of the previous day, the morning is blessedly cool. He walks to where the grass meets the trees and finds the hoofprints of the buffalo from the previous night. A flower has fallen into one of the indentations left by the creature. He lifts it to his face. Small and white, with yellow anthers, the flower releases an alluring scent when he rubs it.

He hears the rustle of wings behind him, the scrape of talons on dry leaves.

"You are leaving today?"

Ichiro turns, the monk has appeared as though out of nowhere. "I will pack some provisions for your return journey."

"We are in your debt."

Knowing it is meaningless to offer money, he asks if there is work the two of them may instead perform before their departure.

"There is no need," says Julian. "Your temporary help will only remind me how short-handed I am the rest of the year."

༺༻

FOLLOWING PACKING, JULIAN INSISTS on escorting them to the main road. As they venture out into the whiskey-smooth sunlight wearing only their undershirts over their trousers, Julian points to the general area of Tadashi's midsection.

"What is it that you're wearing?"

"This is called a Senninbari, Holy One," says Tadashi. "When we become enlisted, our mothers stand on the street asking women walking by to tie a knot that is then sewn into the sash. Once a thousand are gathered, the sash is considered finished. Senninbari protect us from gunfire on the battlefield."

"What do those two characters on it say?"

運命

"That is *unmei,* meaning 'destiny,'" says Tadashi. "The Chinese pronounce it 'ming yun,' and read it left to right rather than the other way as we do, but that is their prerogative, given that they invented the characters."

Julian leads them deeper into the forest, a place of silence and leaf-strained light. Barefoot and dressed in maroon robes as the day before, he carries a bamboo stick to aid his hiking.

It is another hour's march before the trees thin out and they are walking on scrubland, eventually reaching the paved main road.

"You have our gratitude," says Ichiro, standing at the edge of the camber. "For everything."

Julian joins his hands together and bows to the men. "I merely drew up that which was below the surface."

Tadashi unfastens his sash with a ceremonial slowness and offers it to the monk—a soldier surrendering his sword to a conquering general. "Holy One, honor me by accepting this."

Julian gently pushes the offering back. "I am honored enough by your gesture. Besides, do you not need it more than I do?"

Tadashi appears wounded. "If you will not accept my sash, will you at least bless us?"

Julian considers. "I believe in knowledge, not blessings. If you ask, I can teach to you that which was taught to me."

Knowing the formal response to this ancient offer, Tadashi says, "We ask. Please teach."

"Stand beside me," Julian says.

The men obey.

He bends and uses the tip of his walking stick to etch on the ground a curling bipartite symbol, and once complete, kneels to blow away the dust gathered above the furrows so that the flowing curves and alien proportions are clear against the red earth.

Yet when they crowd in for a closer look he says, "I'm not done."

As the monk draws a circle around his work, Ichiro feels the world tremble and subside, the ground thrumming as though a mystic circuit has been completed, the rune within coursing with power and mystery.

"*Aum* is the cosmic sound," Julian says. "The beginning and the end of the universe, the fixed axis upon which it turns as well as the void that pervades. It is composed of four syllables, four parts: Think of a fish jumping up from a hidden lake, miles below the earth. Think of the creature's face breaking the water, the brief shining moment in which it is suspended in the air, its return to the lake, and of course the water that surrounds it. A lifetime of study will reveal only a fraction of the secrets of this sound, unlock a scintilla of its possibilities. For you right now, it will be most useful as a tool for meditation, focus. A way to access the transcendent in a time of need."

The men stare long at the rune, repeat its name under their breaths. Commit it to visual and auditory memory.

Ichiro bows to Julian, and then, remembering something the monk said the previous night, asks a question. "Julian, the village of your birth . . ."

"Ranshofen, in Braunau am Inn."

"Yes, I cannot place it, but I have heard the name before. Is it famous?"

"For just one thing," Julian's face clouds. "As the birthplace of the man Germany and Austria now follow. *Der Führer.*"

Ichiro nods. "It is remarkable that two men coming from the same village would choose such different paths in life."

"He is driven by fear and desire. That leads to destruction and sorrow. After my passing, no one will remember me. That is what I sought."

～～

THEY SAY GOOD-BYE AND resume their trudge. They have until late afternoon to reach their camp, when their leave is set to expire. They speak little, taking small sips from a bladder to conserve water. The noon heat is monstrous, their horizons wavering, the trees stock still and dry as though ready to burst into flames.

They march on. Hours pass in which the road remains desolate, unfurling into the glassy, shimmering distance. When they finally see a sign stating that their camp is near, Ichiro stops and waits for Tadashi, who tarries behind, walking with a dreamlike expression on his face.

The air burning in his lungs, Ichiro takes a long sip of water. "Why try to give away your sash?"

"A piece of cloth. What use do I have for it?"

"Your mother made it."

Tadashi laughs. "My mother or the government? Maybe I was trying to protect the sash by leaving it in a safer home. I should have done it a long time ago. Or I should give it to an infantryman.

They need it more, neh? And that way, I'll increase my chances of ending up in Yasukuni Shrine."

"Should I give my things away as well?"

"No. You will see your mother again."

Ichiro stops, chilled by Tadashi's words. "What're you saying? What manner of pessimism is this?"

The two friends stare at each other. They are within sight of camp. Shouted instructions to stop and raise their hands reach them from the sentry towers. The guards begin a count from one to ten, following which, they warn, they will shoot.

Ichiro puts his hands up, holding his military identification in one and yelling his name, rank and number. But the soldiers do not lower their weapons, as Tadashi is still walking forward, his manner casual, arms at his side, his expression focused on something only he can see.

"What are you doing?" Ichiro shouts.

But Tadashi does not appear to hear him, much less the soldiers who continue to count down—FIVE, FOUR, THREE . . . a warning siren goes on and soldiers mobilize in the camp in a controlled frenzy. Tadashi turns to him. Ichiro recognizes his expression of pure and primal intensity. It is faith.

"Ask my mother to forgive me."

※

ICHIRO ASCENDS THE SKIES above Bengal, just past the Burmese-Indian border. He flies a Kawasaki Ki-48, affectionately called "Lili" by the pilots. His drop zone is in Chittagong, more than two hundred miles from their camp. Originally Tadashi's, his mission is to drop a payload of propaganda leaflets near a small fishing village by the shore.

They dare not breach the city limits where the British are likely to have instituted anti-air defense. Still, it is the farthest a Japanese bomber has traveled into British-Indian territory, the prelude to a planned strike on Chittagong.

Since his friend fell a week ago, riddled with bullets, breathing out his last in Ichiro's arms, Ichiro's life has been a nightmare of interrogations, recriminations and threats from Command. He was told that he would be court-martialed, dishonorably discharged, and at points even threatened with swift execution for treason. Ironically, the utterly bizarre circumstances of Tadashi's death were what saved him in the end, as the commander could not decide under which violation of the army code he could put Ichiro in remand before proceeding to court martial. It also helped that he was one of the few experienced pilots remaining in a division now short of one.

The monk had scattered the seeds of his ideas across both their minds, yet it was in Tadashi that they found the more fertile ground, took root, took him. He wishes that he could weep for his friend, but finds that this grief is not like air—it will not expand to fill whatever space it is released into. Its brittle edges do not fit the shape of his days; its weight demands a fortitude that he cannot offer.

He pushes down on the flight yoke to sink the aircraft into the blanket of clouds that cover Bengal. His break through the cumulus is gentle, cushioned by the rush of wind shear. Now he can see the land from a height of ten thousand feet—it is fissured with broad rivers and estuaries, giving Bengal the appearance of a great green hand reaching into the bay. He descends farther and the land comes into sharper relief—a brilliant patchwork of golden fields, green rice paddies and water flashing silver in the late-day sun.

Four thousand feet . . . soon three. He is minutes from his drop zone, and close enough to the ground to see the thatch-roofed, mud-walled houses clustered around ponds and demarcated by tall areca

nut trees. At the sound of his plane, men look up, scatter. The coni-
cal hats they wear remind him of those worn by farmers back home.

The altimeter steadily ticks down

Fifteen hundred . . . fourteen . . . he is less than a minute away

Thirteen hundred

Twelve hundred

Eleven hundred . . . he releases the flight yoke and settles the
plane on cruise

He is fifteen seconds from the drop zone when he sees the
girl—a tiny figure in white. He scrambles for his binoculars to
look. She is not more than six or seven years of age, frozen in fear.
In one hand she holds a pail, presumably for fetching water. For a
mad moment, he feels their eyes lock.

Ten seconds

She is the only human figure visible

Five seconds

She is directly at the center of the drop zone, an audience of
one for Japan's propaganda to Bengal. He pulls the lever to release
the payload. Leaflets by the thousands plume out in the plane's
slipstream, a whirling cloud of red, yellow and black that reminds
him of monarch butterflies.

He has moments to admire the view before needing to lift the
plane out of the low glide, skirting a line of trees with seconds to
spare. Against the might of the wind shear, pulling back on the
yoke takes much of his strength, and he feels drained.

There are two sounds just then—one a rapid burst of coughs,
followed by the whine of the cabin depressurizing. It feels as though
someone has just punched him hard on his side. The pain hot and
screaming. His right shoulder is soaked with blood. Bullets have
pierced the fuselage, and at least one has pierced him. The British
have installed anti-air defenses much farther from the city than
anticipated.

He watches his fuel gauge drop precipitously. His plane is on a steady downward course. His vision dims. His grip on the yoke slackens.

In a scrabbling grip for purchase as it tumbles off the cliffs of memory, his rapidly fading consciousness casts back, latches onto a symbol. A sound.

Aum.

The pain dulls somewhat as the word leaves his mouth. The fog before his vision lifts as he pictures the symbol Julian drew on the ground. He banks the plane left to follow the water, the white-capped waves frozen into miniature Mount Everests. He descends closer to the beach, almost skimming the grainy sand. He is only a hundred feet from the ground. He hopes that by landing in the water, he can reduce the chance of fire, minimize civilian casualties, perhaps his own.

A line of hillocks rushes up and he wrenches the yoke again. As the sound of tearing metal fills his ears, Ichiro's last thoughts are of a fish bursting out of the water. Diving back into the blackness.

BOOK II

Eye

Shahryar & Anna

Washington, DC
September 2004

Dragonfly is easy to miss—a second-floor walk-up on a side street, recessed to accommodate a front-facing patio. Once upstairs, Shar can see that it is longer than it is wide, with a bar at the far end.

The floor thumps with the deep bass of Ambient music. An invisible projector throws Japanese anime against the wall. A woman clad in all black greets him. "Just one?"

"Two, but I can wait at the bar."

He is a half hour early. He consults the menu and orders a Ramune soda, wanting to keep a clear head.

As the appointed hour of seven approaches, Dragonfly begins to fill with a steady trickle of DC's bright, beautiful and young.

Seven fifteen. Then seven thirty. By now the club is almost full, buzzing with conversation. He is about to ask the bartender for the bill when Katerina arrives, sees him across the room and walks over with a quick wave. She is dressed in a slim black cocktail dress that reaches her knees but leaves her shoulders bare. Her hair is piled on her head in a stack of thick gold. Earrings, long and sparkling, swing with every step she takes. She greets him with kisses on each cheek. This close, he can smell the faint perfume of lilacs on her skin, see the effort she has put into her makeup. If she were walking down the street, she would merit a second glance from most men she passed.

She places a clutch on the counter—slim and black like her dress. "Did you have trouble finding this place?"

"No. Are you um . . . going somewhere after this?"

"No. Why do you ask?"

"Your outfit."

She laughs. "A girl should look nice on a Friday night, don't you think?"

She catches the bartender's eye. "I'll have a vodka sour. You?"

"Dark and stormy," says Shar.

The bartender returns before long with drinks that Shar and Katerina sip facing forward, watching each other's reflections in the glass panels behind the bar amidst an unnatural silence.

"Is it normal practice for you to meet with your clients like this, after work?"

"It's not normal. But neither is your case, Mr. Choudhury."

"What's so difficult about it?"

"I didn't say 'difficult.'"

"You said 'not normal.'"

"That's not the same as difficult. Difficult things don't have a lot of solutions."

"So it's simple?"

"On the face of it, it actually is very simple. Since you can't marry someone, the only way for you to stay back in America is through a job. But you still need luck on your side."

"I've tried everything," says Shar. Which is true. He has sent out resumes widely, for positions such as researcher, lecturer, executive assistant, program designer and policy analyst. But even the smallest flames of interest that he kindled were extinguished when he had to answer that one question—*Are you permitted to work in the United States?*

"Maybe not everything. No one ever has tried everything. That's what we're here for. Mr. Ahmed will find a way for you. I know it."

He smiles. "You have a lot of faith in him."

"I've my reasons."

"What do you mean?"

She assesses the state of the club. The noise in Dragonfly is reaching a crescendo, the clientele spilling from the packed tables onto the dance floor, where a sunglassed, headphoned DJ spins J-pop.

She places twenty dollars on the counter. "Take a walk with me."

THEY TAKE A STROLL around Adams Morgan. The night is warm. The steamy remnants of the day's rains halo against the streetlights. Walking up 18th Street, they must push past gallivanting crowds of college students and revelers.

They turn into Ontario Road, free from pedestrians and lined with tall, darkened townhomes. In the empty parkette at its terminus, they find a bench to sit on.

"Do you know what a K-1 visa is, Mr. Choudhury?" Katerina asks.

"No."

"Then this will require an explanation. Around three years ago, my mother and I lived in Kiev, in one of those many khrushchyovka apartments built in the fifties. My father was a civil engineer. He died when I was a teenager. He received a small pension from the government. That, along with some scholarships, was enough for me to complete a master's in Electrical Engineering from the University of Kiev. I spoke good English, had a good degree from a good university, but there was just one problem—there were no jobs in Kiev, or Ukraine in general. I took part-time work as a receptionist in an Internet firm, kept looking for work.

"It was a friend of mine who told me about a site—there were so many of them popping up back then. The way she explained it, it didn't sound like much of a commitment. I would have to write a paragraph about myself (or the website would do it for me), post my best pictures, and who knows, maybe I'd meet a kind gentleman in America, Canada or Western Europe. I thought about it. Did it. But I also kept my life going. If something happened, it'd be like winning the lottery, I told myself.

"But something did happen. I uploaded my best pictures. And there was interest from men. From many men. I'm not boasting, but this was something I had time to get used to in my life. Most were jerks. Perverts. I'd gotten enough lewd messages and pictures that I was close to deleting my profile and moving on when Howard contacted me. He was about forty-three. So, much older. He had his own private electronics repair business in Virginia. He had been married before, and had two teenage daughters. He was tall, fit for his age. Maybe not too good-looking, but he dressed well, had a kind face. Most importantly, his first message to me was to comment not on my body or face, but my name. Saying that it was the name of his grand-mother, who came over to America from Sweden.

"We moved on to video calls over the Internet. He had that American way. Loud laugh that made you feel at ease with yourself. Warm. I didn't fall in love with him, but I thought I could at some point.

"He applied for a K-1 visa for me. That's what's called a 'fian-cée visa.' You like a woman (can be a man I guess, but mostly it is women), you apply for a visa for her to come to America, and when she arrives, the two of you have ninety days to figure out if you want to go through with it.

"Howard did his part, filed a Petition for an Alien Fiancée in Herndon, Virginia. It was approved in a month, and the paper-work was sent over to Kiev. We were both jumping for joy on the web-camera. My family was excited, frightened. I was too.

"Then one day in January, I took a thick file folder of all my vital documents: passport, driver's license, birth certificates, police certificates, medical examinations, my diplomas and degrees, the copy of every email and letter Howard and I had sent each other. I stood in line for four hours on a freezing morning in Kiev in front of the American Embassy—which is big and blocky like a prison. When I got in, I was interrogated by this thin unsmiling woman who did everything except say that I was a fraud who was going to America just for a green card.

"But I must have convinced her. Because they granted my visa. And less than a month later, my Aeroflot flight was touching down in Dulles.

"Howard was the same man up close as I'd seen from far away. Just as kind, funny, charming and sweet. In just the first month, we visited New York City, Disney World, Chicago. I thought I was living in a dream. It didn't seem that I'd have to convince myself to love him. Everything just seemed easier to do in this country. It was the air, I thought. It had to be the air.

"One night, over dinner, I built up the courage to tell him what I had been hiding for the last six months." Katerina opens her clutch. The entire time she was speaking, she was staring ahead, too invested in her recollections to acknowledge him. Now she searches her purse until she finds an accordion-style picture holder. It unfurls from her hand, swinging in the mild breeze.

He takes it. The pictures are of a little girl. Blond, bearing a strong resemblance to the woman who sits next to him.

"What's her name?"

"Ilyana. She's nine now. She's in Kiev, with my mother."

"What was Howard's reaction?"

"You can guess. He didn't take it well. All the sweetness and kindness vanished overnight. Told me that it wasn't that I had a kid. It was my dishonesty. He just couldn't trust me anymore.

"I had to move into a hotel. I had very little money. I cried myself to sleep that night. Because I had no one else to blame. I had made the decisions. I owned every mistake. I thought I could bring Ilyana here. That we could build a life together. I was just too frightened to tell Howard at the start; I thought it'd scare him away. Then I just kept finding excuses, kept convincing myself that when we met in person, he'd find it easier to forgive me. I was good at that. Convincing myself.

"I found Mr. Ahmed's advertisement in the paper, went to see him, and he said the same thing to me that he said to you—that this was going to be difficult, but that he would find a way for me to stay. But he couldn't. In the end he made me an offer to stay on as his assistant. He would sponsor me himself until I got my green card. I could attend Strayer to become a legal clerk in the meanwhile. I go there Tuesday and Thursday nights now. I finish in May. I talk to my daughter every day. Sometimes we see each other on the web camera. But the Internet is not so good in the Ukraine.

"Do you know what my biggest fear is, Mr. Choudhury?"

"That you won't be able to bring her here?"

"No. That something will change. And she will not feel the same about me anymore. That feeling between a parent and a child, it's so . . . delicate, like a spider web. It can be okay for so long, and then one mistake and it's broken."

She looks to him. Her eyes glisten, and she wipes them.

"What about you?"

"What do you mean?"

"You have a daughter. But you're not married to her mother. What happened there?"

"It's not a happy story. But my daughter's in my life. For now at least."

"Would you feel better if you shared it with me?"

He looks at her. She leans forward, her mouth slightly open. In the light, in this setting, her beauty is heartbreaking.

He looks away, takes a deep breath, and begins to speak.

SHAHRYAR

Over the Atlantic Ocean
August 1993

At one point during the six-hour flight from Heathrow to Washington, DC, he awakes to darkness, the squeak of the flight attendant's food trolley. He lifts up the window shade to peer outside. The plane has lost its chase of the setting sun. The ocean churns a deep blue beneath the clouds.

He has led a sheltered life—shuttled to and from school and university in a chauffeured car like so many others of his class and generation. Going out on weekends to play football (the international kind), cricket or to the cinema with friends from similarly well-groomed families.

Even by the conservative standards of a Muslim Bangladeshi family, he is a late bloomer. He has had paramours, but never one serious enough to ask his parents to have "the chat" with hers. Other than the occasional cigarette—whose evidence he diligently destroyed by chewing leaves from the guava tree in their garden before returning home at the end of the day—he has never been bad, never even had a drink.

In Dhaka, he was woken every morning by Rina, the woman who has cared for him for as long as he can remember, the one woman he is closest to apart from his mother. After greeting him with his customary cup of hot milk tea, Rina would lay out Shar's clothes while he bathed. Once dressed, he would join his parents for breakfast at a dining table long as a river, often thinking of their low, cultured tones as vocal accompaniments to the music of clinking plates, glasses and spoon.

With his stocky build and dark skin, he bears little resemblance to his mother and father, who are both tall and slim, bearing the hooked noses and fair skin of Mughal aristocrats. A year before India was carved into three distinct wings—an event of great magnitude and unforeseen consequences that history has dubbed Partition—his parents journeyed across the border from one nation-to-be to another, from India to what would become East Pakistan and then Bangladesh. They were comfortably into middle age when Shar was born to them, twenty-one years later.

That is why his mother calls him her little miracle.

THE IMMIGRATION AGENT IN Washington, DC, is a black man with gray hair and kind eyes, the first he has encountered in the flesh. He peers at Shar over his half-moon glasses, scrutinizing him. "What will you study at Georgetown, young man?"

"Economics, sir."

"And you're doing your bachelor's?"

"Master's, actually."

The agent hoists his eyebrows with surprise. "But you look so young!"

He collects his lone suitcase and steps out of the terminal at Dulles. He walks to the bus stop, where the view is ugly and drab and intimidating, where swooping lines of concrete block out the sky and wide yellow cabs skirmish with red-and-white buses for space. There are other passengers waiting for the bus, an array of faces of all shapes, sizes and colors waiting to be whisked away into this new world.

He shrinks into a corner of the shelter. Under a canopy of cloudy plastic that looks out to a placid Virginia sky, he makes himself as small and invisible as he can.

༄

FOLLOWING A FEW WEEKS in a run-down rooming house in Kalorama, he seeks a more permanent home. An advertisement affixed to the bulletin board in his department catches his eye. Written in a fine, spidery hand, it reads—*Responsible boarder sought. Well-appointed room. Laundry and separate bathroom provided. Must be quiet and studious. Possibility of meals. No horseplay.*

The address is in Georgetown. One of the innumerable townhouses. After making a call to ensure that the space is still available, he arranges for a visit. The proprietor is an elderly gentleman named Karl Laurson, who meets Shar at the door and escorts him up to examine the room he might occupy. Located at the end of a hallway on the second floor, it is large and sun-lit, and looks as though the occupant is only out for the day. Hockey and lacrosse sticks cling to the wall like tangible graffiti; the desk shelters dog-eared copies of *The Catcher in the Rye*, *The Stranger* and *Heart of Darkness.*

The room reminds him of the one he left behind in Bangladesh, except that his walls were adorned with cricket bats and badminton rackets, while his desk held the works of Tagore, Islam and Guha.

They sit in the living room to discuss the details. Across a meandering hour-long conversation, he learns that Karl Laurson is from Wisconsin, from a line of Norwegians who settled in the area in the nineteenth century. A series of photographs on the wall shows Karl and his slim, dark-haired wife standing behind three boys and two girls who grow steadily taller and older. The latest series features a phalanx of grandchildren, but his wife is absent from the final two photographs.

"They're scattered all over the country now," he says, noticing Shar's interest. He sees them twice a year, he says, at Christmas and Thanksgiving. His oldest son, Patrick, whose room Shar may rent, is now a civil engineer in Phoenix.

Shar feels a twinge of sympathy. He thinks of Dhaka—crowded and boisterous. Of waking up on Eid mornings with his parents, going to mosque, hurtling down the city's suddenly barren roads in their car, visiting over the course of the day the few relations and friends they have in the city. Like most Bengalis, the thought of a child voluntarily and permanently distancing himself from a parent is unthinkable to him, the importance of family in his culture so paramount that there is a word for it—*ekannoborti*—a family of fifty-one.

Karl clearly seeks a boarder not for income but company. As a former economist for the Bureau of Labor Statistics, he has earned enough of a pension to lead a comfortable retirement.

"You seem a good sort," he says to Shar. "A boy who keeps his nose stuck in a book and out of trouble."

They rise together, embark on an extended tour of Mr. Laurson's home, which is surprisingly large. Heavy wooden furniture (made by Shakers, assures Karl) huddles in room after spacious room, the desks and chairs refugees from past decades, fearful of a modern world. Shar likes the large house, imagining it to be a modern incarnation of the home in *Wuthering Heights*. He is certain to be productive here.

"Do you require a deposit?" he asks.

ᘓᘐᘓ

HE MOVES IN AND establishes his identity around the edges of Patrick's, whose Dire Straits and Genesis albums dwarf Shar's Miles and Souls LPs. Whose dusty Robert Ludlum and Stephen King hardcovers lean against his Siddiqua Kabir cookbooks and poetry collections. Whose frozen pendulums of swimming and wrestling medals gain the rustic backdrops of Bangladeshi macramé Shar brought from home.

Finally settled in America, he falls into a routine of bagels with cream cheese for breakfast while perusing the *Post*. He jogs, working off the softness settled around his belly during his first month in the country, even though the steep grade of the Georgetown streets makes his ankles ache. Karl takes an interest in his studies. Some mornings, he finds stories clipped from the business section on the dining room table, Karl's commentary on economic theory penciled in the margins.

He purchases a used car, a 1983 Chevrolet Malibu. Small but rust-free, Shar finds it more assured on city streets than on the highway, where—going past seventy—it shakes like a malarial patient, swaying dangerously in the wake of semis rushing past.

It is on this precarious mode of transport that he takes a white-knuckled drive up I-95, headed for New England during the Christmas holidays, determined to witness a real winter in bucolic America. There, he rents a cabin from a farmer in Stowe, Vermont, and watches the snow smother the town until it piles high on hats and caps, streets and eaves, the branches of maple, birch and oak. For the first time in months—as he witnesses this silent, relentless accumulation in the deep loneliness of December—he realizes how far he is from home.

HE IS LESS ADVENTUROUS when the new year arrives, holing up in Patrick's bedroom to complete his thesis—on Hayek's Theory of Spontaneous Order as it relates to disaster response. Although he has promised his thesis supervisor a research proposal by early April, by February it becomes clear that this deadline was much too ambitious, thanks to his tendency to procrastinate on big projects. He begins waking to a sense of palpable dread, spends evening after evening at Lauinger Library, having convinced the librarian to grant him the use of study carrels normally reserved for doctoral students. Tucked into these wooden nooks, he plies himself with coffee and chips as he pores over textbooks, loses count of the dawns he emerges bleary-eyed, the light in the east only beginning to leak across the sky.

One such night in early March, he is reading one of Hayek's more inscrutable works when he nods off. He wakes two hours later, the pages of his notebook embossed on his face. He rereads the last two pages of practically nonsensical notes, barks a laugh, and stands to stretch. Lauinger appears abandoned, but he can see a pair of Chuck Taylors peeking out from under a carrel by the window.

"Hello," he says to their owner, this other lone citizen of the library. "Would you mind keeping an eye on my bag? I'm just going to get a coffee."

Halfway through his request, he realizes that he knows the man. "Hi. How are you?" He nods to acknowledge their acquaintance. *Nikhil? Nitesh?* The man is Indian-American, bearing a shaved head that Shar remembers being told is for the intramural swim team.

"I'm good, man," the man says, smiling. "Happy to look after your stuff. Don't take too long, though. I might fall asleep."

Niten. He remembers his name as he walks out to a gray morning. He is from Niagara Falls, where his parents run a motel. He has mentioned how he spends his summers helping them manage it, often driving across the border to Toronto on the weekends.

After buying coffee for himself and Niten at Peet's, he returns to find the library entrance blocked by a campus tour group. The leader, a woman in a maroon duffle coat and a Hoyas cap, addresses the group in an upbeat voice that contrasts with the cold, depressing conditions.

Despite the chill, he does not go in. He stands, sipping his coffee, listening as the woman recounts the history of the Lauinger Library. Her auburn hair is pulled back into a ponytail, a striped muffler wrapped thick and high around her neck. She has green eyes. He cannot stop watching her, but when their gazes lock, she offers him nothing more than a quick impersonal smile. Remembering that Niten is still watching his bag, Shar goes in, and does not think of the woman in the Hoyas cap again.

A MONTH LATER, HAVING made progress on a serviceable draft of his thesis, he comes home to find a letter. The stamp of an eagle appears on its top-right corner, the words *Selective Service* printed below in green ink. His own (egregiously misspelled) name greets him in the plastic window.

He rips the seal open and reads the letter, and then again, all the while wearing his backpack.

He finds Karl reading the *New Yorker* in the study, his glasses perched halfway down his nose. He barely glances at the missive and accompanying form when handed them.

"It's a Selective Service request," he explains. "The United States maintains records of men who are potentially subject to conscription. Those of a certain age are required to register."

"Conscription?"

"The draft. For military service."

"It must be a mistake."

"They likely didn't know that you're international," Karl says, licking an index finger and using it to turn a page. "I don't think you need to send it in."

But he is unable to dismiss the summons so lightly. He sits at his desk that evening, a copy of *Invisible Cities* open before him, the letter claiming a space on his desk. At the edge of his vision, stiff from its folds, it has the weight and presence of a corpse.

He reads it again. The penalty for not returning the form can be a fine of up to a quarter million dollars. Or five years in prison. Or both.

༄

HE VISITS THE INTERNATIONAL student office the next morning, signs in and waits for his turn to speak to a counselor. Two others are ahead of him in the queue: a tall blond man in black and a woman in a hijab. They are summoned by their last names—first *Harakka*, then *Yilan*.

After a long wait, Yilan emerges from the counselor's office, offering him an apologetic smile as she walks past.

The counselor, a red-haired woman, comes through the door, consults the list.

"Chou-dhu-ry?" She motions him to follow.

The carpeted office is spare and neat. A window looks out to the Potomac, the concrete arches of the Key Bridge skipping across. She gestures to an empty chair. "How can I help you today?"

He looks away momentarily, trying to remember where he has seen that smile. Then, remembering that avoiding eye contact is rude in America, he tells her why he is there.

"Can I see it?" She puts out a hand, freckled like her face and shoulders. Locks of her auburn hair are tucked behind her ears; her eyes are tilted and green.

She scrutinizes the letter for a full minute, pursing her lips. She admits with an embarrassed shrug that she has no idea what it is. She leaves the room with the promise to consult her colleague. She returns soon.

"Colin says that you can just fill it out and return it. You won't get sent off to war," she chuckles.

He laughs too, abashed at how ridiculous his fears seem in the light of day.

"Anything else I can help you with?"

"Maybe you can help me remember where we met before? You seem very familiar."

"The tour group in front of Lauinger, I think. About a month ago."

The day returns to him. "Yes. You're right. You were buried under that hat and scarf."

He holds out a hand. "I'm Shar."

She takes it. "I'm Val."

ᙅᙏᙣ

VAL'S SMILE, THE FIRM press of her hand in his, consume his thoughts all evening. Impulsively, he had asked for her card before leaving the office—in case of more questions he might have—grinning sheepishly at the flimsy excuse.

Over the course of the next day, he opens the wallet and studies the card multiple times. *Valerie Neider.* The continued presence of her name in his pocket reassures him, a receipt acknowledging their chemistry.

He has begun to spend more time with Niten since that day in the library; now he consults his American friend on how to proceed. Niten suggests that he just call Val and ask her out, but Shar balks. His affairs back home were all products of months, and sometimes years, of unacknowledged attraction between him and the girls he pursued.

"Just rip off the Band-Aid," Niten insists.

ᙅᙏᙣ

HE WAKES ONE MORNING soon after and heads to a pay phone in a quiet corner of the campus. It rained the previous night; the puddles on the sidewalk are filled with leaves and sunshine, the air clean.

He punches in the seven digits of her number on the square

aluminum buttons, the carved numbers grimy with use, each confirming tone a bell tolling his doom. It is 9:35. Her office has been open for five minutes.

She answers on the third ring. "International students' office. Valerie Neider speaking."

He freezes. A part of him hoped to find the answering machine on the other side, the synchronicity of an actual conversation making rejection that much more painful. But his voice is steady when he speaks.

"Hi. It's Shar. I came by your office last week."

"Oh, hi! How are you?" she asks, the recognition and enthusiasm seemingly unfeigned.

"I'm good. I was wondering if you wanted to go out for a coffee sometime," he says in a rush.

There is a pause. "I don't drink coffee."

He flounders in space. He expected rejection to feel painful, but at that moment, it just feels like nothing.

"So, how about I have a tea with you instead?"

He leans against the pay phone and closes his eyes, the cool metal soothing his forehead, the hammering of his heart overwhelms his senses, but by the end of it they have somehow agreed to meet at Peet's on Friday.

NITEN IS LESS IMPRESSED when briefed over lunch at Food Factory in Arlington, with platters of pink tandoori chicken, spicy raita and naan spread before them.

"Just coffee? That's it?"

"It's a first date. Isn't that what's done here? I don't want to—how do you say it—come on too strong?"

"But it's clear that you both like each other. So why do something so wimpy as coffee?"

His appetite vanishes. "I hadn't thought of that. Maybe we should go to the movies?"

Niten dips a drumstick into the raita and brings it to his mouth without spilling a drop. He chews thoughtfully and swallows. "That's not great either. It's your first date. And you're going to sit and stare at a screen for two hours without getting to know each other?"

"Why don't you give me some ideas then, Mr. Dating Guru?"

"Well, maybe you can go to a later show. Have dinner first."

In the end, he takes none of the options offered, instead calling her on the day of their date to suggest a late afternoon stroll along the Mall, to which Val agrees readily.

On the day, she is waiting for him on a bench along the crushed gravel pathway that lines the Reflecting Pool. She rises and smiles as he approaches, taller than he remembers, standing shoulder to shoulder with him.

A gray screen of clouds drapes the horizon behind the Lincoln Memorial, hiding a melting sun. Val's hands are thrust into the pockets of her wool duffel coat, the same one from that day in front of Lauinger. As they walk in the general direction of the Washington Monument, he finds that his nervousness has disappeared.

She tells him that she is from Reading, Pennsylvania, which is between a small town and a city in size. Has he heard of it? No? John Updike is one of its famous sons, she reveals.

He knows the name, having found *Rabbit, Run* as a teenager in a pile of old books in his father's closet. It was the 1963 Penguin edition. The cover, composed of a red background juxtaposed behind sketches of a man's face and a woman's bare torso, had intrigued him, though after reading through a quarter he abandoned it in favor of the science fiction, fantasy and horror novels that held his attention in those days.

But fearful of inviting further questions, he tells her that he has not heard of Updike.

She is in the second year of a master's in International Development. She was in Bhopal, India, on an internship the previous summer—a difficult time in which she contracted chikungunya and pinworms and was briefly hospitalized.

She asks him about Bangladesh, questions that make it clear she knows much more about the country than the average American: Are the people still resentful toward the Pakistanis after the war? What is the country's current relationship with India? Has he visited the Hill Tracts in the south where the aboriginal populations reside?

She knows of Muhammad Yunus, she tells Shar, who founded a bank with the aim of providing financial services to the poor. Of Fazle Hasan Abed, who built a rival organization called BRAC—serving millions around the country.

He tells her that he met Yunus when their families lived in the same neighborhood in north Dhaka.

"You're shitting me!" she exclaims, and immediately blushes.

He laughs. "Bangladesh is both large and small. Like Reading in that sense. Slightly more crowded, though. Imagine if half of America decided to move to Iowa."

They stroll past the Mall, time left behind in the slipstream of conversation. Evening falls and against the streetlights, the loose hairs on Val's ponytail glow like filaments. They find a Peruvian restaurant on Eye Street and continue their conversation over ceviche, lomo saltado and beer.

Val's parents divorced when she was nine, her brother ten. Her father was an auto mechanic who moved to Shippensburg to live with his girlfriend afterward. Val's mother dated but never married or settled into a long-term relationship. For eight years, she dutifully drove Val and her brother to Shippensburg every other weekend. Val remembers hot summers in her father's backyard, limeades served by her father's girlfriend, Jeanie, as sour and bitter as the beverages she made.

"Why international development?" he asks to change the subject.

"I wanted to get away," she says, her eyes on the empty beer bottle, which she rotates by its base. "Going to school here instead of Penn or Pittsburgh was the first step."

"Why natural disasters?" she asks in turn, referring to the topic of his thesis.

"Our country has a love-hate relationship with water. Bangladesh is flat, just a few meters above sea level, and we have all these incredibly wide, long rivers that dive toward our country from the springboard of the Himalayas, bringing the rich alluvial soil that makes Bangladesh so fertile that it can sustain a hundred million people, the same rivers that flood every summer with the monsoon rains and displace millions. But the storms are much worse in terms of death tolls. They lash our southern coast every year. The damage is unthinkable sometimes. The storm in November 1970 killed a half million people overnight because no one was warned."

She raises a hand to her mouth. "My god. That's horrible."

He nods. "Indian ships had warning that Tropical Storm Nora was developing into a typhoon and headed to the coast of East Pakistan—as Bangladesh was called back then. But the relationship between India and Pakistan was so bad that the warnings were not passed on, or maybe they were and ignored. The West Pakistanis dominated the East back then, and even in the aftermath of the typhoon, with hundreds of thousands of corpses and livestock rotting in the sun, they took slow, grudging relief measures. They even turned down assistance from India, which we could have used badly. Many scholars think that is what really planted the seed for the Bangladesh War of Liberation that happened five months later."

He does not tell her of another precursor to his interest, his childhood memory of the seashore, a day of black skies and keening winds—and running hand in hand with an unknown figure toward a great house to escape a storm. His parents have gently dismissed this memory as the work of his imagination whenever he has mentioned it, and over time, he has convinced himself that it must be so.

When the bill arrives, she reaches for her wallet without hesitation. He raises a hand. "Can I get this one?"

"No! Really? I'm perfectly capable and happy to pay."

"Then why don't you get the next one?"

"So, there's going to be a next time?"

He smiles.

The server arrives—a young woman in white and black, her ash-blond hair tied in a ponytail. They thank her for the service and food. She leans over to collect the check.

"I just want to say that I think you two are adorable. Your children are going to be beautiful."

They laugh—uneasy with the compliment—and head for the door.

"I should've left a bigger tip," he says.

THE FOLLOWING WEEK, THEY go to see *Four Weddings and a Funeral* at Loews at Waterfront. Later, walking up an alley and before late-night kabobs at Moby Dick, they kiss on a bridge over the canals.

They spend weekends walking from one end of the vast Smithsonian network to the other, browsing the outdoor stalls at Eastern Market, where he buys for her a shawl of gold brocade on blue, amusing her by demonstrating the stylish way men wrap them around their shoulders in Bangladesh. After she makes him excavate the Bangla books stored in a trunk in his closet, they spend an afternoon drinking milk tea as he helps her trace the characters on parchment paper, spelling her name in his native letters, practicing until the shaky pencil outlines gain the thickness of confidence and they must switch the lights on to continue.

During their courtship, he worries about things he cannot control—disapproval that he spots in the eyes of shopkeepers and pedestrians, minute scowls or the tiny bending back of lips at the sight of them holding hands or kissing, often so brief and subtle he wonders if he is imagining it. She tells him of her Indian boyfriend—the son of the head of a local NGO—whom she met while volunteering for flood relief, over the course of several rainy afternoons. Their romance was brief, covert, and ended when she left India. But stored in a shoebox in her closet she keeps photographs of the two of them. Seeing these, Shar feels jealous that Val was once so close to someone who, at least superficially, resembles him.

In these early days, the canvas of their relationship is a blameless white, but as the weeks and months pass, he begins to sketch on them dark and troubled visions of how his parents might receive the news of him dating a foreigner. He summons himself to the witness box to testify to his motives for dating Val—are his feelings genuine, or merely fueled by the thrill of dating an American? His imaginary prosecutor poses the same questions to Val—asking whether Shar is the understudy, a pale(r) stand-in for the man she left behind in India. The one she really loves. When they sleep together, the indecency of the act, his lifestyle in this new country, inculcated in him through a lifetime of steeping in the amorphous brand of Islamic morality that permeates his homeland, overwhelms the sense of intimacy and love that it should engender.

He confesses these fears to her, including his concern about the fate of their relationship once his program at Georgetown ends. Her response, that they will cross that bridge when they come to it, he finds less than reassuring.

She seems to be standing still, so he runs closer to her instead. One night he tells her of a dream he has had since childhood—of waking in a hut, the sunlight shining through many blazing apertures in the thatch roof. Playing with chickens in a dirt courtyard, his feet nestled in the hot sand of an unnamed beach, holding the hand of a woman whose dark skin makes the green of her eyes starker still.

"That is a strange dream," she says. "How many times have you had it?"

"Too many to count," he says. They are lying in bed. A feeble July breeze crawls through the window of her Tenleytown efficiency. The sheets stick to their backs.

"Maybe it's from something you read once? A movie you saw?"

"No." He shakes his head, unable to find the words to express that this dream, like that of him running to escape a storm, does not feel imagined, the product of a mind alone. They are relics washed up on the shores of his being.

Other than his parents and now Val, he has only spoken of this dream to Rina, the woman who helped raise him. She told him to pay it no mind.

⌒‿⌒

ON A SATURDAY IN September, they take a long drive through the Blue Ridge Parkway in a rented convertible. There is a touch of coolness in the morning air as they follow the road, twisting around peaks, rising above a valley covered in cloaks of mist run ragged in places by trees crowned with fall's incipient fire. They have a picnic lunch in a meadow recumbent on a mountain, spreading their blanket on grass brilliantly green in the sunshine and shot through with wildflowers. Here they sit and eat homemade chicken sandwiches—a recipe he learned from his mother—with diced chicken and cucumber sautéed in butter, salt and black pepper.

The day concludes when they pull into a bed-and-breakfast nestled on a ridgeway, where, following dinner, Shar and Val walk out to a back porch opening out to an expansive vista of the valley below. Sitting on wooden chairs as dusk falls and the fire in the brazier before them subsides to glowing embers, they sip red wine that stains their mouths the color of the evening sky, wrap themselves in a silence that Shar interprets as one borne of familiarity and contentment.

He wishes to tell her that he loves her, that he can not only imagine a life with her but sees it as inevitable. He opens his mouth, only to hesitate as last-second nerves overtake his resolve. But the hard, square press of the box in his jacket pocket—one he intends to reveal to Val in moments—reassures him. He forges on through the uncertainty.

He takes her hand. She turns to offer him a smile. In the dying light, he cannot see that it is strained, that it does not reach her eyes.

"I've something to ask you," he says.

VALERIE

Washington, DC
September 1994

They decide to drive back the same night, forgoing the room they had booked for the weekend at the inn. This time the rental's canvas top stays up, the atmosphere in the car sullen and stormy. Shar drives in silence as Val quietly cries, her face turned away from him. His proposal caught her completely unawares. In recent days she had been gathering the nerve to gently end their relationship, because despite caring about him a great deal and cherishing his sweetness, she could not see a future together. They are opposites in the most important ways—while she craves adventure, he prizes safety. While she strains to leave home, he cannot wait to return to his.

Even if they were to somehow reconcile those differences, at only twenty-five, she is not ready to leave so many future doors unopened. She had hoped that after these months together there would be a natural separation that would ease matters, a widening fork between them as they approached the ends of their respective programs. She has told him how excited she is to have received an internship with the World Bank, shared her enthusiasm for her Arabic classes, clues to which he remained cheerfully immune. She saw the weekend getaway to Blue Ridge as an opportunity to bring their relationship to an amicable close. But Shar had other ideas.

These were the thoughts she tried to marshal and articulate when he started to speak on the porch, a moment when her heart and mind clenched in panic as she recognized what was coming, rendering what emerged from her mouth halting, inconsiderate, abrupt. As she spoke, she could see him shatter and crumble before her eyes, and found her tenderness toward him tempered by irritation at his obliviousness, his self-absorption. *God, how could you not know, Shar?*

She hated herself for that.

They come to a gliding stop before her apartment building in Tenleytown, the street abandoned this late at night, drenched in the sodium glow of the streetlamps. Shar alights and goes to the trunk to unload her luggage. She steps out to the sidewalk. He wheels the small American Tourister suitcase to her.

"Do you need a hand to take it up?" he asks, his first words in two hours.

She shakes her head, her eyes still red. "Shar, I'm sorry that . . ."

He raises a hand. "It's okay. Don't apologize. I should have seen it coming. I'm sorry to have put you in that position."

"I won't say something trite like 'let's stay friends,' but it's an option for us, one I'd very much like to take."

He nods, not looking her in the eyes. "Thank you. Yes, sure. Maybe."

He walks over to the driver's side. "I'll wait until you're inside."

True to his word, he drives away as soon as she closes the door to the foyer behind her, not waiting a second longer than he needs to.

DAYS PASS IN WHICH she does not hear from him, a period in which she is also circumspect about reaching out, respectful of the space and time he needs to recover. One evening, a week to the day since that fateful evening in the Blue Ridge Mountains, she is contemplating a friendly call to see how he is faring when her phone rings. She answers it to find Shar on the other end. Her joy and relief are soon replaced by concern when he speaks.

"Val, I just got a call from Dhaka," he says, his voice cracking under the strain. "It's about my father."

He contacted her immediately after receiving the call about the heart attack. Rahim was in the hospital, conscious and recovering, but Shar was still frantic with worry. Rina called him with the news—Rahim and Zahira were sitting on the wrought iron swing in the back lawn, sipping their morning tea. Upon hearing the newspaper man ring the front bell of their gate, Zahira left her husband's side. When she returned, a copy of the *Daily Star* tucked under one arm, she found him kneeling on the ground, his face contorted with pain, the legs of his perfectly white slacks stained by grass and tea.

"I spoke to the doctor over the phone," he tells her. "He said it was a 'garden variety' heart attack. Can you believe it? Like it's some species of snail."

She drives over to see him the same night. She takes her usual route through Mass Avenue, the road mostly free at this time of the evening, all the while trying to ignore the headache pulsing at her left temple. All week she has dealt with a low-grade fever and nausea. It could be the flu.

Karl greets her at the door to Shar's house. "He's upstairs, packing his bags."

He lays a fatherly hand on her shoulder as she is about to start up the stairs. "He's a good boy. You're lucky to have each other."

She nods and continues her ascent, aware of his regard, uncomfortable with the burden of expectations. *I guess Shar hasn't told him.*

In his room, he is filling a suitcase on his bed. He embraces her when she enters. "Thank you for coming."

"Don't be silly." She feels the room darken for a bit, and sways. "Are you alright?"

"Sorry, just tired." When he continues to stare, she says, "Don't worry about me. Focus on your packing. Have you booked tickets?"

"Yes. Expensive as hell, but I had no choice. My flight is in the morning."

"I'll take you to the airport," she says, then goes over to hold him again, unsure of what else to add. "It's going to be fine. I know it. How's your dad now?"

"He's better, but can't talk yet. At least Mother and Rina are by his side."

"That's the nanny who raised you, right?"

"Yes. She's always been a part of our family. My mother calls her the prime minister to her president." He laughs.

The curtains flutter from a cold breeze, the soft hiss of rain. "Do you want some food? I have sandwiches."

"No, but I can get them for you." She starts to head down to the kitchen.

"Val, do you want to stay here tonight?"

She hesitates. "Shar, of course I can, and want to, but as a friend. I hope we're still on the same page on this."

He nods. "You can stay in the guest bedroom. I'll talk to Karl. I'm sure he's okay with it. I haven't told him what happened yet, but I guess this would be a good time."

She smiles. "Then I'll stay."

THEY DRIVE TO DULLES in the morning. His flight is Dragon Air 216, at eleven. Going the *wrong way* to Bangladesh—LA to Tokyo to Bangkok to Dhaka. A forty-hour trip.

He does not have time to inform his thesis supervisor about his father, so Val volunteers to deliver his letter explaining the situation. Karl, who insisted on accompanying them, is the lone backseat passenger. Niten, Shar's closest friend in America, is in Niagara Falls, visiting his parents.

"I don't think I'll be gone that long," he says, in better spirits this morning. He called home again over the course of the night and learned that his father was already stronger, better, sitting up in bed and talking. The doctors assured his family that the danger of a second heart attack was minimal. Rahim would be home within the week.

They arrive well ahead of schedule, finish checking in and decide to have breakfast at a Johnny Rockets in the terminal. They order. Shar declines the bacon—a stricture that always amuses Val, given his lack of inhibitions toward alcohol. He denies any hypocrisy in the act—*I just can't, no matter how delicious. Eating something versus drinking something is totally different.*

He devours his eggs and hash browns, talking excitedly about how much he misses his family, Rina, Dhaka. She takes half-hearted bites of her cream cheese bagel. They rise together when his flight is announced on the overhead speakers. Karl tells them to go ahead without him, shaking Shar's hand, wishing his father a quick recovery. Val recognizes the kindness of the gesture, intended to give the couple a measure of privacy during their good-bye. But a part of her wishes he had not.

She gives him a kiss on the cheek at the gate, wishes him a safe trip. He goes through the gate. Turns to wave. Before long, the 737 is lumbering to the runway. Val stands and watches it ascend the horizon until it is a shining metal shard in the sky. Only then does she go to the bathroom so she can throw up her breakfast.

~

SHAR CALLS HER SOON after reaching Dhaka. His father is back home, "but I've never seen Abba this serious," he says, his voice low. "He said he has something important to tell me. I told him it can wait. It's probably about his will. I think his heart attack scared him."

"That's understandable."

"How are you feeling?"

"Better," she lies. In a corner of Val's mind where she dare not look yet, a small but persistent realization is growing.

"Tell me about Dhaka," she says.

He does. It is not even two years since he left, but the city already feels different to him, like a young cousin who has crossed into puberty in his absence. Billboards advertising cell-phone service line the highway. Late-model cars choke the roads, darken the horizon with smog. He must reacclimatize to being chauffeured around instead of driving himself, to the subtleties of tea rather than the bluntness of coffee.

They chat some more. It is late at night in DC and early morning in Dhaka. Val is yawning. Shar promises to call again soon.

THE NEXT DAY IS a busy one for Val. She spends four hours in the morning at her World Bank internship, attends Arabic class in the afternoon. Feeling much better, she eats a full order of basil fried rice for lunch and meets a friend for drinks in the evening. She and Jennie—a fellow Drexel grad who is now a junior accountant in the city—meet on the second floor at Lindy's Red Lion, where the windows look out to Pennsylvania Avenue.

Jennie's hair is tied up in a professional bun. In her dark pantsuit she looks older than her twenty-four years. Val shrinks slightly, aware of the contrast her gray sweatpants draw—she was at the Bally Total Fitness nearby for a quick workout on the StairMaster, but could only manage twenty minutes before losing her breath.

Jennie shakes loose her hair and stretches her finger-entwined palms toward the ceiling until her joints crack. "Jesus, I need a beer!"

"Jesus is right on that. Long day at work?"

"You've no idea." Jennie leans forward. "A whole day spent reviewing dumb P-and-L statements, all that on top of studying for my CPA. You're lucky you can take the time to smell the roses while you figure stuff out."

Val is defensive. "It's not exactly a vacation." What is it about women that the most innocuous things they say to each other still seem barbed? Or is she being too sensitive? "I have the internship, classes, learning Arabic . . ."

"Uh-huh." Jennie is looking past her shoulder. "I think that guy's checking you out."

"It's you he's checking out. No one would look at me twice the way I'm dressed."

Her friend is still preoccupied with her alleged suitor. Her head swivels back to Val. "He's cute!"

"Buy him a drink." She wonders where the server is. She and Jennie became friends at Drexel because they ran in the same circles. But she always found her self-involved. Apparently, little has changed since then.

"Looks like a senior out with first real ID. I probably look like his mom to him. Besides, he was looking at you, babe. Turn around and see."

"I'll pass."

"Oh right, you're dating that Indian guy. What's his name again?"

"He's from Bangladesh, not India."

"Sorry. Where's that anyway?"

"Right next door. It used to be a part of India before the British left."

Jennie shakes her head. "You know so much random stuff. I

can't believe you actually went and lived there." She shudders. "I could never do that."

Their server arrives—a harried young woman in T-shirt and jeans. "Hi, did you want some food today?"

Jennie orders a burger. Val, fries.

"Anything to drink?"

"I'll have a pint of Heineken," Jennie says.

The server looks to Val. "I'll just have a club soda and lime." She turns to Jennie, who is nonplussed. "Sorry, a bit too much to drink last night. Still nursing a hangover."

"You do look a bit pale. Must've been a good party."

"Something like that."

"So what about this guy? You see a future with him?"

"We broke up, actually. Just last week."

"Oh, sorry, babe. How come?"

"It's a long story." She tells Jennie the general outlines of her reasoning, excluding what happened at Blue Ridge Mountain to protect Shar's dignity. Airing her misgivings about the relationship to Jennie feels like a betrayal, selling a precious memento in a yard sale. Perhaps she is the one at fault. Her mother's divorce poisoned her faith in relationships, marriage and children. The responsibility of raising her and her brother occupied every last precious corner of her mother's selfhood. She wishes she could reimburse her mother for the time she lost.

Their drinks arrive. Then food. She shepherds the conversation toward safer pastures: Jennie's career, her classes. Jennie becomes even more demonstrative and brazen by her second beer, and Val begins to enjoy herself at last, the stresses of the last few days dissipating.

At ten they step out to streets full of carousing students, dodge a laughing couple chasing each other.

"You taking the metro?"

"I am, but go ahead. I need to pick up some contact-lens solution."

"This late at night?"

Val forces a laugh. "I'm afraid it can't wait."

～～

THREE HOURS LATER, HER hand trembling on the receiver, she calls Shar. Partway through, as she is inputting the plus sign and the area code for Bangladesh—880—it dimly occurs to her that she should have bought a phone card for this call. She does not have an international plan and has no idea the rate MCI will charge her.

She is in no state of mind to note his subdued tone when he answers, his lack of surprise that it is her calling him rather than the reverse. "I really need to talk to you about something," she says. "Is this a good time?"

His tone is flat. "I actually need to talk to you too."

"Okay. You go first."

He does. He speaks for more than an hour, during which she does not, cannot interrupt him, during which the news she has called him with becomes no more than the daytime moon to the sun of his own revelations. Present, but unseen.

He says that the night before, his parents summoned him and Rina into the drawing room. Holding hands, his father and mother told him that he was the son of a man and woman he may no longer remember. He laughed at first, thinking it a joke, that his parents were recreating the melodramatic reveals from the Indian serials that had recently taken over Bangladeshi television. Then he began to wonder if they had simply gone mad from the stress of his father's illness and Shar's prolonged absence from Bangladesh. But he saw the determination in their eyes as they continued speaking, as they brought out a cloth bag containing the two artifacts that belonged to his birth parents.

For more than two decades, Rahim, Zahira and Rina had been burdened with the secret they carried. They had endlessly debated whether and when to tell him, but as he grew taller and stronger and his memories of the hut by the beach, of his mother and father, faded, the lie became easier to maintain, the truth more difficult to explain.

"I . . . I don't know what to say, Shar," is what Val manages when he finally stops speaking. "What're you going to do?"

"I don't know. I've been pinching myself all morning. They've left me alone, as though I'm some dangerous animal that'll bite if they get close. They're overwhelmed with guilt. The burden is heaviest with my . . . with Rahim. He said he took so long to tell because he couldn't forgive himself for what he did to my birth mother. He was afraid I'd judge him for betraying her."

"And do you?"

"I don't know what to feel. A part of me is angry, sure, but another asks what I'd have done in if I were in their place."

"What was in the bag?"

He tells her.

"That's so unusual. Do you have any idea where they came from?"

"Rahim knew a little about one of them. The other we're not sure of, yet. All I know is that it was sent with me when I came for shelter that day."

"You'll need some time to process this—"

He tramples over her words. "I've talked to Rina. Told her that I want her to take me to Chittagong. To the village. I want to see where I was born."

"That's understandable."

"I'm sorry. I interrupted you. You called to tell me something."

"It's not important."

"Tell me."

She takes a long breath. "Do you want me to take your car for an oil change? It's due per the sticker."

"Oh, okay. Yes, sure. Thanks."

Seconds pass in which neither speaks.

"Val?"

"Yes?"

"I think I'll have to be here until I've figured out what this all means. I don't know how long that will take. I guess in that sense, what happened that night at Blue Ridge was a good thing."

She squeezes her eyes shut, making tears race to the bottom of her cheeks and drip onto her gray hoodie. But when she speaks, her voice is calm. Warm and strong. "Yes. It was for the best."

"I care for you very much."

"And I you."

"Thanks, Val. Was there anything else?"

"Not for now. Get some rest. Keep me updated on what's going on."

She puts the phone down. It's two in the morning. A light breeze blows through the window of her kitchen. The dim light above her stove is the only one on in her apartment.

On the dining table before her are five home pregnancy test kits that—in a fit of obsessive compulsion—she arranged in neat alternating rows. In the small window at the center of each kit floats a blue "plus" icon.

Valerie Neider, alone in Washington, DC, and eight thousand miles from the father of her child, puts her face in her hands and begins to sob.

※

SHE WAKES SOMETIME AFTER eight, following a fitful night. She forgot to pull the blinds down and the sunlight streaming through the window holds all the final promises of summer, but it takes only a few seconds for her new reality to crash down on her.

She disrobes from the sweats she slept in and takes a long hot shower. She focuses her mind on the mundane rituals of cleansing. During the process, when her hand gets close to her belly she finds it scurrying away, as though that area of her body is alienated from her now. As though she is invading space belonging to another.

She shuts off the tap and leans her head against the glass. The steady drip of the tap and her breath the only sounds. No heart beating but her own. But she feels watched.

There is no nausea this morning, ironically. As though her symptoms just needed her to know the cause before abating. She boils oatmeal even though she is not hungry, and after tossing the kits in the trash, eats at the same dining table she sobbed on the previous night.

This is not her first scare—there was that one time in her final year of high school, and another as a college sophomore. The second time her period was late enough that she took the test. That was with Paul. He was on the dean's list, the intramural squash team—a man who turned heads and had his sights set far beyond her when they ended things. He is a corporate lawyer on Wall Street now. They have spoken on the phone a few times, even planned to meet for lunch once when she was visiting New York, but somehow that did not end up happening.

She never told him.

She tosses the bowl into the sink and dials Shar's number. She lost her nerve in the face of his revelation the previous night, but now she must tell him. By her calculations, it is around nine at night in Dhaka. She remembers him telling her that Bengalis like to eat late, joking that they wait for the national flag to appear on their television screens before they set (or in his case, someone else sets) the table. He may be sitting down to dinner right now.

The phone rings fifteen times and is picked up just when she is about to hang up.

"Hello?" says an unfamiliar male voice.

She freezes. Why did she assume that Shar would answer? Her voice sounds timid and whingy to her ears when she speaks. "H-hello . . . can I speak to Shahryar please?"

"I'm afraid he's not here," says the man, his voice raspy but the English impeccable. "May I take a message?"

"Oh, you must be Mr. Choudhury. I'm so glad to hear you're better, sir."

"Thank you, my dear. Are you a friend of my son's?"

Yes. And he knocked me up. She stifles a mad giggle. "Yes, my name is Valerie."

"Oh. He speaks so fondly of you. Valerie, I'm afraid he's gone to Chittagong, do you—"

"Yes, I know where that is, Mr. Choudhury. Is there a way to reach him there?"

"There's no number I can give you. He's in a very rural area, you see. Is this urgent?"

You can say that. "No. I just wanted to say hello. Do you know when he'll be back?"

"I'm afraid I have no idea."

෴

SHE WOULD KEEP CALLING.

In those first weeks when she is frantic to reach him there are times when she wants to scream at his parents—who become steadily more confused by the frequency of her calls—that she is carrying his child, that she is frightened and cannot do this alone, even do this at all. But she always demurs at the edges of these confessional precipices. At one point she even suspects that his parents have quietly surmised what is happening, can sense the question on the edge of their lips in the abiding uncomfortable silences that fall. She would welcome it. Would tell them if they just ask. But they never do.

She writes letters. Letters that she sends everywhere that Shar might possibly be—his home in Dhaka, in Chittagong, even their old address in Calcutta in the vain hope that the search for his past might take him there. Such is her need to reach him that she painstakingly writes the address and name on the envelopes in Bangla, learned from a book she finds on a dusty shelf in the local library. The letters sent to his home in Dhaka are left respectfully on his desk by his parents. The others are like stones dropped into the abyss.

She shares the news of her pregnancy with no one at first. Not her friends, and especially not her mother, the one person she is most frightened of becoming if she has a child now. She always wanted a child, but at a time and place of her choosing, and every day that she does not hear from Shar, this choice recedes like a shore falling away from a fast-moving vessel, for it is not hers to make alone.

She finishes the fall semester and submits a request for a deferral a week before the Christmas holidays. When she finally calls home, her mother makes the three-hour drive from Reading to DC the same night.

She spends the winter in Pennsylvania, then spring. At points, when reconnecting with old friends she had left behind for college, relatives to whom she must explain her life and choices, she wonders if she has made a mistake in returning.

More sober about the prospects of an international career, she busies herself with night courses at a local college in the new year, focusing on a fast-track finance degree. All the while the child within her grows, a placid, benign acceleration other than for the occasional morning sickness. On some nights, the being makes itself known, an errant limb or the head pressing against her until its outlines can be seen across her belly. Feeling mischievous during these sightings, Val gently pushes down against the protrusion with a finger until it disappears again in the depths of her womb, like a startled fish.

One morning, her mother leaves for her part-time volunteer position at the local library, reminding Val that she is expecting a package, so when the doorbell rings around half past ten, she descends the stairs with hurried but careful steps, one hand bracing her belly, worried that if she missed the FedEx truck they would have to drive to the warehouse located in the outskirts of town, twenty miles away.

She opens the door and the words with which she planned to greet the delivery person wither on her lips.

Shar stands before her, dressed simply in an olive green T-shirt and jeans, a canvas backpack slung over his shoulder. On the driveway behind him sits a gray Buick that he has presumably rented to drive to her.

He makes no motion to approach. His hair is long now, his cheekbones more prominent, the arms and elbows honed sharper. He does not smile. His eyes are hooded and wary. Buried below the man she knew was another, and his emergence is nearly complete.

"When did you get here?" she manages to ask.

"I landed in DC a few days ago. I thought you'd still be there. I had to track you down. You didn't leave a forwarding address."

"I didn't hear from you, so I stopped writing. I didn't think anyone would come looking for me."

He stares at her belly. "Do you know if it's a boy or a girl?"

She shakes her head. "I asked them not to tell me. Felt like a measure of control over the process."

"How long are you here for?" she asks him.

"My visa's good for three months."

She still has not moved out of his way, nor has he moved a step closer since they began speaking. Val sighs and leans her head against the doorframe.

"Well, my friend, just what the heck do we do now?"

Shahryar & Anna

Washington, DC
September 2004

Shar stops to catch his breath, nearly an hour after he began
speaking. All that time, Katerina has not interrupted him once.
It is cooler now, their breaths just beginning to fog in the air. Faint
sounds of revelry drift in from Dupont Circle. A dog barks nearby,
insistent at first, then trailing into silence. A raccoon, back arched
and wary, steps out of a driveway across the street, and upon spot-
ting them, retreats into the dark.

He notices Katerina wrap her shawl closer. Embarrassed that
it took him so long, he offers her his jacket. She accepts with gratitude.

"Your story is unbelievable, Shar," she says, zipping the leather
jacket halfway up. "I mean in a good way. Not in the way that I don't
believe you. Why did it take you so long to get back, though?"

"After finding out about my birth parents it felt like nothing
was real anymore, except for them. I had to know more, I had to.
I spent months in that village, talking to everyone and anyone
who knew them, who might have known them. And all that time,
it was as if the rest of the world had disappeared. But I had to
come back home at some point, if only to convince my parents
that I hadn't completely lost my mind. They told me that Val had
been calling, showed me her letters. After I read the first one, I

immediately applied for a visa to the States, which normally takes months to get, but my father pulled all the strings he could. I left two weeks later."

"Were you there for the birth of your daughter?"

"I was, but Val and I couldn't work out how we wanted to be in each other's lives. Those first few months, things were tense. It was everyone's fault and no one's."

Katerina inches closer. "I know we discussed this at Mr. Ahmed's office, but was reconciliation not possible?"

"We discussed it. I didn't want to leave so soon after Anna was born. I offered it. We would have had to get married for me to stay back. But she said no, saying that we didn't have a good foundation on which to build a relationship, but that I could be in Anna's life in whatever capacity or extent that I wanted."

"When did she meet her boyfriend?"

"A couple of years later." He tells Katerina how Val worked during the days at places like Pottery Barn and Williams-Sonoma while Anna was watched by her grandmother, all the while taking night classes for her finance degree. An executive track MBA at Drexel and a CA certification followed. She secured a position at ING in Maryland, rising quickly to become a senior financial analyst, then finance manager.

It was in Baltimore, one day after work, when Val's car would not start in a Trader Joe's parking lot. The man in the BMW beside her offered a jump-start, and when that did not work, drove her to the babysitter's residence so that she could collect Anna. Finally, he gave them a ride home, a business card on which he wrote his cell-phone number. A number that Val would dial three days later, proposing a walk in Rock Creek Park. She mentioned that she would find a sitter for Anna, but Jeremy insisted that she bring her daughter along. Anna was a little over two years old at the time.

Shar was working in a small NGO near Chittagong by then,

finding time to research his roots in his spare moments, all the while keeping up regular correspondence with Val and Anna. He was also realizing the unsustainability of his lifestyle and trying to find a way to be closer to his daughter. Applying for a doctorate, with proposed research on the lives of the fishermen of the Bangladeshi coast, presented itself as a possibility, and he applied to the Social Anthropology program at GW, receiving an acceptance letter four months later.

Val broke the news about Jeremy to him gently. A few weeks after he moved back to America and began his doctoral classes at George Washington, she invited him for grilled-cheese sandwiches and coleslaw at her apartment one Saturday afternoon, told him that she had been seeing Jeremy for some time, that she and Anna were planning to move in with him.

I want you to know that this does not in any way diminish your role in Anna's life, she said. *I think it'll be good for her to be in such a loving environment. Jeremy and I can provide that. And you'll of course be a big part of it.*

He sat for some moments, blindsided by the news. When he spoke, his words were enveloped in a quiet fury. *I could have provided that. I offered, twice. You said no both times.*

This seemed to be an accusation she had prepared for. *I did. It's true,* she said. *The first time, I wasn't ready. But the second time, it was you. I could see the relief in your face when I said no then. You couldn't hide it. You weren't done with your past, and even Anna wasn't enough reason for you to remain here. I know you would have stayed back if I'd made you, but unhappily. I don't blame you for that. I can't imagine being caught between the past and the future the way you are . . . were.*

She reached across the table and entwined her fingers with his. *This is for the best, Shar. I swear. It's no small thing you've done in moving back here. I know it. Jeremy knows it, and when Anna's older, she'll know it too.*

ڡﯔ

AND NOW, KATERINA LAYS an arm on his, recreating the past. "She was right, you know. You're not alone in this. I know just as much as you how painful it is to not see your child. And we're both lucky to have Mr. Ahmed on our side."

"I know," he says. "Thank you." He gently takes his arm away. He has spoken longer and in more detail than he thought he would. Now he feels a glaze of shame to have laid out so much of his life before this woman who is barely more than a stranger.

Katerina stares at him intently. He breaks the eye contact, reminding himself how easily beauty and charm can be weaponized.

"Mr. Ahmed's going to work his fingers to the bone for you, Shar, but he also needs your help in return."

"I don't have a lot of money, but I can do my best to—"

"No, no. That's not what I mean."

Katerina's shoulders are tensed, as though she is steeling herself for what comes next. Her voice is barely above a whisper when she speaks.

"Do you know who Pablo Aguilar is?"

ڡﯔ

HE TAKES A TAXI home from Dupont Circle to his apartment, too weary to be frugal this night. Before he left, Katerina urged him to consider carefully what she proposed—the fee that was Faisal Ahmed's demand.

He sits at his desk and turns on his laptop to search for Pablo Aguilar.

The very first result is his official US Senate web page, with a picture of the handsome young senator in the upper right corner.

He returns to the list of search results and clicks on the second entry—an article from the *New York Times*. Less than a year old, it concerns the growing political chatter around the young Republican senator from Maryland as a potential presidential candidate in 2008. Originally a state senator, Aguilar was nominated to the US Senate by Maryland's Republican governor to replace a long-serving Democrat forced to resign due to scandal.

One of Aguilar's priorities is to introduce a comprehensive immigration bill within the next year, and to this end, the young senator has been building consensus across both sides of the aisle. The article concludes with quotes from an anonymous source on the number of policy experts already collaborating with Aguilar to refine the proposed legislation in a way that will be palatable to both Democrats and Republicans.

One of them is Albert Volcker, the director of the Institute for Policy Dialogue, where Shar works.

BOOK III

Surging

ICHIRO

Chittagong, East Bengal (Bangladesh)
April 1942

He wakes sightless and bound. He is blind, he decides. Blue
skies, light-flecked waves, the flicker of wings through the
trees—all will become memories.

He twists, moans as movement coaxes blood to his limbs. There
is the chafe of ropes around his wrists, ankles. They are tied to the
posts of a bed.

"He's coming around," says a woman in English, and he knows
that he is captured. A man's voice, nasal and crisp, confirms this.
"You are now a prisoner of His Majesty's Army. You will be interned
under the conventions stipulated by the military tribunal for de-
tainment of enemy soldiers. You will be held indefinitely, or until a
necessary prisoner exchange occurs with your government. Do you
understand?"

The man stops speaking as another translates his words into
rough, accented Japanese.

"Do you understand?" the man and the interpreter repeat
when he does not respond.

Still he says nothing.

A hand seizes his hair and pulls up his head. "Do you, *Jap*?"

The woman interrupts. "Selwyn, I don't think this fellow's recovered enough for such rough stuff."

"How well do you think these gooks would treat us if the tables were turned?"

"None too well, I imagine. But they don't set our standards, do they? And I assume if he's valuable you want him at full strength when he's interrogated."

Selwyn releases Ichiro's hair, and his head flops back onto the pillow. A rage courses through him at this indignity. He channels it through to his clenched fists under the sheets, his jaws, teeth that he clamps down hard on his cheeks.

"I suggest you give him what he needs and no more. It makes me sick that our boys are out in the halls while he gets a cabin." Selwyn and his interpreter exit the cabin with the sharp metered cadence of soldiers.

He takes a slow trembling breath, unclenches his fists and relaxes his jaw until the coppery taste of blood floods his mouth. The world is dark still; he hears the moans and cries of other wounded soldiers. The door to the room must be ajar.

The woman remains.

"I've something that belongs to you," she says. "I think it's your diary. It's in Japanese, but I saw German and English as well. I know it wasn't proper to look inside but . . . I know you understand me," she hazards.

He does not speak. What if this woman and the man who spoke before are collaborators in a trap? Is Selwyn lurking just beyond the door? Smirking at his naïveté? Ichiro has been told to expect no mercy from the British if he were captured, advised to swaddle his heart and mind in stoicism to withstand the torture that would be inflicted on him, then take his own life and die with dignity at the first opportunity.

"You've nothing to fear while you're under my care. My name is Claire. May I know yours?"

Her tone hardens when he remains silent. "Very well. If you

won't speak, you won't get your diary back. When you're ready, you can ask for it. *In English.*"

Claire leaves the room in determined footsteps. He listens to the sound of her heels echoing down the hallway.

He would have told her everything if she asked just once more.

☙❧

IN THE SIGHTLESS DAYS that follow, his nose charts the scents of the hospital: the astringent scent of Dettol in his cabin; the must of smoke in the evening air from the burning hay of the paddy fields; the manure supply's pungent arrival on a creaking cow-cart in the morning, outside his window. His ears tally the sharp footsteps of the British sisters rapping over the hallways like steady reports from a pistol, the soft swish of whatever footwear that their Indian counterparts don; the dull clang of the shift bells.

His tongue is less clever in comparison—barely able to discern the morning porridge from the evening's potato mash, the idiosyncrasies of the chalky pills he is forced to swallow.

The sclerotic officer from the first day returns twice more over the course of the week. He questions Ichiro intently each time, and each time, Claire oversees the process.

He continues his silence during these ordeals. Already blind, he has little to lose by feigning deafness. After the third pointless interrogation, Selwyn asks Claire when Ichiro can be released into military custody.

"Well, you can see that he's not recovered. We're yet to even take the bandage off his eyes."

Ichiro receives a hard poke in the ribs from what feels like a baton. He grunts in pain and surprise. "He seems fine to me."

"Even if he were, it's not as though he'll suddenly be able to speak English. I don't understand the rush."

"Being married to Drake gives you no protection or privileges, Claire. If this is about what happened back in Rangoon—"

"Not at all," Claire interrupts. "I'm simply speaking as a doctor. I'm on your side, Selwyn. Surely you agree that if I release him before his time he'll just be back here again after a few days. I'm saving you from wasting time."

There is the rustle of paper as Selwyn produces a document. "Ready or not, we're moving him to the mobile interrogation center in a week, then he'll be shifted to the Delhi Cantonment for further questioning."

"That's too soon."

Selwyn's tone turns a shade kinder. "Look, Claire, I understand that you see his hairless face and you think of someone's son, brother. But you can't imagine what they've done. I've seen it firsthand. He's no innocent just because he's a pilot. His hands are as bloody as any."

All warmth has fled Claire's voice when she responds. "I know what they've done, Selwyn. I see it around me every day. And did you forget why we had to flee Burma? I'll take the order under advisement."

"Just remember—a week and no more." Selwyn departs.

Seconds pass. With a lack of warning that makes Ichiro shudder, Claire pours a desperate whisper into his ear. "If you don't talk, then there is nothing more I can do to help you. And I'll have to surrender your journal."

He tastes the rust of unpracticed English on his tongue. "And why would you want to help me?"

She edges close again, flooding his senses with lavender and sunshine. "I knew it."

She undoes the straps around his wrists and his hands tingle as the blood rushes back in. She places something on them and his fingers scrabble across its hard leather surface, caressing again the smooth warm grain, tracing the shape of a heron in flight that is embossed on the cover. He knows that it is pictured as though from above, the tips of its wings meeting in a point before its head to form a graceful circle, the white feathers reminiscent of chrysanthemum petals.

His father had bought the journal for him when on a visit to Tokushima. A month before his enlistment.

He sighs and thrusts the journal back in Claire's general direction. "Thank you. Will you please keep it safe? It is of no use to me in this state."

She takes it.

HE HEARS UNIDENTIFIED FOOTSTEPS approach him the next day. Heavy. Masculine. They belong to a doctor who informs him that the bandages from his eyes are to be removed.

"He's suffered retinal damage from the explosion," he says to another in the room. "We've done our best to save his vision, but God only knows what he will or won't see after we take the bandages off."

The hand on his face is rougher and thicker than Claire's but still gentle. He keeps his eyes closed as the bandages are removed.

"You can try opening your eyes," the doctor says. "We've drawn the shades."

When Ichiro does not respond, the doctor taps his eyelids lightly to make him understand.

He opens them just a sliver before the blazing light overwhelms them. How can there be so much of it if they have drawn the shades?

It is as though the sun has left the heavens to visit his room. Did they lie? Is this a cruel punishment devised for his state? He turns his head to the side, wanting no part of this painfully bright world.

"Seems a good sign." The doctor's voice holds grudging approval. Ichiro is afraid to peep again, his vision scalded by light on his first effort, but he forces himself. Gradually, the shining mist that first shrouded his world begins to lift. The light's burning intensity becomes bearable, until the images of his new world telescope into clarity.

He is—as he already deduced—in a hospital cabin. And it is also true that they have drawn the shades, their outlines etched bright by the sun. A floor lamp shines dim yellow above him, illuminating little—a twin to the IV drip on the other side. And there are blurred figures—what seems a tall man with a mustache. The other is near the window. A woman. He cannot discern her face but has no doubt who she is.

～

HE SEES HER AGAIN when she walks through his door the next day and closes it behind her. He wishes her a good morning in English, and adds, "Happy Easter."

About to reach over to check his bandages, she stops. "And a Happy Easter to you," she says, surprised.

She resumes replacing his bandages, disposing of them in a bucket by her feet. They are spotted dark with blood. His shoulder aches less now.

"How did you know that today is Easter?"

"I've kept count of the days since my crash. Besides, I am a Christian."

She pauses again, her green eyes narrowed. "Do you truly mean that?"

"Yes."

She shakes her head. "All the things we've been told about your lot were about the differences, not the similarities."

She takes the bowl of porridge on the side table, clotted now into an ugly lump. She is about to feed a spoonful into his mouth when she stops again. "Can you name the twelve apostles of Christ?"

He names them all, enunciating with care, and sees the distrust on her face melt steadily. At the end, she stands with the spoonful of porridge still hovering near his mouth. She appears embarrassed.

"Did I name them correctly?"

"I'm not sure," she says. "You named eight more than I could."

HE WAKES TO THE patter of rain in the morning. A cool wind blows in through the window. The past few days were hot and dry. The trees grimy with dust. But now the rain has washed the world and he can see its true colors—the deep green leaves, the rust-red bricks that line the path to the hospital, the beds of coral roses in the front garden.

The too-close skies and oppressive air of Burma feel a world away, and Japan, with its frigid winter nights and mountain slopes strewn with milk vetch, another lifetime. He has entered a new world in old skin. The plane's fire has not burned out his doubts. The bullets that pierced him have not bled him free of weakness. It is hard, so hard and frightening to be brave. He wants to plunge back into the depthless pool of beauty that is this world.

Claire does not come in during the day. His breakfast, lunch and medication are delivered by a nurse with dark hair and pouting lips painted red. This nurse—whose name he will later learn is Rachel—is beautiful in her own way. But whatever pity that Claire has extended him, Rachel does not share, her antipathy to him clear in the way she looks at him, the brusque manner in which she inspects his bandages. He finds this reassuring, because it is what he expected all along.

Claire visits him at dusk. He can hear the low of cows returning home, strange chants that have a religious cadence. This is not the first time he has heard it, so he asks her what it is.

"The Moslem call to prayer. It happens five times a day, beginning at dawn."

"It has a strange beauty," he says. "It is almost—"

"Haunting?"

"Yes. It is haunting. But I heard other sounds as well. Horns being blown. Was that Moslem also?"

"Conch shells. The Hindoos offering prayers to their many gods and goddesses."

She does the requisite inspection of his wounds, a test of his vision where she holds out her fingers in different numbers and at different distances. He passes.

"Do you need to visit the loo?"

He wavers. There is a protocol to be followed. Each time he needs to use the toilet, the doctor or nurse-in-charge has fetched two soldiers who keep their rifles aimed at him as he is released from his restraints. They then follow him into the bathroom with guns pointed at his back or face depending on the nature of his business there.

But this day she walks to the door, peeks outside and then locks it.

"What are you doing?"

She begins to undo his restraints. "I'm going to trust that you won't try to harm me when I release you. Or escape. Think of this as a courtesy, both to you and the soldiers who have to accompany you."

He rubs his wrists in relieved wonder. She has moved on to his legs. For a moment, his soldier's heart surges. He quickly considers the chances and potential consequences of pushing her away and trying to escape, dismissing the feasibility by the time she finishes.

He is too weak to even overpower an unarmed woman, not to mention that the hospital is crawling with soldiers.

But most importantly, he does not want any harm to come to her.

Traces of this calculation must have risen to his face. Because when she looks at it, she stands straight and crucifies him with a stare. "Am I going to regret this?"

He shakes his head.

The bathroom has a thin towel hanging on the rack, a bar of soap on the holder, and toilet paper. The rest is bolted down, including the "mirror"—a sheet of stainless steel polished to a reflective finish and riveted to the wall.

He opens his mouth and examines its dark expanse before the mirror. The molar that is the second from the back on the left lower side is larger than the others, its color off. He takes the towel and, wrapping it around his index finger and thumb, uses it to wiggle the tooth from side to side.

It takes more effort than he expects, but he manages to detach it from his gum. It sits on the towel, surrounded by a bloody corona. Using his now long nails, he fishes out the tiny glass capsule within.

Like the tooth, it is marred by his blood. He washes it clean so that it shines in the wan light; the liquid inside clear and unassuming until it forms a murderous partnership with the glass that contains it, the glass that will cut him once broken in his mouth, providing egress to his blood so the cyanide can shut down his cells one at a time. Choking them of air. The scent of bitter almonds will fill his senses and within five minutes of ingestion he will convulse on the floor. Within ten he will know eternity.

He will no longer wonder what he will face at the British prison camp, about the disgrace of his mother and father as parents to a captured soldier. About love, marriage, children.

Death. That glacier perched on a mountain. In a slow slide to-

ward him every day, its cold breath was on his face now. This is
what is expected. To lay his life down without question and sacri-
fice himself at the altar of Pride and Shame—the dark gods who
rule Japan, loom behind the Emperor's throne, their monstrous,
bloated bodies slumped over his nation, their terrible wings block-
ing out the light.

A hammering upon the bathroom door. Urgent and insistent.
Claire's voice is tinged with panic. "What are you doing in there?"

Startled, he turns. The capsule drops from his hand, strikes
the floor with an audible *clink* and rolls toward the drainage hole
in the corner.

"I am almost done!" He scrambles on the floor to stop the pill,
but his grasping fingers send it skittering even closer to the gaping
hole. He lunges, stopping it a bare inch from the edge.

His heart pounds in his chest. He has ripped his stitches. He
can feel fresh blood seep into his shoulder.

Claire speaks again. Her mouth must be right on the door, for
her voice is resonant against the wood. Her words a plea clothed as
threat. "I'm giving you another minute to come out. If you don't, I
will . . . I will have to call for help."

"There is no need. I am coming out." He stands with effort and
returns the capsule to his tooth, the tooth to his jaw.

She is standing back from the door when he opens it. She ap-
praises him from head to toe. He sits on the bed and positions his
feet to be once again restrained.

"That can wait," she says, venturing into the bathroom.

She returns after a minute. Her fists are on her hips. A mother's
pose. He is amused despite his pain.

"What happened?"

"I fell down."

"How?"

"There was water on the floor. I slipped."

"I didn't see any water."

"I used the towel to wipe it."

"I see." She peels back the collar of his gown to examine his shoulder, frowning. She touches him there, ever so softly, but he flinches and so does she. They stare at each other, a moment meant to frame an act of duty become something else. She blushes, red invading her pale features so that her face echoes the color of her hair. She steps back, eyes on him as though she fears an attack. She goes to the table by the wall and returns with Dettol, fresh dressing, gauze, tape and scissors.

Once more she cleanses his wounds, bandages them with care. When she finishes, she says, "I have to tie your arms again. Stay still, please, or you'll rip the stitches again."

Once finished, she produces two small pills from her apron, holds a glass of water to his lips. "These will help you rest."

He swallows them. He wants oblivion.

❧

THE DARK-HAIRED NURSE DOES not return the next day. The sunlight wakes him instead, so bright and clean that it is as though he was never asleep. Claire comes early. She locks the door behind her, removes his restraints and places before him a bowl of hot runny porridge.

"Why do you show such kindness toward me?" he asks her.

"I have been doing my duty."

"More than that. If not for you, Selwyn would have had me transferred to the prison camp much sooner."

"As long as you are in one of these beds you are a patient, no matter the flag you were born under."

"Even though our nations are at war?"

She stops in the act of adjusting his drip. "I don't need to be reminded. I was in Rangoon when the Ja—the Japanese invaded."

"The British invaded these shores as well. They just did it a few hundred years before us."

Her eyes flash too quickly for him to recognize whether it was from anger, regret or another emotion, but her voice is even when she speaks. "I suppose we did. I don't defend the past, nor use it to justify the present."

"Is that the difference between us?"

"Between the British and the Japanese or you and me?"

"You decide."

"The fundamental difference between you and me—long before we can consider the flags under which we were born—is that I'm a woman and you're a man. Every morning when I wake up, there're a thousand obstacles that either don't exist for you or are invisible. A hundred considerations I have to make before I open my mouth, decide where I can go and can't."

"I am certain that being British gives you certain advantages. The world is your playground."

"As a woman, I have no country. As a woman, I want no country. As a woman, my country is the whole world."

"Who said that?"

She laughs. "Virginia Woolf. Perhaps you should read more women writers."

She asks him about his diary, wanting to know why it is in English.

"I will be punished severely if my commanding officers read my journal. I write in English to protect myself."

"Where did you learn to speak it so well, though?"

"We were required to learn two foreign languages apart from classical Latin in First Higher School. I had to pick between German, English and French. I chose the first two. I learned French on my own, but I am less skilled in it."

She nods, impressed. "We just learn English at school. Latin, of course, if you're learning the classics. A little French if you fancy it.

"Are all Japanese soldiers as well-spoken as you?" she asks after a while.

"I don't know. But many of us joined directly from university, so we are usually well-read." He thinks of his friends, the many bright flames that will be extinguished in this war before they can burn their brightest.

"You're not the way I thought you'd be."

"Because I speak your language?"

"No, because you are thoughtful."

"Death makes philosophers of soldiers."

"Are all Orientals so fatalistic?"

The word is new to him, but he can guess at the meaning from the German counterword—*fatalistisch*. He asks her what it means nonetheless, and she tells him—"to be a servant to fate."

"We are all servants to fate whether we accept it or not."

"Not I," she says, and stiffens because voices have drifted close to the door. She relaxes only when they move on. "What is the last memory you have of home?"

He closes his eyes and casts his mind back. "A spring morning. I woke to birdsong. We had breakfast together: my mother, father, younger brother and me. Later, I took a walk in the woods, up a mountain path. Just by myself."

"Do you not remember leaving? Saying good-bye?"

"I am telling you what I chose to remember. It was the last day of an old life. I began a new one at university. Another in the army. What of you? What do you remember of home?"

"A cold rainy morning. Warblers sitting fat and soaked in the trees. Milk tea with my mother and sisters. Getting married the same day. The hem of my wedding gown was trimmed with mud. That's stayed with me."

He remembers then that Bengal is home to neither of them, Claire no more an extension of this place than he. Perhaps that is what lies behind the British frenzy for building monuments on strange shores, he thinks, laying train tracks that span a thousand miles, binding the land with roads and highways as though subduing a wild creature. They were both island nations, frantic to leave their blue prisons—to leave marks on lands that do not want them.

"You are married."

"His name is Theodore. He's stationed in Imphal." Reaching into her apron, she takes out his journal. And a pen. "These are for you. Given that your eyes are working just fine now."

He examines the latter. A silver-and-gold Parker 51, with a black barrel. It has a pleasing heft in his hand.

She notices his admiration. "A cousin brought it for me from New York. The ink dries fast. It's really quite lovely to write with."

"Thank you."

"Well, you can only have it until you're finished writing." She heads for the door. "I'll be back to check on you in three hours. I have the key today, so don't worry about someone else walking in."

⁓

HE WRITES. NOT ONCE does he look up from his journal, the only sound in the room the scratch of his pen against the page.

Claire enters minutes after the bell clangs to announce noon, and he looks up, smiling, shaking his hand to rid it of the cramp that always seems to settle in. "Sorry. I had to recall several days' worth of memories."

He holds out the journal and pen to her. "I would be grateful if you kept these. In fact, I have a further request. On the last page, I have written down the address of my friend's mother. Once I am moved to the camp, would you be kind enough to send this to her?"

"I shall. But I must go now. There are other patients waiting."

He bows his head. "Thank you. I have another favor to ask of you. Please release me so that I may use the WC?"

"You promise me that there will be no more of that silliness from the last time?"

"I do."

"Very well." She undoes his restraints.

He goes in, putters about in the bathroom, making the noises expected of him—sitting down on the commode, working the flush; the tap at the washbasin.

He stands before the mirror, staring at the haggard apparition before him. Has it only been two years since he joined the army?

He has never been religious. He has visited church more out of love of family than fear of judgment. He loves Jesus, but as a man and not the Son of God. He believes his soul to be eternal, redeemable, yet the Japanese side of him demands death, to plunge into the black without a backward glance. If he swallows the pill, will his spirit wander this world forever? A moaning hungry ghost as the Buddhists describe? A scrap of ash swirling in the wind but never breaking apart?

There is only one way to find out.

He opens his mouth and begins to pull out the false tooth again.

Shahryar & Anna

Washington, DC
September 2004

He meets Katerina again the next day, this time in Lafayette Square. He sends her a text message and in fifteen minutes, she is skirting around the statue of a mounted Andrew Jackson to approach him. Her hair is tied back in a tight bun today, her cream-and-white dress cinched with a gold belt. She reminds him of a Patrick Nagel print.

"I've looked him up," he says when she sits down. "What we're talking about here is very serious. This could be jail time."

"What is the bigger risk, Shar? This, or going back to Bangladesh not knowing if you will ever be able to see your daughter again?"

"I could always get another visa to come see her."

"You could. We're not discounting that. But this is the post-nine-eleven world we live in. You're a Muslim male that fits the profile. Bangladesh is not on the list of countries that sponsor terrorism, but who knows what could happen in the future? It's just not a guarantee."

He considers her argument. Even though three years have passed since those dark weeks and months that followed 9/11, that febrile air of fear, confusion and mistrust remains in America, as if the entire nation caught a disease that even after a cure, leaves one weaker, disfigured.

In just the past year, he has been called a "raghead" and a "Paki," both those times when emerging after Friday prayers from a small mosque on Eye Street, near GW. First was a homeless man who called Shar the epithet and then cackled through a toothless mouth. The second was a well-dressed businessman driving a Corvette who just missed him on the crosswalk as he took a fast right turn. Red-faced and swearing, he left in a squeal of tires.

"Be that as it may," he says, "it's a guarantee I'll go to a federal prison if I get caught."

"An extremely small chance. Mr. Ahmed will do his best to make sure that it doesn't happen."

"That's something I had a question about, actually."

"What do you mean?"

"You told me that Mr. Ahmed hired you to be a paralegal, when your fiancée visa fell through, right?"

"Yes . . ."

"Wouldn't you have to leave the country first to change your visa?"

Wary until now, Katerina becomes indignant. "Are you calling me a liar?"

"No . . . no, I just . . ."

"What is more important here, Shar? What happened to me, or what will happen to you in a few weeks? As for me, yes, you have to leave the country to change visas, but Mr. Ahmed has ways of making things happen. He was afraid that if I left the country I'd never be let in again."

He speaks quietly. "That wouldn't be so bad, would it? You'd get to see your daughter again."

She rises. "That's it. I'm not going to sit here and let you insult me."

He takes her wrist. "Look, I'm sorry. I take it back. Please sit down."

She does, scowling.

"I'm not saying yes or no, but tell me what this involves again."

She once again unearths an artifact from her purse, this time an object about the size of his thumb. "This is a USB flash drive. Thirty-two megabyte capacity. Volcker's computer, if it's built in the last ten years—and we think it is—will have a USB port right in front. All you have to do is stick this in and copy the files. Very simple."

"And these are the files that concern the immigration bill Aguilar's pushing?"

"Yes. And even beyond. Any correspondence between the two will be useful. Emails, white papers, decision notes. Anything."

They sit, their eyes trained front. Across from them, beyond the strolling tourists, joggers and office workers out for lunchtime strolls, is the White House. A group of protestors hold up *Free Tibet* banners near its fence.

"Can I ask you something?"

"Of course."

"Why does Faisal Ahmed need this?"

Katerina rises, sweeps her dress smooth with both hands. "I don't ask these questions, Shar. All I know is that he is a good man. And that he will keep his word."

She bends down and gives Shar a quick kiss on his cheek before walking away. Soon, she is swallowed up by the milling crowds.

༄༅༅

FAISAL AHMED CALLS HIM later that evening. "Hello, Shar. How are you?"

"I'm good. Just trying to understand what is being asked of me and why."

Ahmed sighs. A weary parent dealing with a difficult child. "I understand that you have questions and concerns, Shar. Trust me, I do as well. But as Katerina promised, none of this will get back to you. That I can promise."

"I don't even know why you want this information, I mean—"

"Let's keep the discussion general, Shar, shall we?" Ahmed sharply interrupts, then continues in a softer tone. "I think my interest in this matter is rather understandable, don't you think? I've been an immigration lawyer for well over twenty years now. I'm president of the American Institute of Immigration Lawyers. I've served thousands of young men and women like you, who asked for nothing more than a chance at the American dream. If there's anything in this upcoming bill that might jeopardize the work I do, of course I'd like to know about it. You're one of my clients now. If anything, this helps you."

"And you can't find out by reading the paper, like everyone else?"

"Time is of the essence."

"It's just a huge risk."

"I'm asking for a lot, but offering you a lot in return. I've spoken to one of my friends. We can get you hired as a trainee manager at a Wendy's franchise as soon as next week."

"What?"

"Hear me out. I'll get you a job as a policy analyst in a DC firm, but that'll take time and the pulling of many strings. In the meantime, you'll have to do something to support yourself. This is temporary, I assure you."

Shar closes his eyes. Six years of post-graduate work, a PhD obtained with distinction from George Washington University—tracks of achievement that now converge on a grill assembling burgers.

"Tell me it's at least close to DC."

"Depends on your definition of 'close.' It's in Huntington."

"Huntington, Virginia?" He tries to find solace in this. Huntington is a fifteen-minute drive from Anna's house.

"No. Huntington, *West* Virginia."

"What?" His laptop screen is open before him. He types in the city name and state in Google. "Oh my god. That's basically Ohio."

"Beggars can't be choosers, Shar."

"What's to stop me from saying no to you and just working under the table somewhere?"

"Nothing, but that's a life in the shadows. Cowering. On the run. You won't be able to file taxes, renew your driver's license, rent an apartment or visit your parents in Bangladesh. If you stay back as an illegal, you forfeit seeing them. You'll be choosing your child over your parents. I'm offering you a life in the sun. You don't have to choose; you can have it all. That's the American way, isn't it?"

"Can I think about it?"

"Yes," Ahmed says. "You have a week."

⟳

BUT THE NEXT MORNING, he receives a text from Niten asking to meet near Shar's work at noon. The brevity of the message underlines its urgency; Niten promises to explain more when they see each other.

Shar awaits his friend at the Starbucks on M Street, and he arrives at the stroke of twelve, looking perturbed and carrying, of all things, a briefcase.

"Can I get you something?" Shar asks. Since college, Niten has developed in the opposite direction of most men: he has lost weight and has grown out his shaved head so that he now sports a thick crop of hair going prematurely gray, cut short and swept neatly to the side in the manner of a news anchor.

"Just a green tea, man, thanks."

Shar buys a tea and returns with it to the table, upon which Niten has placed a stack of papers. "I've been looking into this Faisal Ahmed guy."

He hands Shar a printout of a newspaper article from the *Baltimore Sun* titled, "Complaints Mount about Gaithersburg Immigration Lawyer." It occupies a single page, with a black-and-white picture of a younger Ahmed as an inset. Shar reads the article from beginning to end, then looks up at Niten.

"This is what this guy does, Shar. He sets up people in dodgy job enterprises with the promise of getting them legal papers. That's when he's not setting them up for fake weddings for green cards. If there have already been complaints about him, then my feeling is that the government's been looking into this for a while. I'd be very careful if I were you."

Shar sets the paper aside. "In that case, you should know what's going on."

He proceeds to tell Niten of his dealings with Ahmed so far. His interactions with Katerina. What is being requested of him in exchange for employment in America.

Niten stares at him open-mouthed by the end. "For the love of God don't tell me you're considering this."

"I'd rather not. But what choice do I have? If nothing turns up in the next month, I either have to leave here or stay illegally."

"Can't you get a tourist visa and come back?"

"That's not a guarantee. Ever since nine-eleven, I get hassled at the airport coming back in from Bangladesh, even with a valid student visa. And even if I got the tourist visa and came back, I still wouldn't be able to work here."

"So you're gonna break federal law and risk how many years of jail instead?"

He is morose. "I didn't say this was the perfect plan."

"No shit. What's he supposed to do with this information anyway?"

"He said he needs it to understand what's on the horizon for immigration law. But I think that's bullshit."

"I agree." Looking thoughtful, Niten rifles through the stack of paper. "Just hold on a minute, though . . ."

He finds his quarry. He places between them another printout, one that features a picture of a group of people in a hotel lobby. "You said he wanted correspondence between Aguilar and Volcker, right?"

"Anything relating to the immigration plan especially. But yes, more or less."

"Then read this."

The picture shows an older, more recognizable Ahmed shaking hands with another man, taller and silver-haired. The two are in the center of a throng of people.

"What am I looking at?'

"The tall guy is Clarence Cummings. He's the current Maryland AG. This was at an event in January where he announced that he's running against Aguilar this fall."

"So?"

"Think about it. What does an attorney general do?"

"Advise the state government on the law?"

"Keep going."

"You're the one who went to law school, my friend."

"Among a host of other duties, a state AG is the one that decides who to prosecute on behalf of the state." Niten leans forward. "Do you see what I'm getting at?"

"Ahmed's trying to curry favor with Cummings?"

"Most likely in the hopes that he doesn't bring charges. The Maryland Justice Department is probably investigating him."

"But how?"

Niten places the articles in question side by side. "Put two and two together."

"Cummings is running for the Senate in the special election against Aguilar . . ."

"Who was appointed by the Republican governor. As a Democrat, Cummings can't hope for support."

"So he needs dirt on Aguilar?"

"And?"

"And Ahmed is providing him with details on Aguilar's signature bill in the hopes that Cummings won't prosecute?"

"Well, he's selling you that angle, but I think that's a red herring. He probably doesn't care about the immigration bill. Otherwise he wouldn't be asking for his emails. He's likely hoping to find something incriminating or salacious in it that Cummings can use. From what I read in the *Post* today, the race is tight. Aguilar's just a few points ahead of Cummings—within the margin of error. Cummings is looking for any advantage he can get. When you let slip that you work at IPD, Ahmed probably sent Katerina after you with her sob story to soften you up. Maybe he thought you're a sucker for a pretty face."

"I suppose. Although it sounds like a very Rube Goldberg way of going about it."

"Got a better theory?"

"No."

Niten puts the sheaf of papers in a dossier and pushes it toward him. "Never underestimate a man facing jail time. Before you do anything rash, I suggest you do a bit of digging on Ahmed on your own. See if you can find out more about him."

"I think I know just the place," Shar says.

CLAIRE

Chittagong, East Bengal (Bangladesh)
April 1942

She forces herself to sit. Her heart is racing, her neck damp. She relaxes when she hears the toilet flush, the tap run, but only a little. She holds her breath for the interminable minute that follows, until its end is marked by a stream of curses from Ichiro.

He emerges. "What have you done?"

"Please be calm," she says, getting up.

Ichiro does not approach. His expression is unreadable. She eyes the door, steps away. She could run, call for help. But he need only move to his left to cut her off.

"What have you done?"

"Those sedatives I gave you that evening, they knocked you out. I feared that you'd try to kill yourself again. I had to search your person, and the only way I could do that was if you were in a deep sleep."

"You found the capsule in my tooth?"

"I looked through the keyhole. I could see you reaching into your mouth."

"Why did you do this? It is not for you to decide if I should live or die."

"Nor you. Do you value your life so little that you'd take it so easily?"

192

"It is *because* I value my life that I wish to choose the manner of my own ending. Even if I am someday released from the prison camp, my life is finished. There is no greater shame in Japan than that of a soldier who has let himself be captured. Or to have such a soldier as a member of your family. My government has made sure that death and shame are my only options."

He staggers to the bed and sits with his head bowed. "That choice was the only thing I had. And now you have taken it from me."

SHE ARRIVES AT THE ward at two past eight in the morning the next day, after a sleepless night at the end of which she came to an important decision. She stands before Ichiro's door, debating whether to enter, when someone clears a throat behind her.

Rachel stands with a tray in her arms.

"I thought you had the day off?"

"I did, but Ivy came down with something. Is everything alright with you, dear? You look a bit funny."

Claire laughs, the sound strained to her ears. "Just tired, I suppose."

"More reason for us to get a tipple at the club. I don't think I've even had a chance to chat with you since this Oriental fellow fell into our laps."

She opens the door for Rachel. They walk in to find Ichiro in bed exactly as Claire had left him the night before. Tied to the bedposts. As he looks from one face to the other, his expression is bland and submissive.

As Rachel turns her back to put the tray on a rolling trolley, Claire tips over Ichiro's IV drip. The glass shatters with a resounding crash.

"Sorry, dear. I'm such an oaf." Claire looks sheepish.

Rachel clucks with annoyance. "The stuff's everywhere. Not to worry. I'll get the orderly."

She follows Rachel out, watches her lithe figure canter to the far end of the hallway.

She rushes back into the room and undoes his restraints as fast as she is able. "We're just on the second floor. But directly underneath the window is a flower bed. Can you jump down?"

He sits up rubbing his wrists. "Yes, but—"

"No time. I'm going to pull the fire alarm. When you hear it, you can run out in the confusion. Everyone else is going to be gathered on the front lawn." She hands him a map. "You have to go due east. Meet me at the top of the hill marked by the *X*. It's the tallest—you can't miss it. There's a temple at its summit. I'll meet you there tonight."

THE KLAXON BLARE OF the alarm draws the staff and patients to the front lawn in minutes. There they jostle and fret. Though they are accustomed to the air-raid sirens by now, this is the first fire alarm in months. Those too ailing to move have remained inside, attended to by a handful of staff.

A vanguard of C8s arrives before the fire trucks. Selwyn alights from one, surveys the crowd until he spots Claire and walks over, swallowing the distance between them with long strides.

"What happened?"

"The fire alarm went off. We followed procedures."

He rushes into the hospital. Returns in minutes, his pale features screwed into lines of rage under his army cap. He jabs a finger in her face and bellows, "If you followed procedures, you'd know that someone was supposed to stay with him in case of a fire. He's gone."

"Who?"

"You bloody well know who."

"The prisoner of war? I'm sorry to hear that."

"Are you?" He looms over her. There is a dark band of sweat at the lining of his cap.

"There're more than fifty soldiers in my ward. My first thought was to evacuate everyone safely. It's likely that in the rush I forgot to lock the door. I'm sorry, again. But I'm sure he can't have gone far."

The crowd's attention is on them. Selwyn glares at her, clenches and unclenches his fists. "He was supposed to be strapped to his bed at all times. Your forgetting to lock a door shouldn't have made a difference."

"I know," she says, finding Rachel in the crowd, standing at a distance to them. Her expression is sullen, that of someone made to play a fool.

"I know."

CLAIRE RETURNS TO A silent and empty house at the end of the day. Her staff have the day off, and she is all alone, exhausted, despite knowing that much remains to be done.

Selwyn spent two hours interrogating her in the matron's office, his aggression eventually moving the older woman to ask if Dr. Drake could kindly return to her rounds. He left, face twisted with suspicion, and Claire knew she would have to choose her next moves wisely. So she put her mind to going about her tasks for the remainder of the day, a mental eye always on the clock, an ear trained to the hammerings of the shift bell.

At home, she packs a tiffin carrier filled with food, a flask of water, a small knife and an army blanket into a haversack. An envelope containing her first month's salary from the hospital she places into one of Teddie's old wallets and wraps it tightly—along with a handwritten letter—in a cut-up old waterproof. Finally, she pulls out the bottom drawer of the wardrobe in her bedroom and removes a neat pile of her husband's clothes to reveal a Luger P08. Left behind for her protection, she has never dared touch it until now. It confronts her like a dark, coiled snake. She buries it under the shirts again and closes the drawer.

She sorts through Teddie's clothes. Not finding a black sweater to wear, she makes do with navy blue. She trims a pair of his charcoal trousers with kitchen shears and slips them on. She twists her hair into a tight bun and shoves it under a cap. She stands before the mirror and assesses her appearance. The clothes smell of him still and suddenly she is overwhelmed with loneliness, desperate for the crutch of his strength, his presence.

The too bright moon prevents her departure, so she sits in her drawing room and hoards nerve. The Moslem call to prayer drifts in through the windows, along with the warm heavy scent of evening jasmines. It feels like both her first and last night in this land, like the betrayal of her people, husband and family. It feels right.

She prays for darkness to arrive, aware that each additional minute is a conspirator against her. Thankfully, clouds amass before the moon and she steals out through the back door, a small but powerful electric torchlight in one hand, the haversack slung over a shoulder. The woods lie beyond the small meadow annexed by her backyard, but she must first pass by the row of the servant's quarters, whose windows emit soft yellow light, the low murmurs of conversation and the tinkle and clatter of the evening unfolding life within. Should anyone look out at that very moment, she would be spotted.

But she manages to rush through this treacherous stretch without incident. In the safety of the trees, she risks a light to find her bearings. The temple sits at the edge of a forest atop a moderately steep hill, not far, but deep in the wilderness. On a walk to explore their new home in the first week, she and Teddie discovered the temple by accident, a brooding reward for their trek up the hill.

She walks there now, praying that he has made it. It takes her an hour's trudge and climb before she stands—out of breath—at the foot of the temple, which appears as a gaping hole scissored out of the night sky.

She crouches in the shelter of the trees. A clearing stands between the edge of the woods and the edifice. She flashes the torchlight three times in quick succession. In moments, a shadow detaches itself from the temple's side and walks toward her.

"I didn't think you'd come," Ichiro says when he sees her.

"Well, I gave you my word, didn't I?"

They step into the temple together. She swings her torchlight around, and the beam falls on a vicious face at the far end. She freezes with fear, then remembers who it is. A seven-foot-tall woman with midnight skin stands against the wall, unclothed but for a garland of severed limbs around her waist. The goddess Kali. She of the gold-rimmed eyes and lolling red tongue that reaches beyond her chin. Incubating in darkness for so long, the light has brought her to life.

"She is quite extraordinary, isn't she?" Ichiro says. "I feel safer with her here."

She nods and moves the light to reveal walls encrusted with vines, underneath which she can spy elaborate carvings—elephants, horses, humans with features of both men and women, copulating figures. Above them, the holes on the roof look out to a star-spattered sky. It is just the two of them there, under the watch of an ageless deity.

"Let's have a seat." She moves toward the wall. The enormity of her responsibilities is registering. A man's fate, and more, rests in her hands. This is no game.

They sit with their backs against the bumpy walls, listen to the sounds of their breathing—erratic and unsynchronized—fall into the same rhythm.

Ichiro's profile is silhouetted by the moon and starlight. "When I was little, we lived in mountain regions. I went out to the woods all day and stayed there until it was very dark. Night sounds don't bother me so much. When I listen to symphonies, they remind me of being in the forest."

"Night sounds didn't bother me so much in England, just 'cause it's so bloody quiet. But here they do." She looks to the statue. "The nights are so alive here. Did you see any snakes?"

"No. Why?"

"No reason." Her first and only time seeing one was when she was six. They were in Dorset on summer holiday when she saw an adder slithering through the grass at Corfe Castle, its skin—a variegated gold-brown—glistening in the sun. She had screamed and run to her father, hysterical with fear.

"I want to thank you for helping me escape," Ichiro says. "For helping save my life. As long as I was captured I was determined to end it."

"Why?"

"In Japan, there is much madness that we have made normal in the name of honor. I can see through those masks more and more. We call it *gyokusai*. The term is from an ancient Chinese text—*The Book of Northern Qi*. It means 'shattered jade.'"

"I don't understand."

"The wider meaning is that a soldier who dies in battle or kills himself is a shattered jewel. A prisoner of war who lives is a whole roof tile. The Japanese think it is better to be the first thing. The Chinese, at least now, have evolved to a different, more reasonable view. They don't see the need for uselessly throwing away the lives of men for the sake of honor and tradition."

She mulls the concept. "You wanted to be a shattered jewel?"

"The last few days, I was."

"We are all shattered jewels in a way," she says.

"What do you mean?"

"We are all broken in a way. But while the Japanese see it as an end, not just to be accepted but embraced, the English see a path back, a way to pick up the pieces and make something of them."

She removes the food from the haversack.

"What is this?"

"A tiffin carrier. Indians call it a 'dabba.'" She opens the lid, places the three compartments on the floor.

He whistles. "Very clever. We have bento boxes in Japan. But these appear better for carrying."

"That nurse. Rachel. Is she a friend of yours?" he asks.

"The closest thing to it. At least when we first met. But we've been drifting as of late. And now when I look at her, I feel like maybe I don't know her that well at all."

"Do you have many friends here? Outside of England, I mean."

"I had a good one in Rangoon," she says, after a pause. "We were . . . separated during the fall of the city."

"I am sorry."

"What about you?"

"I had a good one as well."

He proceeds to tell her about Tadashi, about everything that happened before the temple, and after. It takes the better part of an hour.

"What happened to his sash after you took it?" she says at the end, then hastily adds, "I mean. I'm sorry. I know that shouldn't be the first concern . . ."

"I was wondering that as well," he said. "When you first gave me the journal, I was going to ask you about it."

"Why didn't you?"

He turns to her. "Because that's when I remembered the girl."

She stares at him. The night has gotten cooler now, the light of the moon dimmed. "What girl?"

"When I was about to release the leaflets. There was a girl standing in the drop zone. Just . . . standing there. Frozen. When I looked at her through my binos, it felt like she was looking directly at me. And then when I crashed. She was there too."

"Doing what?"

"I don't remember the immediate moments after crashing, but I must have somehow crawled away from the plane, because when I opened my eyes I was lying on the ground, not far from the burning wreckage. My eyes were blurred and painful from the explosion, but through them I could see the girl standing above me. Maybe she had dragged me a little as well. I had wrapped my friend's sash around my arm; I don't know why, but I tried to give it to her. Perhaps I didn't want it to perish with me. But she did something unexpected. She soaked it in the water she carried in her pail, held it against my mouth, and it was cool sweetness. It was heaven. She stood over me for a while, yet all I remember are her eyes—a deep gray. They stood out like jewels against her dark skin."

"Do you think she has your friend's sash?"

"It is likely. Perhaps something scared her, the arrival of the British soldiers. I don't mind if she kept it. I'm forever grateful to her."

She does not speak in the wake of his story for some time, preferring to take solace in her meal rather than dwell upon the extraordinary circumstances that brought them together. A quiet falls between them and grows until she feels compelled to break it.

"I realize that you can't hide out here forever," she says between mouthfuls of food.

"Is there more to your plan?"

"There never was much of a plan in the first place. I came in this morning not knowing what I was going to do, but that you'd be free at the end of it. What I did with the IV drip, that was all improvised."

"So, what do we do now?"

They have emptied the first level of the tiffin carrier, the one with the roti and aloo bhaji. She begins to refill her haversack. "We return to where we first met."

"The hospital?"

"Not quite. We're going back to the beach."

"Why?"

"Because it's Sunday."

IT TAKES THEM MORE than two hours to reach the dark, roaring shore. There they sit on the sand, listening, girding themselves for disappointment. When the sky begins to brighten to lighter shades, they rise and walk east.

A sliver of sun is leaching pink and bruised purple into the sky when she reaches the boat. Hashim stands among other men, wide-shouldered and stocky, applying tar to the hull with a brush and bucket. When he sees them, he ends his work and rises to his feet. Claire removes her hat and shakes out her hair.

Hashim hands the brush and bucket to another and approaches, wiping his hands on a rag.

"Hello, Hashim. Do you remember me?"

He nods immediately. "I take madam on boat ride."

When she tells him what she requires of him, he looks at her as though he has misheard. She repeats her request and he barks a laugh, turns to his crew to share the mirth. They join in on the derision, shaking their heads.

"Burma far, madam. One full day . . ." he mimics the act of rowing, "to there." He points south. "If go, still bad. Army . . . big problem."

She takes Ichiro's hand. "Please, Hashim. It is a matter of life and death."

But the dodginess of their request is clear to Hashim. As she tries to persuade him again, she can see the physical signs of her impending defeat—his robust arms cross against his chest, the uncommonly direct gaze shifts above, and his features begin squeezing into implacable lines. The crew gawks, turning their heads from her to Hashim as though witnessing a match of tennis.

He points to the leaden skies when she finishes. "See sky? Big, big, storm come."

She removes the roll of money stuffed deep inside her haversack. "Please, Hashim. I am willing to pay. Please take him. It's very important."

"Memsahib not understand. Can buy boat. Cannot buy life. Storm coming."

But the money on offer is like petrol on the fire their appearance has already lit in the crew. One of them approaches Hashim and looks to be attempting to convince him to take the pilot. The others join until he is surrounded by a chorus of encouragement and urgency. Through it all, the fisherman keeps shaking his head.

After minutes of loud debate, he raises his hands to quiet the men, and turns to Claire. "They say take the money, we take man. But I say no."

He drops his head. His back to the sea, the wind blows his shoulder-length hair forward until it forms a black curtain, hiding his face. Water flecks her skin, the ocean fidgeting like a restless dog.

Hashim looks up again. His eyes hold a sadness, and she knows she has gotten her way once again, unaware of what a bitter victory this will be.

He points to Ichiro. "Me and he. *Just we go.*"

He takes the wad of bills, retains half and divides the remainder among his crew. But the protests continue once he finishes. Evidently, they are now opposed to Hashim going alone.

A spectator until now, Ichiro bows deeply to the boatman. "Thank you. I am so grateful."

He points to the bucket of tar and brush. "May I use them?"

The boatman nods, puzzled.

His knees planted on the sand, Ichiro paints on the prow. First on one side, then the other. He finishes in minutes.

"What are they?" she asks.

The boat stares south with graceful, wicked eyes. Beneath each is a single character in a foreign script. With simple strokes of a tar brush, Ichiro has brought the vessel to life. Now it quivers on the surf, eager to take flight.

"Eyes of the dragon. And the characters underneath mean 'destiny.' For good luck."

Hashim is less impressed. He points to the roiling skies. "No more time. If go. We go now."

They have been hurtling toward this moment like twigs in a waterfall. The crew stare and whisper furtively among each other as Claire and Ichiro say their farewells. As they embrace.

"I am forever grateful," he says. "If there is ever anything I can do to repay you . . ."

"Actually, there is." She takes out the waterproofed wallet and letter from her haversack. She tells him what she requires of him.

He nods. "I will not rest until it is done."

"You'd better not. Or I might come after you."

The two men push off and jump into the boat, its prow teetering and slamming against the surf. Ichiro seizes an oar and rows alongside Hashim. The strokes smooth and strong. Only when the boat is no more than a speck against the iron-gray horizon does he stand and turn to the shore. He waves to her until she can no longer see him.

Hashim's crew disperses then, muttering and shaking heads. In seconds, only their footprints and the deep, long gash left by the boat remain on the beach. She takes off her waterlogged shoes and sits on the sand. Every part of her cold. The wind keening. The water edging to her feet before falling away.

She smells the petrol belch of the C8s before she hears them. She stands and watches them approach. A group of soldiers descend from one. Selwyn and Rachel from the other.

The pair stand back. Selwyn's face is so pale that it glows white under the overcast skies. Rachel is a step behind, but close to him, the space between them dense with meaning.

"How long have you two been an item?"

Rachel looks down at the ground.

"How long have you been spying on me?"

"It was for your own good, Claire. Look at the mess you're in now."

Selwyn approaches, his manner controlled, his voice at the edge of conversational. "So, was this your revenge?"

She looks to the sea, thinks of the waterproofed bundle that Ichiro now carries across the heart of the bay, to Burma, one that contains the letter she wrote on the train that night, asking for Myint's forgiveness for leaving her behind, along with the wallet full of sterlings that she hopes will make a difference in her friend's life.

I pray he finds his way to you, Myint.

She looks Selwyn in the eye.

"No," she says. "This was my penance."

Shahryar & Anna

Washington, DC
September 2004

At the DC Bangla School that afternoon, as Anna attends her penmanship class, Shar marches to the front desk. A pleasant-faced woman dressed in kurta and jeans greets him, her hair cresting in a bun.

He speaks to her in Bangla. "I'm wondering if you can help me out. It's a bit embarrassing. I met a gentleman here the other day. He gave me his card but I've lost it. I just need his number to give him a call about a potential business transaction."

She is wary of the request. Looking around, she says, "I'm not supposed to do that. There've been complaints from the parents about these kinds of things."

He offers her his most charming smile. "You know what, I think you're right. I would be upset also if someone were giving out this kind of information so frivolously. However, if you could do me just this little favor—I don't even need the number. Can you just tell me if I've got his name right?"

She heaves a sigh. "Alright, but you can't tell anyone, okay?"

"Of course."

Her fingers hover over her keyboard. "What's the name?"

"Faisal Ahmed."

She types it in. Frowns. "Any other spelling?"

205

"No, but try the first name with an *o* if you don't mind. If that doesn't work, the last name without an *h*."

She fulfills these requests in the course of thirty seconds. "I don't see anyone by that name. Are you sure he's a parent here?"

"That's what he . . ." he stops as something catches his attention.

"Thank you so much. You've been very helpful," he says to the receptionist and walks over to one of the Ping-Pong tables where Ahmed's son is involved in an intense game with another teenager.

After a particularly involved point, when he sees Shar standing expectantly behind him, the young man stops in the act of retrieving his ball. "Hi."

"Hi there. I was wondering if your father was going to pick you up today. I met him here the other day and wanted to continue our conversation."

The young man is quizzical. "I always come here on my own. Are you sure it's my dad you met?"

"Your dad isn't Faisal Ahmed?"

"No."

"I must have made a mistake. Sorry!"

He has an hour to stew over his discoveries before Anna emerges from the classroom. She holds a large piece of paper in her hands.

"What was today's project?"

"Not too hard." She hands him what has occupied her afternoon.

"What's this?"

"We have to write our names in Bangla for our first assignment. Can you help me?"

"Of course." He studies her work, impressed.

"I see that you've already got *A* down."

He shows her that when one adds that little straight line going down next to অ—*shorey* "aw"—one gets আ—*shorey* "ah"—the first half of her name, *Ah*-na.

She hangs her head. "This'll take forever, won't it?"

"No. You've done really well. And I'll help you as soon as I take you home."

"Are we going home now?"

"Yes, but I have to make a quick call first."

He fortifies Anna with quarters for the vending machine, and after installing her in front of one, steps outside.

Faisal Ahmed picks up on the first ring.

"Shar. I'm glad to hear from you."

"You'll never guess where I am," Shar says.

"Uh, okay . . ."

"The DC Bangla School."

"The DC . . ."

"I'm surprised you don't recall. We first met here just a month ago. You struck up a conversation with me. Remember?"

A tinge of irritation enters Ahmed's voice. "Right. Of course I do. Shar, I really don't see how this is germane to what we were discussing the last time we spoke."

"I asked them about you. And your name doesn't appear on the member list."

"That's probably because I'm not a member."

"You're not?"

"No. And I never said I was. You don't have to be a member there to enjoy their facilities."

"Then how do you explain that the boy who you said was your son doesn't even know who you are?"

"What did this boy look like?"

Shar describes him.

"There were two boys playing that day. Did you ever think that you approached the wrong one, Shar?"

He did not, so he reaches into his quiver for his final arrow—confronts Ahmed with everything he learned from Niten about him.

Ahmed sighs when he finishes. "Shar, that's quite a conspiracy theory you've drawn up based on very circumstantial evidence. I've helped thousands of people over the years. People who were asking for nothing more than to escape a desperate situation or have a chance at a better life. Katerina can provide you with a whole list of individuals, families even, that you can talk to if you don't believe me. And as for Cummings, sure, I probably did meet him at some fundraiser or another, but I go to several of those a year."

"You're right in that I don't believe you."

"Need I remind you that it was you who asked for my help when I told you I was an immigration lawyer?"

"My name and profile are up on the IPD website. You guessed that I was Bangladeshi and stalked me to the Bangla School."

Ahmed laughs. "You're in the wrong line of work, Shar. Someone of your imagination should become a writer. I'm going to hang up now. When you come to your senses, you know how to reach me."

༄

JEREMY GREETS HIM AT the door when they arrive at Anna's house, an hour following his conversation with Faisal Ahmed.

"Hey," Shar reaches out and they exchange a stiff handshake. Jeremy is in a navy-blue suit, the tie loose around an unbuttoned collar.

"Val and I were wondering if we could have a quick chat. Anna, honey, can you go up to your room? Shar will be up to tuck you in soon."

Shar follows him into the living room. Val is sitting on the sofa, in work clothes also—a striped blouse and a pencil skirt. She stands up when the two enter, lending more formality to the proceedings.

"Hi, Shar."

"Hi." He takes a seat on the single wingback chair. Jeremy joins Val at the sofa. The configuration makes him feel like a couple's therapist.

She wastes little time on pleasantries. "What's going on with the visa situation?"

He thinks back to the conversation with Ahmed this afternoon. His last real option. "It's not looking good."

Val has taken to wearing glasses over the past few years. Black, slim-framed ones that she peers over now, her gaze pin-sharp.

"What about getting enrolled in another study program and staying on as a student?"

"I have to leave the country first to get a new student visa. And that's not a guarantee either. I can't afford to live here without a job indefinitely."

"Can't you just stay back then?"

"Illegally, you mean?"

"Whatever you want to call it. You wouldn't be the first to do it."

He enumerates all the risks associated with that option, listing the disadvantages the way Faisal Ahmed had explained to him.

Val sits back in the sofa. Jeremy—leaning forward with his elbows on his knees—complements her. It all looks oddly right in that moment to Shar, the two of them fitting together like lock and key.

"I think we're ignoring the elephant in the room here," Jeremy says.

"No," Shar says, surmising his meaning instantly. "No. We can't. It wouldn't be right."

"Think about it," Jeremy says. "You two have a child together. You have history. It won't be hard to convince the government that it's a real marriage."

Val turns to him, her face unreadable. "You'd be okay with it?"

Jeremy laughs, wryly. "Provided it's temporary, of course. I'm sorry, babe, I should have run it by you first. It just popped into my head now. You and I can keep things discreet. I think you and Shar would have to show things like a joint bank account, a shared address. I haven't thought it all the way through. After Shar gets his green card, the two of you can get a divorce."

Val and Jeremy look at each other; something passes between them, a Rubicon breached, a decision made and communicated in the unspoken language of couples. They nod and turn to him.

"I . . . I don't know what to say," he stammers.

Val is looking at him intently. "Do you *want* to stay?"

He reaches deep in himself for the answer and is satisfied with what emerges as the unvarnished truth. "I've made my peace with the past. I want to stay. But how is this going to affect the two of you?"

"Well, that's the thing, isn't it?" Jeremy says. "It's not just about us. It's about Anna."

ZAHIRA

Calcutta, India
August 1946

Zahira walks to the back of the house, where Motaleb is to meet her. In a nod to disguise, she has marked the space between her brows with a large red circle, but has not changed her clothes apart from wearing her sari in the looser, more billowy style of an upper-class Hindu woman.

More than an hour has passed since Inspector Nandi left, and since she and the driver arrived at an important decision regarding Rahim's rescue. The dark has descended fully outside in the meantime, the night blooming into life around them.

At the foot of the stairs that terminate in the rear courtyard, Motaleb blinks at her in the murky light. Earlier, he argued vehemently against her accompanying him to meet the abductors, citing the dangers and risks inherent, but relented once he saw how adamant she was.

"Begum sahiba, if I didn't know who you were, I'd take you for the ginni of a high Brahmin household."

He says this even though he too has transformed, donning a dhoti as opposed to his usual trousers. With the thick streak of vermillion on his brow and an orange turban, he looks just like a Hindu man.

"Don't call me 'begum sahiba,' you fool, and enough of your sycophancy. It's getting dark already, and I'm beginning to question the wisdom of all this."

"Evening is when the sadhus congregate at the ashram and smoke. This is the best time to go. Did you bring the ransom?"

She shows him the bag.

"Good."

ꙮ

INSPECTOR NANDI'S LONE CONSTABLE is posted at the main door, so they slip out the back gate, which opens into an alley, and hail a cycle rickshaw.

Zahira stumbles climbing up onto it, the bag of ransom jingling in her hand; Motaleb hops up with a quickness that belies his age and tells the rickshawallah where they intend to go.

The man, who has thinning hair and sunken cheeks despite likely being no more than thirty, gives a firm shake of his head. "Are you mad? Going into that neighborhood at this hour?"

"What's wrong with it?" asks Zahira.

"A den of thieves and dacoits is what's wrong with it. The best I can do is drop you a few streets away."

"That's fine. Just get us there quickly."

The man presses all of his meager weight onto the right pedal to push off, then the left. Zahira gives Motaleb a sideways glance. The old driver's eyes are feverish in the dark, as though he wants to pull the rickshaw himself. As an alternative, he leans on the rickshawallah's back as a jockey would a horse.

She whispers to him. "You said you have an idea of who the abductors are, Motaleb. How is that?"

"Huh? Oh." He looks briefly lost. "I saw the tripundra on their foreheads. A sign of the Aghoris. A most dangerous cult, begum sahiba. Wrapped up in all manner of dark, unnatural things. I've heard that the gang roams about an ashram nearby Hungerford. With Direct Action Day tomorrow, I wouldn't be surprised if whatever rogue sadhu these men patronize wants to start a ruckus."

"And kidnapping a rich Muslim man is the way to accomplish that? Most sadhus I've known are men of peace."

"Begum sahiba, do not be so quick to know what lies in the hearts of men. Muslim, Hindu, Buddhist, Jain, Brahma, Jew or Christian—it doesn't matter your God. They say that too much faith ruins a man, but it is really men who ruin faith, always. A man enters a religion with his whole self, and all the putrid things that he brings with him, all the darkness. It infects the faith. The riots we've seen, the senseless killings, it's not religion that is to blame, but the men who practice it."

"And where do we find these devious men of faith?"

The sarcasm is lost on Motaleb. "If anyone knows of those goons, it'd be the people in the ashram. We will go in and ask questions—two devotees looking for words of wisdom from a baba."

"I'm having doubts, Motaleb. Inspector Nandi said—"

"Begum sahiba, if we're talking risk, what do you think is the greater threat to sahib? Us bringing the ransom to those who hold him, or arriving with a contingent of police?"

The city is well in the arms of darkness when they turn into unfamiliar streets. Here, the alleys are lined with gnarled mango and lychee trees, behind them the boundary walls of old houses whose scabrous patches reveal the brickwork beneath. They loom like dead things, and in a snatch of thought, she wonders about the inhabitants of these homes, about the feet that pressed on their steps, the hands that pushed open the doors, their own secret histories of laughter and pain.

They escape the knot of alleys to enter the mouth of a wide avenue. There is more traffic here—rickshaws with hurricane lanterns lighting their undercarriage and even the occasional car that rolls by. Two clearly intoxicated young men with their arms around each other's shoulders catcall in Zahira's direction and make an obscene gesture as they pass by.

They disembark at a corner in Barabazar, at the southern end of which, under a cavalcade of lights, is the Sri Krishna Pramahansha Ashram. Ostensibly, the grounds are for worshippers of Kali but on occasion freelance sadhus—holy men who roam Calcutta and its surroundings and live off the kindness of the public—stop by to sit beneath the massive banyans and chat, smoke ganja and toss nuggets of wisdom to men and women who seek it.

The yard is steeped in shadows when they step into it, the air inscribed with incense and ganja, punctuated by the twang of ektaras plucked. They melt into the crowds of men and women, rich and poor, going from tree to tree under which sit mostly male (and mostly naked) gurus with impressive dreadlocks, their bodies smeared with ash, glassy-eyed from ganja, facing parabolas of congregants and cronies.

They pass by sadhus who represent different sects and factions within Hinduism, and Zahira is soon lost about the differences among them, until Motaleb begins to narrate: Here are the Vaishnavas, worshippers of Vishnu, their foreheads marked with a great *U* in white with a red dot in the middle; Shakti priests bearing only a red dot on their foreheads symbolizing the third eye, and Smartists, unbound to any one God, with a smear of ash on their faces, a painted *Aum* on their foreheads.

"How is it that you know so much about the Hindu religion?" she asks as she recalls her own readings on the religion as a child, imprints that have faded with time.

He gives her a shy smile. "I don't know. I've always found their stories so fascinating. There is so much color in their faith."

She scans the surroundings. "We've visited every tree, but we haven't seen any men or sadhus that have the symbol on their forehead that you described. The tripundra."

Motaleb looks anxious. "That is odd. They told me they would be here. At this hour."

"What about him, Motaleb?"

"Who?"

She points to a knot of people. "There, the monk with the shaved head, in maroon robes. He looks as though he is hunting for a space. Do you not see him?"

"He has the tripundra on his forehead?"

"No, on his satchel."

"On his . . ."

But she is already running to the monk before Motaleb can finish his question.

"I beg your pardon, Baba," she says when she reaches him and the monk turns.

"*Yes?*" The man replies in English.

She stammers, lost for words. The man is European, his clear blue eyes sparkling, lines radiating from a lean, strong face. And she can also observe that what she thought was the tripundra is another symbol entirely—a background of white composed of a solid rectangle rather than of three stripes, the red central circle proportionally larger than the one Motaleb drew earlier in the day.

She points. "That symbol you carry, is it a flag?"

The monk looks at it, makes a noise of pleased exclamation. "That would be the work of my apprentice. When bored, he will sometimes spend time sewing patches and symbols onto my satchel. This was a gift from him as I set out to visit Lumbini in Nepal, the birthplace of the Buddha. In threads of red and white, he thought to sew a flag of Japan on my satchel."

"I see," she says, dejected.

"I am sorry. Was it not the symbol you sought?"

"No, Baba," she says in a hushed and strained tone.

"Years before, when I myself needed answers, a wise man told me to travel east, perhaps your answers lie there as well."

Her throat is dry. "East? You believe I should go there?" She thinks of home. East Bengal. She cannot help but look in that general direction.

When no answer comes, she turns to find that the monk is nowhere to be seen.

"Did you see him leave, Motaleb?"

"Forgive me, begum sahiba. I was looking where you were. I didn't understand what the two of you were saying."

Feeling eyes on her, she looks up and freezes.

On the lowest branch of the banyan tree nearest to them sits a large raven, just like the one she encountered on the balcony in the morning. The body a black clot against the tree trunk, its large, wedge-shaped head is cocked toward them, the eyes lambent in the reflected lights of the ashram.

It holds her gaze for a moment more before hopping off the branch. On a low, straight path it flies into the gloom that lies beyond the iron gates on the eastern side.

Motaleb, mystified by her sudden catatonia, inquires, "What are you looking at, begum sahiba?"

"Follow me," she says.

The ashram is large and soon she is running toward the gates, Motaleb a few steps behind, his breathing ragged.

Reaching the gates, Zahira secures the bag of ransom under her armpit, grabs hold of the handle and twists. It takes most of her strength and an almighty shriek of metal-on-metal to loosen the bolt.

They step into a small orchard shrouded in darkness, no larger than a plot of land for a middle-class home. The air here is warm and thick, exuded by the trees.

She is about to tell Motaleb that perhaps they have made a mistake when there is the squeal of metal again. Three men enter and close the gate behind them. The man at the head of the group is the tallest, his silhouette long and slender, his face obscured from the lights behind him. He stands and observes before walking over in big strides. The other two linger at the gate, presumably to keep a lookout.

Up close, she can see the knife scar on the man's chin, the mark of the tripundra on his forehead.

He smirks. "What's this? Playing as devotees? You fool no one."

Later, she would marvel at the courage she finds to say what she does, having seen the long curved knife he wears on his belt, shoved into a leather holster. A Nepali kukri.

"Neither do you. Where is my husband?"

The man is amused by her bravado. "His fate is in your hands, literally. Have you brought the ransom?"

She gives him the bag. He rifles through the stacks of notes inside, bites each gold piece.

Eventually, he says, "This is only half of what we asked for."

"The rest you'll get when you hand over my husband safe and unharmed."

The man yawns. "I can't be bothered with all that. This will have to do."

He tosses his scabbarded knife to one of his comrades. "Take care of them. I'll go deal with her husband."

Motaleb, who has appeared to be mesmerized by the proceedings, now releases a strangled cry. "That was not part of the agreement. You told me no harm would come to us."

The man continues to walk away. "Forgive me, but I've decided to keep your cut of the money. You should think hard before striking bargains with the likes of us."

Seizing a handful of Motaleb's shirt, Zahira slaps him hard enough to make her hand ache. "You bastard. This is how you repay us?"

Motaleb deflates against her fist, weeping. "I'm sorry. I'm so sorry. I thought you two were leaving. I didn't know what would happen to me, my family. I've run up so much debt gambling."

"Then you ask us. You ask!" She releases him and he collapses on the ground, clutching his chest and complaining that he cannot breathe. The other two thugs are advancing on them. One holds the unsheathed knife in his hand, gleaming in the moonlight. Their smiles are sadistic. She wonders what her fate will be. It occurs to her that she should scream, but even the act of opening her mouth seems to take forever.

The ear-splitting noise of a police whistle shatters the evening air instead, followed by the rush of feet, shouted commands. The thugs stop and look behind them. A group of men have entered the orchard, uniformed, armed with pistols that they point at the abductors. The thin man is apprehended first by two burly constables. His accomplices drop their weapons and when ordered, lie prostrate on the ground.

Dusting off his uniform as though he took a tumble, Inspector Nandi emerges from behind the constables. "There you are, madam. You gave us quite a fright."

"You . . . how . . . what?"

The inspector removes his cap and runs a hand through his sweaty, brush-cut hair. "The constable we left at your house noticed your and your driver's absence and notified me immediately. We narrowed down where you might be to here, but even then, if it weren't for a random monk telling us where you were we might not have found you in time."

"This monk. What did he look like?"

"That's the oddest thing. He was a *firangi*, a European." Nandi looks around. "He was behind us just a moment ago."

She sits on the ground, the events of the day finally overcoming her. "Is Rahim safe?"

"Yes. And we are certain that he is nearby. We just have to . . . squeeze these three and we'll know exactly where."

"Why would they do this?"

"I don't know. But this is a conspiracy we have just begun to uncover. It likely originated somewhere beyond the men here. Your driver was the go-between. The motives are what we intend to find out."

A voice speaks up behind them. "I'm not sure that will be possible, sir."

They turn to find one of the constables holding up Motaleb's hand as though taking his pulse. They shine a light on his face. The driver's eyes are open but the pupils still and dull. A rope of drool hangs from his mouth, joining him to the dusty ground. The constable closes Motaleb's eyes, bringing peace to his face.

"I fear this one is beyond questioning."

Shahryar & Anna

Washington, DC
September 2004

After the conversation with Jeremy and Val, he goes up to his daughter's room. Anna is asleep. But when he kisses her forehead she immediately opens her eyes.

"Hey, Baba," she says in a sleep-saddled voice.

"Hi there."

"Why're you so late?"

"I was talking to your mom . . . and dad. We were discussing some important things."

"About staying here?"

"Something like that."

"What did they say?"

"I was doing most of the talking, actually."

"Is that good or bad?"

"I don't know. How was school today?"

"It was alright. Hey, you wanna see something?"

"Sure."

She removes from her bookshelf a large paper rolled up and secured with a rubber band. She spreads it out on the bed.

"I remember this! You've made some progress, young lady."

On the same page from earlier in the day, Anna has indeed managed to complete inscribing her first name:

আনা

"This is really good."

In his mind, her achievement is impressive enough to eclipse the earlier discussion with Jeremy and Val. "How did you figure out how to write the rest?"

"I remembered what you said about adding that little line after *n*—so that it becomes *na*."

It brings him joy to see her interest in writing Bangla, to see her work on the project unprodded.

He ruffles her hair. "You're a natural."

She looks up, beaming. "Really? I guess I get it from my grandpa and grandma then."

He smiles. "Something like that."

じじじ

AN HOUR LATER, HE tucks her into bed and walks downstairs. When he sees neither Val nor Jeremy, he steps out to the driveway, his mind in turmoil. A piece of paper tossed into the swirling winds, buffeted by possibilities, dangers. He thrusts his hand into the pocket of his jeans, desperate for the calming poison of a cigarette. The box of Camels he pulls out is squashed and empty. He swears in Bangla.

It is cooler than in the day now, everything a deep shade of blue, spackled with the warm yellow light spilling from the houses in the neighborhood—the Violet Hour.

Footsteps behind him. Jeremy, in a T-shirt and jeans now, but somehow more dapper than earlier in the evening.

He smiles. "You want a lift to the subway?"

In his BMW, Jeremy turns the silver knob until they tune into a station playing British pop. Shar struggles with how to broach the subject of what happened earlier in the evening.

"I want to thank you for what you proposed. It's incredibly generous of you."

"Let's sit down and plan this a bit more. I'm sure there's a lot of scrutiny around these things."

"You're taking a pretty big risk."

"We all are. Are you having second thoughts?"

"I . . . I don't know. Not because I don't want to stay, but I ask myself sometimes what my role is here. The three of you, you're a unit. I'm on the outside, looking in. You're the one who held Anna's bike when she first took off the training wheels. You'll be the one to interview boyfriends. Take her on tours of college campuses. Set up her dorm room."

"That bothers you?"

"It shouldn't, but it does. And it makes me feel ashamed. Petty. You were there when I couldn't be. Anything you get from Anna, any love, you've earned."

They stop at a red light. Jeremy lowers the volume of the radio. "You've done the same, Shar. You've been here for the last six years. She'll always be your daughter. Her last name won't change. She'll always look like you. I'll be more like a traditional dad, that's true. But you'll be something I'll probably never be—her friend. You'll always be the one she can't get enough of."

They begin to move again. He looks out the window to the dark vistas rushing past, thinking about this purgatorial decade, an existence where he is both with a family and without, a child and an orphan, a father and a bachelor.

"What about you and Val?" he asks Jeremy. "Don't you want to get married someday?"

Jeremy laughs. "It's been more than six years, so any day now. My parents have given up badgering us about it. I've brought it up more times than I can count, but Val's in no hurry. She says people get married because they don't feel safe, when they're afraid of the future. She says she feels too safe with me to feel the need."

"How do you feel about that?"

"I'd love to marry Val. She and Anna are the best things that've ever happened to me."

He looks at Shar. "Don't tell her, but I bought a ring a month ago. I was planning to propose on her birthday, in October."

"Jesus. Jeremy . . ."

"Don't worry about it. The ring's not going anywhere. Neither's Val. Sooner or later, she and I will get married. I know it."

They arrive at the subway station, the BMW gliding to a smooth stop at the kiss-and-ride. Shar steps out, overwhelmed by gratitude, guilt at all the envy he has silently emitted at this man over the years. How well would he handle matters were their places reversed? How hard was it to raise another man's child? One who carried his name, looked so little like you? One whose father was still very much in the picture?

"Jeremy. I . . . just, thank you. Thank you for everything," he says. Jeremy flashes a thumbs-up sign before driving away.

He sits thinking the entire journey across the Blue Line, as the train flies over the Potomac and dives below the city, only to emerge again near Eastern Market. And by the time he walks into his apartment he has made a decision. He sits at his kitchen table and dials the first of the two calls he must make this night.

Faisal Ahmed is curt when he answers. "Mr. Choudhury. How can I help you?"

"I'm calling to apologize for earlier today," Shar says. "I've been under a lot of stress lately, and I think I let it get to me."

When Ahmed does not respond, Shar says, "I'm hoping that the offer is still on the table."

"It is," Ahmed says eventually, and Shar releases the breath he has been holding. "But Shar, you'll have to promise me that there will be no further outbursts. You must put your faith in me going forward, or this won't work."

"Thank you, Mr. Ahmed. I will be at work tomorrow. If you can give me a couple of days, I should be able to collect what you need."

"Good."

He calls Jeremy next.

"Hello?" Jeremy's tone indicates that Shar's number is not saved on his cell phone.

"It's Shar. Sorry to call so late. I just came home and checked my email. One of the job interviews that I was pinning all my hopes on came through. For now, I can use that to get an extension on my OPT visa, but down the road they should be able to sponsor me for a green card."

"Really? That's awesome. I'll have to tell Val the good news. What kind of a job is it?"

"Oh, just a policy analyst. It's a little far, but I don't mind the commute given the long-term benefits. Best of all, we don't have to go through with what we discussed."

Jeremy laughs. "I was thinking about this on the drive back. It was a pretty crazy idea, huh? I was actually starting to get cold feet, if it's possible to get cold feet for someone else's marriage. So, maybe this is for the best."

Shar smiles. "Yes, I really think it is."

RAHIM

Chittagong, Bangladesh (East Bengal)
September 1946

L ying tied up on the filthy floor of a lean-to near the ashram, Rahim hears voices approach the door. Thinking his abductors have come to finish the job, he braces himself for the worst, hoping that if death must come, it arrives swiftly. But the first face he sees across the door is his wife's. He bursts into tears of relief, as does she at the sight of his bruised and battered face, his torn clothes.

But upon hearing of the capture of the abductors, the betrayal and demise of his driver, he has no appetite for interrogations from the police. They wisely let him alone.

He has little time to convalesce, for on the day following his rescue, the city descends into chaos. The protestors dispatched by the Muslim League clash with their Hindu counterparts. Riots rage around the city.

They spend the day locked in their bedroom, feeling as though they have escaped the proverbial frying pan and are barely avoiding the fire, an audience of two to the symphony of violence conducted outside—the screams, shouts and sirens. On occasion, they peek through the shuttered windows to discern the sources of the monstrous sounds. Among the many horrors they witness that day, the image of a man with a bloody face, running from an armed mob, stands out. He runs up to the main gate, which Zahira had asked the guards to chain the previous night. The bloodied man shakes it so hard they hear the locks clanging from their room. Even in his debilitated state Rahim is about to run out to help, the key to the gate in hand, when his wife stops him.

"It's too late." She indicates the mob already set upon the man, who disappears in a maelstrom of whirling fists and sticks that became redder by the second.

It is during the second straight day of captivity that Rahim decides to leave for East Bengal, a decision refracted through a kaleidoscope of disappointments—in his city, his country, in harmony between Hindus and Muslims, forever promised but always elusive. In himself—the brittleness of his loyalty to the country of his birth.

In all, four thousand perish in riots across the city over the course of seven nightmare days. At the end of the Week of the Long Knives, carts piled deep with corpses leave Calcutta for the charnel grounds, mass graves. In the aftermath, newspapers report on tales of violence and horror so depraved that Rahim and Zahira cannot bring themselves to read them.

He sends a telegram to the zamindar in Chittagong, who is relieved to hear that Rahim has reconsidered and agrees immediately to expedite the house exchange. Rahim and Zahira apply for the right paperwork, as he submits his resignation to a disappointed but supportive Theodore Drake. They gather up their life in Calcutta. As the day of departure approaches, they write to Zahira's father to inform him of their decision. They receive a terse cable in response—*Will await at train station on expected date.*

The preparations take another month. They hire a tonga on the day of their departure. Rahim frowns when he sees the horse—ribs clearly visible beneath a dull brown coat—consigned to pull the carriage. But with an affirmative slap on its rump, the kochwan assures him that the animal is up to the task.

"I fed her just this morning, sahib. She'll have you at the station before you can take two breaths."

It is unclear if the horse—who gives a desultory flick of her tail in response—shares the owner's confidence.

Zahira is surprised by the attachment she feels to Choudhury Manzil, mostly unexpected and only manifesting itself now that her departure is inevitable. As the carriage is being loaded, she takes a final tour of the house, which, with its shutters firmly tied with rope and emptied of furniture, is gloomier than ever.

She visits the fretworked balcony, where Calcutta unfurls before her in all its familiarity—yellow with dust, green with coconut trees, craggy from the spires of British buildings that crowd the sky. But she feels alienated from the humanity that surges in its streets now that she knows of what it is capable.

Her footsteps echo on the stairway during her descent. At one point her hand ventures too close to the limestone walls and they mark her knuckles with white. She stares at them, and when she resumes, pushes them harder and harder against the wall, until they burn and bleed. She studies them again and sees that the white is now stained with red, like vermillion.

House, now we have marked each other, but we will not begin a life together, but end one.

She steps out to bright sunshine, shielding her eyes from the sun and hiding her damaged hand from an impatient Rahim, who wears an unadorned white punjabi that makes him fairly shine in the light.

"How handsome you look," she whispers in his ear, not daring to place a hand on his chest.

Everyone—from the carriage driver to the servants—watches. Their bearer, Mintu, is the sole member of their staff to accompany them to East Bengal. For those remaining, Rahim has arranged for employment among his circle of friends and acquaintances in the city, or has provided compensation worth several years of their salaries.

"If only he had asked," Zahira says again, so many times since that night of Rahim's abduction that they have lost count.

He knows who she means. But Motaleb was dead, and the only path forward was paved with forgiveness, they had concluded. So they had paid for the driver's funeral, even arranged for a stipend for his youngest son—still studying for his matriculation.

"Have you said all your good-byes?" Rahim asks her as they mount the carriage.

"Yes," she says, after a final look at Choudhury Manzil. "I have."

ON THE HOUR-LONG RIDE to Howrah Rail Station, they breathe in deeply the final dregs of the city. The streets are no longer littered with bodies, the smoke seeping out of the burnt-out tenements extinguished by rain, the blood-smeared boundary walls hastily covered over with quicklime, the tops no longer lined with vultures come to feast on the corpses. Calcutta is back to a semblance of its old self. But now, it seems like a trusted comrade who has slipped off his mask to show the demon's face beneath.

"Who could have thought that so many people were killed here just a few weeks ago," Rahim muses.

She takes his hand. Having learned early in their marriage that his was the gentler soul, she pooled within herself a reservoir of strength and grit that would suffice for two. The world's ugliness and injustice always shocked him. Once a girl and now a woman, she has come to expect it.

They arrive at Howrah to find chaos—families, hawkers and station guards clog the platforms. Conductors—resplendent in white uniforms—shout themselves hoarse trying to maintain order but soon throw up their hands in futility as the trains fill to capacity through every cavity. The Week of the Long Knives has hastened the pace of departures of Muslims from West Bengal, as well as the arrivals of Hindus from the East.

"Like ants attacking a dead cockroach," Zahira whispers to Rahim in dismay. But in the madness he identifies pockets of co-operation: a group of men hauling to a window the massive trunks of a woman traveling alone, faceless in a dark burqa; a pair of constables reuniting with her family a child lost in the bedlam; coolies forgoing their baksheesh to assist the old and destitute. He is momentarily lifted by hope for the prospects of East Bengal.

Zahira carries her own luggage; Rahim shares the load of a heavy trunk with Mintu. The three trace a path through the crowds to the first-class cabins located at the front. They wait patiently to board, but arrive at their cabin to find it occupied. A heavyset man is ladling out the contents of a tiffin carrier to two young girls. A woman sits on the bench with her feet tucked underneath.

Rahim and Zahira look to each other in distress, too polite to accost the squatters. Mintu engages the man on their behalf. "This is sir and madam's cabin."

The usurper acknowledges them with a quick nod before returning to supper distribution. "Arey bhai, there's room enough for all of us. Come. I'll make space for you in a moment."

Mintu takes his employers' silence as consent to escalate. "Let me see your tickets."

"Why? Are you the conductor?"

Mintu extracts the tickets from his pocket and displays them to the man. "I don't know if you can read, but this says 'First Class Cabin F.'"

A bluff, as Mintu himself is illiterate.

The man's family collectively cringes, but he laughs. "You're

Muslims like us, no? Leaving to settle in East Bengal? When we leave the country of our birth with tails between our legs, brother, we're all traveling third class."

Mintu takes a step forward at the insult, but Rahim restrains him. "That's alright. This gentleman is correct. There's enough room here for all of us."

"But sir—"

"Go to your seat, Mintu," Zahira says. "We can manage."

∽

WHILE THEY WAIT IN the sweltering cabin for the train to depart, their cabinmates utilize the delay for a family nap, the father laying out blankets across the benches and floor. Rahim and Zahira sit stiffly, resisting calls of nature in fear of stepping on an errant limb on their way to the toilet. Only after two hours, when the train suddenly awakens and lurches eastward, leaving behind a sun that dissolves in a glob of orange and red over the city, does the family rise and stretch in unison.

"We are wise to leave early, before the rest," their cabinmate proclaims. "The true nightmares will come when they actually divide the country, whether it's now or the next year."

"How are you so sure?" Irritated by the man's smugness, Zahira feels the need to dispute his dark prediction. The children look out the window, their excitement rising as the train saws through the quick-falling gloom. She looks away from them. Below the blue-black sky, a strip of yellow lines the horizon. The jaundiced skin of a sick world.

The lights switch off.

"Perhaps it's the conductor's doing," the man nods sagely. "You know, so we're not attacked."

Pale moonlight slices in through the window, makes his eyes shine like, like . . . *like a crow's*, the thought comes unbidden to Zahira.

The man lights a cigarette after begging Zahira's leave and solicitously offering one to Rahim, who refuses. The man's wife, curled up on a bench with her back to them, is yet to speak a word.

"Has either brother or sister ever lived across the river before? On the other side?"

"I'm from there," Zahira says. "Mymensingh District."

"Near the capital then. Dhaka isn't as big or grand as Calcutta, but if you prefer the city life, you'll like it there. It's a neat and quiet place."

"We won't be living there," Rahim blurts out, earning a warning pinch from Zahira. "We exchanged homes with a man living in Chittagong, near the coast."

"A cousin of mine lived there, when the country was still whole and not broken into pieces. Right by the ocean, it was. The British had a garrison there during the war, until there was a big to-do after a British officer shot a boatman."

"Really?" Zahira is intrigued. She vaguely recalls reading about the incident in the *Statesman*.

"Yes. In 1942 a local boatman took a Japanese pilot, a prisoner of war, over to Burma in his boat. There were many rumors about what happened—how he seduced an English lady doctor into abetting his escape, killed three British soldiers with his Japanese sword when they got in his way. Supposedly the local commander discovered what happened and went out to the beach to wait for the boatman to return. When he did, *thhash!* An execution. The locals say the man's ghost haunts the shores now. When lightning flashes on stormy nights, some can spy a boat sailing south, the silhouette of a lone figure standing below black sails."

Rahim smiles. "Is the darkness inspiring you to tell us ghost stories, brother?"

The man flings the stub of his cigarette into the murk outside in a shower of orange sparks. "I'm telling you what they say. I don't believe in ghosts. If the dead could return, none of us would fear death."

"Or fear it more than ever."

"You don't have children?" The man asks after a while.

"No." Rahim does not elaborate. Zahira says nothing. There was a time when this question used to bother her, now it just evokes a bland emptiness.

"Good for you, brother! I love my girls, even as much as I would if they were boys. But let me tell you something. You start dying as soon as they are born. If you want to live forever, don't have children."

THEY SPEND A WEEK in Zahira's childhood home in Mymensingh before making the trip south. Her father, Abu Bakar—more skeptical of their decision to relocate to East Bengal than his daughter—is nonetheless overjoyed to see them.

He poses a question to Rahim over tea and biscuits one morning: "What exactly will you be doing there? In Chittagong?"

"I don't know, Abba," Rahim says. "I suppose fisheries is an option. The home swap includes the estate of the old zamindar that I'm replacing. That means hundreds of bighas of sharecropped land, the boats the man would lease to the local fishermen. All that requires management. It's not glamorous, but it's honest work."

Abu Bakar is inscrutable behind his gray whiskers and glasses. "Honest work is done by the farmer sweating under the hot sun, the fisherman knee-deep in the mud. You'll be living off the fat of the land and sea. Also, you're a city boy. With little experience in such matters."

Rahim takes a sip of his tea to gather his thoughts. "I made some inquiries before the swap. The zamindar I will replace was not well-loved among his people. Not necessarily cruel, but ruthless with the bargadars who didn't meet his crop quotas, or fishermen who returned with lean catches. I can try and undo some of the harm he's done to the community. If nothing else, I have time. I've set up a meeting with a fellow named Abbas as soon as I reach there. He's been managing the fishing fleets that are to be mine. He inherited the job after his father passed a few years before."

Rahim's father-in-law sits forward. "Don't misunderstand, my son. I question only because I want what's best for the two of you. I am grateful to have my daughter close to me again. And God knows you're a good man. When I think of what could have happened . . ." He stops, overcome with emotion.

The allusion clear, Rahim is embarrassed by the naked gratitude on display, even though he knows that following three childless years, no one would have blamed him had he remarried.

"You don't have to thank me," he manages.

Abu Bakar shakes his head. "I do. Forgive an old man his emotions, but some debts can't be repaid with words. But perhaps we should discuss matters more urgent. Mainly, what do you know of the house where you will spend the remainder of your lives?"

THEY STAND BEFORE IT the following week. At the gateway to their new home, they gape in awe. Rahim is accustomed to impressive accommodations, but their home-to-be takes even his privileged breath away.

Their seaside mansion's acres of courtyard are enclosed by twelve-foot-high walls of poured cement, meeting at front-gates composed of two massive wings of wrought iron rising to a graceful peak at the middle, with finials of japanned bronze that gleams in the late morning light. Hundreds of yards beyond the gates, the mansion's sandstone bulk shoulders into the sky, with sharp geometries and wide-ramped stairs that recall a Dutch fort.

Zahira points at the pale-yellow circles that dot the lush grass in the yard. "There was something there important enough to take back with them."

"Holy basil plants." Rahim says. The disparity of wealth he was always aware of in Calcutta is heightened here, where this is the only home for miles not made of bamboo or earth. Calcutta, where a fog of noise, smells and activities always permeated. He once found it exasperating, but now he realizes how alive it made him feel. He swings around. A gravel path leads out from the gate, giving way to grass and sand as it approaches the shore. In the pale stretch of beach that divides green from blue, there is not a soul to be seen.

"Who is to let us in?"

The iron gates swing open with a push from his hand. "No one goes into the zamindar's house without permission, and he hasn't left behind anything worth stealing."

THEIR FURNISHINGS (ARRIVING FROM Mymensingh on cow carts) will not be here for another week, when Mintu will also rejoin them following a visit with his relatives. In the meantime, a cantankerous old caretaker visits them with a basket full of fresh vegetables, rice, fish and live chickens with their wings tied back that he slaughters in their backyard, grumbling all the while for having to come in on his off day. That night—in an echoing, barren kitchen—Zahira cooks for her husband. Rahim assists. The scent of spicy chicken curry fills the house.

On the wide, cantilevered balcony that adjoins their bedroom, they light hurricane lanterns and burn a coil to keep the mosquitos at bay. They eat their supper and watch the sun immolate into the sea.

"It feels so different here," she says. "When I knew we'd go back, I could only think of Mymensingh—all flatlands and forests. Here my heart wants to fly across the surface of the ocean like a bird and never return."

"Does that scare you?"

"I think the scary part is over."

She takes his hand. "Let's stay up all night and watch the sun come up like when we were children."

"We didn't know each other then."

"Then we will know each other now."

He smiles. "I'll put the kettle on."

THEIR RESOLVE TO AWAIT the sunrise proves too ambitious, as they wake the next day in bed, clinging to each other, following a night of lovemaking that had an urgency it never did in the city.

"I can't believe there's not a sound in the house," she says, her head on his chest.

"In a few days, there will be. We will need people."

Following a simple breakfast of bhaji and parathas he ventures out for his meeting with Abbas, who recently sent him a detailed overview of his estate in Chittagong, along with a rudimentary map of the area.

He walks out of the main gate and heads in the general direction of Abbas's house as indicated by the map. Earlier, he debated taking a walking cane with him, but Zahira advised against it. "It would seem too imperious. You're a landholder, not a ruler."

The beach is deserted, a gray curve stretching to the end of his vision, lined by green-topped hills to the north. The sunlight is scrubbed clean, the air perfumed with palm, salt and kelp. He follows a stand of short firs on the far side of the beach where clumps of grass cling to the ground. Long runnels of shivering water separate him from the south half of the shore. There, fishing boats sit like black crescent moons.

In a half hour, he reaches Abbas's house, a two-story brick-and-tin affair in the shade of the foothills, a stark contrast to the thatch huts that dot the shore. Rahim pauses at the entrance to consider. It is apparent that Abbas is doing quite well.

The door to the courtyard is open, as is the one to the house proper, across which a heavyset male body moves in a flash of white lungi. Rahim hears the sounds of domesticity seep out—breathes in the scent of a cooking fire.

He steps in.

"Who are you?"

The voice comes from behind him, the tone chill and insolent. Rahim turns to find a boy of about ten standing under an areca nut tree.

"A neighbor of yours. I've come to see your father, I think. Is he home?"

The boy gives him an appraising look. Despite the child's outward unfriendliness, Rahim feels a surge of sympathy seeing the thin face marked by deep craters from what must have been a serious and recent bout of smallpox.

"Manik, is that any way to treat an honored guest?" A broad-shouldered, big-bellied man steps out, hurriedly donning a shirt over his bare torso, his shoulder-length hair swaying as he proffers a quick bow and takes Rahim's hand in his larger rougher ones.

"I am humbled, sahib, to meet my new master, yet ashamed that you were the one to step into my hovel. You only needed to give me the word and I would have to come pay my respects at your new home." He turns to the house and shouts. "Jamila, prepare tea and sweets right away. We are most blessed to host the new zamindar today."

"Just some tea, thank you," Rahim says, repelled by Abbas's unctuous manner. He casts around for a place to sit.

Abbas's son had veered close to his father while he spoke. He receives a smack on his forehead as a reward. "What're you standing around for, you donkey? Go get a kedara for our guest. The big one made of wood. Not the cane one."

"When did your son contract smallpox?" Rahim inquires as the boy beats a sullen retreat to obey.

"Ah, sahib is so kind to ask!" Abbas exclaims. "A few years ago. He was only seven. Thank goodness he escaped with his eyes intact. He likely caught it from some villager's child. You know how dirty they are. Always crawling with disease."

The boy soon returns with a large wooden chair with armrests, his spindly legs wavering under its weight. Rahim walks over to help him, but Abbas intervenes by seizing the chair before he can. "*A, a, a*, what are you doing, sahib? There will be such a curse on my family if I let you lift a finger in my house."

He takes the chair and sets it in the center of the courtyard, bids Rahim to sit while he squats on his haunches on the dirt. A woman—her face hidden behind the long cowl of her sari—ventures out bearing a tray of sweets, winter pittha snacks, a pot of steaming tea and two cups. She sets it before him on a wicker stool and returns inside without a word. Abbas's son stands under the shade of the porch, watching the proceedings with big eyes.

Rahim takes a sip of the overly sweet tea.

"I've come to better understand the business—starting with the boats," he says. "I need the numbers—leased, hired, owned or otherwise. I need the haulage of the fish caught, broken down by each kind if possible, and how much it brings in for the estate every month. Can this be done?"

Abbas throws his head back and laughs. "O-ho. I've heard that sahib is a numbers man. I can get you some of what you require, but I am not as educated as you. I can do simple math, read and write—as you saw from my letter. With my old master, I just handed him the money from our leased boats at the end of the month and showed him how it added up and he was happy. But I can see that that won't be enough for you. I will do my best to get you what you need."

"Thank you." Rahim smiles. Perhaps he was being judgmental earlier about this Abbas fellow. This reflexive cynicism is something he should abandon now that he is no longer in Calcutta, he tells himself.

They chat some more, and Abbas is happy to brief him on the history of the village, important information such as the timing of the tides, the types of fish that proliferate the bay, even the lineage of the mansion that Rahim now occupies, originally built by the former zamindar's great-grandfather, who made his money in indigo until that all ended with the revolt of 1859.

Abbas's knowledge of the locale, Rahim realizes, is encyclopedic.

At this point, Abbas pauses to carefully confirm that they are alone, his son having vanished inside. He leans forward and lowers his voice. "The word has reached us, sahib, of the terrible ordeals you and your family went through before the riots. I am glad to see that you are unharmed. I trust begum sahiba also emerged unscathed."

Rahim is unable to help a grimace as he recalls that day, the bloody week that followed. "How did you hear of it?"

"Oh, the former zamindar, my master, mentioned reading about it in the newspaper," Abbas says quickly. "But there was not much detail, just something about a Hindu gang that was involved."

"I'd rather not get into it."

"Of course. Of course. Please forgive my trespass. I'm sure you have no love lost for that lot."

Now Rahim is puzzled. "And what lot is that?"

"Why, the Hindus, of course."

He is about to rebuke Abbas when a sixth sense tells him to

wait. Careful to keep his tone and expression neutral, he says instead, "I suppose you can say that . . ."

Abbas appears encouraged. "In that case, there actually is a related matter that I've longed to discuss with you."

"Please proceed."

"As you know, sahib, nine out of ten in this village are Hindus, most poor fisherfolk—Namasudra—the lowest of the low. Being distant cousins all—they possess the same last names—Jaladas. They're tight-knit simple folk, superstitious, stubborn and thick. While the old zamindar was here, they had an element of protection and safety, but now that the old man has fled to India, abandoning his brothers and sisters in faith, they are concerned about their future."

Abbas pauses to make eye contact with Rahim to underline the importance of what he is about to say.

"Go on," Rahim says.

"Even as so many Muslims are arriving to our new country from India, almost as many Hindus are crossing over to the other side. But of course this is easier done if you have the capital to make the journey. The fishermen of this village can't afford to leave even if they wish to."

"And what is it that you're proposing?"

The avarice is clear on Abbas's face. "Simple, sahib. Many Hindu fishermen in the area have proposed to sell me their boats—often all they have in the world. All so that they can flee to India. I've been able to buy one or two with my limited means, but with your capital, sahib, we could own a great fleet."

"And if all the fishermen leave, who would man the boats to fish?"

Abbas gives an impatient wave. "There are many of our fellow Muslims for that. They've been waiting ages to have a go at this part of the bay, but never had a chance due to the domination of the

Hindu fishermen here. We can hire them for a fraction of what we now pay."

Rahim smiles. "It seems you've thought this through, Abbas."

"So sahib will consider it?" Abbas rises to his feet from excitement. Rahim follows.

"I already have," Rahim says, his voice cold with fury. "This is the first time we've met, and that is the only reason you still have a job. Approach me with such a vile proposal again and I'll make sure you hunt long and hard to make a living. In case it wasn't clear, I didn't come here to take advantage of poor, fearful Hindus. They will receive from me the same protections and benefactions they did from my predecessor, if not more, given this new climate of fear that has descended after the riots. The same goes for Muslims, Christians, Buddhists and anyone else."

Abbas shrinks during Rahim's tirade like a fish left drying in the sun. "It was just a mad thought that occurred to me one day, sahib, set off by the hot sun beating on my head. Please forgive me and forget we ever spoke of this."

Rahim gestures to his house. "Take care of your family, and put your mind to doing the same for this community. Things are going to change around here."

ꗸ

AT FIRST HE HEADS home, seething, then decides to go the opposite way. The only thing that can cleanse his foul mood is the surf and open air. He walks toward a tiny speck of movement he spots under a copse of palm trees in the distance. Edging closer, he sees that it is a young girl about the same age as Abbas's son. Bare-chested, her hair bleached copper by the sun. She looks up as he approaches but does not greet him.

"Hello!" Rahim says with forced cheer. "What are you doing, child?"

He would say more but is distracted by the girl's eyes, all the more remarkable given the thin, plain face that hosts them. They are gray, as though the oceans of the world have been poured into them.

Never fully at ease with children, the girl's fearless demeanor unsettles him. He answers for her when she does not. "I see you're drawing."

There are indeed scribbles on the ground. Most look like childish attempts at Bangla letters, but there are others that he does not recognize.

"Do you know their meaning?"

Silence. Then, "Who are you?"

"Your new neighbor."

"You're lying. I saw you come into the big house yesterday. You and the lady. You live in the house of the old zamindar. You must be the new one."

He holds out his palms in a gesture of surrender. "You're too clever for me."

He finds himself sitting cross-legged on the ground, pointing to one of the scribbles and saying, "Do you know what that one is?"

"No."

"That's *shorey* 'aw.'" He identifies the first of the Bangla vowels, then names and redraws firmer versions of the other shaky letters the girl has inscribed on the ground—the triangular *kaw* ক, curly *talibo shaw* শ, *jaw* য and *ghaw* ঘ. The girl watches him attentively, but demurs whenever he asks her to replicate his efforts. To coax participation, he finds himself writing down all thirty-six letters before long, in separate sets of vowels and consonants, and then in the many possible variations when two letters are combined into one.

When he looks at his pocket watch again, an hour has passed, and they are at the center of a constellation of letters sketched on the ground. The sun has climbed directly above, steaming the morning's moisture out of the sand. But despite the heat he feels calmer, more relaxed. The hour spent with this child has ground smooth the ragged edges left from his meeting with Abbas.

"Do you go to school, little girl?"

She shakes her head.

"Oh. Are you parents lettered?"

"What does 'lettered' mean?"

"Do they know how to read and write?"

"No."

"Then where did you learn to write these?"

Silence again. The girl shifts her gaze to the ground, tracing her fingers over the characters he has engraved on the shore with her.

"Do you wish to learn more?"

She looks up with those piercing eyes again. Nods.

"Then come to my house tomorrow, since you seem to know where it is. We'll teach you, my wife and I."

He realizes as he speaks that he has volunteered Zahira for this cause without consulting her.

"I'll come," is all she says.

◌◡◌

HE FINDS HIS WIFE at work in a corner of their vast backyard, her back to him. He stands and watches. She is hanging on the clothes-line sets of wide white drapes. They are bright under the sun, billowing like sails whenever they catch the wind, giving Zahira the appearance of a captain on the deck of a ship.

"How was it?" She smiles when she sees him. Her dupatta is cinched across her shoulder and waist; errant locks of hair have escaped her bun and become mired on her sweating forehead. The face she wipes with a sleeve holds a contented glow.

He recounts to her his meeting with Abbas.

"If this is the mentality of those in power here, then things are much worse than I thought," he concludes.

Zahira, who has listened attentively, agrees. "Yes, but we knew this could be a possibility. You were right to warn him, and if there are any suggestions I'd offer for the future, it's that you do it less overtly. Rural people are very concerned about face; the politics here are subtle. It will take you time to adjust."

Her critique is meant to be constructive, but it crystalizes for him the scale of the changes to their lives, the enormity of the challenges ahead.

"Maybe we bit off more than we can chew," he says glumly.

She takes his hand. "Don't lose heart so easily. We lived a nice life in Calcutta, but one very much for ourselves. Here, you and I have the opportunity to do some real good."

"Yes," he says, thinking of the girl with the gray eyes. "Maybe we do."

TRUE TO HER WORD, they find the girl at their main gate the next morning, silent and still until Zahira, looking out the window, notices her. They usher her inside together. Zahira serves her sweet biscuits and tea, and, when she notices the thinness of the girl's wrists, puts on extra rice for the afternoon meal.

The lessons begin immediately after tea. Rahim asks the girl to take a chair at the desk they have set up on the porch.

"What's wrong?" he asks her when she fidgets.

"I want to sit on the floor."

"Very well."

But she is still unhappy. "Now what?"

"The floor is too cold. Can we sit in the yard?"

"We can."

They move to the lawn, sandwiched between sun and grass.

"Do you remember the letters we practiced yesterday?" he asks her.

On the slate provided her, she recreates in chalk every single letter he showed her the day before, the penmanship stunningly improved in the span of a day. He tries not to gape in shock.

"Very good," is all he can manage.

She seems pleased by the reaction she has elicited in him. "I know one you don't."

With unusual care, she draws a new symbol on the slate.

Her claim proves correct, for Rahim stares long at the slate, puzzled. The girl has drawn a strange glyph, a shape emerging from a confluence of sword-like strokes.

運

"Where did you see this?"

"I don't know," the girl says, her gray eyes daring him to challenge an obvious falsehood.

He changes tactics. "I just want to learn from you, as you do from me. Don't you wish to be my teacher?"

She is not so easily swayed. "No."

"Very well." He rubs his temples. Perhaps there are worse fates than being childless. Zahira looks on from her seat at the porch, amused by his frustration.

⁕

BUT WHEN THE GIRL returns the next day, she bears a cloth bag from which she produces a stack of colored paper. Rahim and Zahira gawk at the queer collection of leaflets. One shows a powerful-looking soldier in a helmet and olive uniform, his features twisted into a fierce expression as he charges toward the viewer—*Fight to Free Asia from Colonial Oppression,* declare the Bangla words above his head. In another, two men in turbans crawl on the street while a light-skinned soldier and similarly fair, well-dressed woman walk past—*Humiliated in Their Own Country.* Among many others, a particularly striking one depicts a fanged demon in black, the image of a great edifice set on its chest. Standing on the hands it extends toward the viewer, two figures wearing headdresses (one long and white-tailed and the other multihued) are about to engage in battle—*Do Not Let the Western Colonialists Destroy the Unity of Asia.*

He asks the girl where she found them.

"They fell from the plane." She points to the sky. "I was out in the fields and the plane flew overhead and dropped all these papers on me. I thought they were butterflies at first. That's how I learned letters."

He shakes his head in wonder. The World War is over, but traces of it linger in the most unexpected places.

"And what of the other symbol? The one you said I didn't know. Where did you learn that?"

With a measure of reluctance, the girl reaches into the bag once more, this time pulling forth a folded sash.

Rahim lays it out on the table. He caresses it with wonder. It is a dull yellow, torn, bearing splatters of dark maroon. Emblazoned in the center, along with another, is the character the girl drew the day before.

He directs a question to his wife. "Have you ever seen anything like it?"

Silent until now, Zahira approaches, points to the flag sewn with heavy thread into a corner of the sash—a red sun set against a white backdrop.

"Just that," she says. "On the day I found you."

Shahryar & Anna

Washington, DC
October 2004

When his phone rings at home that Saturday morning, Shar picks it up eagerly. It has only been a few days since his visit to Ahmed's office, when he transferred ownership of the USB drive filled with the digital files of what Ahmed asked for. The act itself felt almost banal because of the ease with which it was accomplished—walking into Volcker's office under the ruse of updating his virus software and instead copying every file he could manage in the ten minutes that his director waited on the sofa, perusing a copy of the *Atlantic*. But the electronic device felt strangely heavy when he handed it over to the lawyer, as though those bytes of data had absorbed his guilt and shame.

Attuned to emotions as lawyers tend to be, Ahmed looked him in the eyes then. "Shahryar, there's no shame in what we do for our children."

He made his escape, Ahmed's promise of quickly pushing through his job ringing in his ears, of calling in just a few days once he has news to share.

But it is Niten's voice that greets him on the phone. "Do you get the *Post*?"

"Yes, but I haven't looked at it yet."

"Do it now. First page of the Metro section."

He turns to the page as instructed and finds the article in question. A sinkhole of fear opens in his stomach as he reads the headline.

"Did you find it?"

"Yes," he says, his voice barely above a whisper.

"Read it."

He does. The article on Faisal Ahmed is short, the thrust of the story contained in the final two paragraphs:

The FBI had been investigating Ahmed for years, following allegations from former clients that he charged them thousands of dollars in exchange for promises of green cards. They allege that Ahmed colluded with a network of business partners who provided paperwork for federal labor applications for workers they would hire on a nominal basis. Ahmed would then provide these business partners with a percentage of the fees garnered from his clients.

Ahmed is reportedly cooperating with the FBI while his practice remains closed. Clarence Cummings, a friend of Ahmed's and a former Maryland attorney general who is running against Pablo Aguilar for the Senate this fall, expressed his shock and dismay at the indictment. He declined further comment by citing the ongoing judicial process. How Faisal Ahmed's indictment will affect the senatorial race, just weeks away, remains to be seen.

"Tell me for the love of God that you didn't go through with what Ahmed asked you to do."

"I wish I could."

There is an audible intake of breath. "Jesus, Shar. What did you do?"

Shar tells him. And when a long silence follows, asks, "What do I do?"

"A lot of this depends on Faisal Ahmed now. There's no way for us to unpack what 'cooperating' means in the article. The one

good thing is that he's been indicted on immigration fraud, and not federal data theft. But I have to assume that the FBI has seized his computers. And if Ahmed was dumb enough to leave your files in there, then that opens a whole different can of worms. The worst thing that could happen from our point of view is that he agrees to a plea bargain, that means Cummings could be a big enough fish for the Feds to focus their energies on. But even then they're bound to ask Ahmed how he got his hands on the files."

The phone receiver grows slick in his grip. "What are the chances of that happening?"

"We don't know. Whatever it is, you need to ask yourself if the risk is worth it."

"What do you mean?"

"Isn't it obvious, Shar? You need to leave the country. You needed to leave yesterday."

༺༅༻

HE WAS SCHEDULED TO visit Anna that afternoon. He arrives early. Fortunately, Val and Jeremy are both at home. He asks if they can sit in the living room to talk.

When they ask why, he says, "My situation has changed."

The discussion lasts more than an hour, and both Jeremy and Val are left shocked and subdued by its end, but understanding of his decision. They agree that he should be the one who tells Anna what is to happen.

She is away at a sleepover, and when they hear a car approach on the driveway, Jeremy and Val withdraw so Shar can greet his daughter at the door.

"Hey, Baba," she embraces him. "How come you're here so early?"

"Couldn't wait to see you. Let's go upstairs."

"Cool. I've got something to show you."

In her room, she hands him a page covered with neat repe-
titions of her first name, in Bangla letters written with care and
grace.

He gasps with admiration. "This is lovely, Anna."

"Yeah, I practiced and practiced until I got it right."

"I think you're ready to write your name in full. But there are
some other things you need to learn first."

He writes on the page—widely spaced—the three consonants
that comprise her last name, which is his last name, and the last
name of Rahim and Zahira.

চ representing the sound *ch* as in *church*

ধ which is an aspirated *d*, as in *dh*

র for *r* (one of three kinds in Bangla)

"Unlike English," he says, "we can't just place the letters next
to each other and have them form a word. Because that would just
read *chdhr*. In Bangla, vowels, when placed between consonants, or
combined with them, change shape."

On the page he writes next the three vowels that must be combined with the consonants he wrote above.

ও as in *ou*

উ which reads *oo*

ঈ like *ee* but originating deeper in the diaphragm

Anna's attention is riveted to the page as he writes. "Don't we
have to capitalize the first letter?"

"Nope. Bangla is very fair in that sense."

He continues. "So, we have to combine চ with ও to get চৌ, or
chou, ধ with উ to get ধু, or *dhu*, and র with ঈ to get রী, or *ry*. The
three syllables that form your last name."

Placing his hand over his daughter's, he guides it on the page until her name reads in full, a stark black against the white of the paper.

আনা চৌধুরী

They stand and admire the result. "It's beautiful, Baba."

"It is. If you keep practicing, you won't even need my help after a while."

She looks up at him. "Yeah, but you're going to be here, right? So, when I need your help I can just ask you."

He sits down on the bed. "About that, sweetheart . . ."

JAMIR

The Bay of Bengal
November 1970

Night has settled in since he started. The boat is anchored, the engines stilled.

He rises to his feet. The scuppers gleam as though new. But his knees hurt. His hands burn with cuts. And his old heart is aching.

He was left alone while immersed in his work. Once, he thought he saw Abbas and Manik in conference in the wheelhouse. But no one has approached him since his conversation with the captain about the letter that he found in the hut.

His work on the scuppers has leached some of the poison from him; he feels lighter as he heads for the galley. He stops when he remembers Gauranga's invitation from earlier in the day. It would not be the worst thing in the world, he decides—caressing the stinger hanging around his neck—to find sympathetic ears.

The turbines silenced, he hears the pop and clank of cooling gears, muffled conversation, as he heads to the engine room.

Gauranga and Humayun are at the far end, sitting on a ratty blanket they have spread on the floor. On it rests a platter of fried fish chunks and a bottle filled two-thirds with a cloudy liquid.

"Finally, the prince has joined us!" Gauranga's slurred voice echoes in the hallway. Humayun's mouth lifts into a half-smile.

Gauranga notices Jamir's scrutiny of the wares on offer. "The

251

finest tari you can get. Old Humayun himself bled his best palm trees, set the sweet juice in a pot in the corner of his hut, and forgot about it for a week. That's all it takes. Sit, have a sip."

"Thank you, perhaps later." Jamir folds down to his haunches between the two men. He assesses the tari. It would not be the first time he has had alcohol, but unlike many other men in the village, has developed no addiction to it.

"Oh, don't be so shy. *Here!*" Gauranga thrusts the bottle in his face. Jamir takes it, has a reluctant sip. The sour liquid blazes down his throat and leaves him coughing.

Gauranga is amused. "It's just burning a path clear. The next ones will go down more smoothly."

Humayun leans back against the corrugated metal wall and hums a ditty about lost love from the cinema. The two men pop fish chunks into their mouths. Jamir is not hungry. He takes another sip of the drink.

"More, more," the older man urges. "Once you're back on land, your woman will harangue you and you will wish you were back here, on water, sipping on life-water."

"And you do not face those troubles?"

"I have a wife, but my hearing has turned to stone over the years. Everything that hits here," he taps his right ear, "just bounces away."

They eat and drink in silence. In the absence of conversation, Jamir feels discontent overtake him once again. Taciturn Humayun, a man Jamir has always thought immune to empathy, surprises by asking what ails him.

"It is . . . regarding my family. If I tell you, you must not repeat it."

"We're fishermen, not fishwives," Gauranga says. "Every word we hear on the boat we drown before we set foot on land."

Jamir's desperation for a second opinion outweighs his mistrust, and he shares with the two men what he discovered in the hut a few weeks ago, though he omits Abbas's assessment of the contents of the letter.

"Well?" Jamir inquires when the two men exchange a look but produce no words, mortified to have potentially traded his secrets for naught.

Gauranga sets down the bottle of tari. Jamir picks it up. "Let me ask you something, my son. What is it you wish to know most about me? I believe I have the answer, but I want to hear it from you."

Jamir's principal curiosity about Gauranga has always revolved around the sailor's missing eye. Unshackled somewhat by the drink, he requests the story behind it.

Humayun chuckles. "Not that story again. Here, give me a sip. I need it."

He wrests the bottle from Jamir.

Gauranga smiles. "I thought as much." He flips his eye-patch to reveal a raw red socket housing the milky remains of his withered left eye. Jamir manages to not flinch.

"Settle down, this will take some time."

As the older man begins his tale, Humayun passes the bottle to Jamir, who takes another gulp. Gauranga speaks loudly but slowly, in the cadence and diction of a wandering *baul*—a singer-storyteller.

"I was seven years old when my father took me to the haat one day. His name was Ram, the same as the god-warrior. And like the god-warrior, he could be both benevolent and frightening, in turn.

"But that day he just wanted to show me the fish he had caught. The big prizes from the sea that he had sold for a high price at the market. He would fish on a steamboat, its purpose identical to the one we are now on. But it was different in the way it ran.

"It was a hot day in the month of Asharh. The rains from the previous night had left the ground squelchy with mud. The sun was hot even early in the day, and the air steamy and heavy. Nonetheless, I recall wanting to skip as we walked past the lime orchards. The fields of aubergines. My father was all mine. During the day, he was different from the man who would stagger home, as he did so many nights, his breath thick and rank with drink.

"We arrived at the haat to find it swarming with people. As it should be on Sundays. My father's catches were spread out evenly among the three biggest fishmongers, but Kartik's shop had the pick of the lot, for he had the deepest pockets.

"While my father and Kartik chatted, I gawked at the catches, told myself then and there that I would be a sea fisherman and not a river one. I could not imagine the depths of the rivers holding anything nearly as wondrous as what I saw before me—the giant morays with their snake-like snouts and evil eyes, the jagged-toothed reef sharks. I made my way to the prize of the lot—a giant stingray that hung from the lintel, its silvery gleam undimmed in death. It was not meant to sell for much, of course, as ray meat can be chewy and tough. Rather, it was there to draw attention to Kartik's shop.

"Kartik and my father were deep in discussion.

"I put my face close to the ray's leathery skin and saw that what I thought was pure silver was actually scored with a smaller repeating pattern of dark gray.

"I gently touched the ray's back, where it met the thick muscular base of the tail, just to feel the rough texture of the creature's skin. It swayed in the breeze, the long, evil-looking stinger hanging just fingers above the ground.

"I touched it once more.

"The creature I thought dead spasmed as though I were God and my finger had given it life. The tail swung like a whip, too quick for me to jump out of the way. Agony more massive and cruel than anything I could imagine exploded on the left half of my face, and I fell to the ground shrieking.

"There were no physicians at the haat to treat my wound, no kabiraj to put on a poultice and draw out the poison. So my father, Ram, ran back with me in his arms the three miles between our house and the haat, passing again the lemon orchards, the fields of aubergines. The sun burning on our faces. I was told later that I was unconscious as he carried me. Barely breathing. My eye was a crater from which a red river ran.

"I burned with a vicious fever the next three days. My mother would tell me I was so hot that she could barely keep her hand on my forehead. My father chased down healers from all the nearby villages. My mother poured buckets of cold well-water on me. But it was not until the fourth day that I woke, my forehead cool and body limp, and asked my mother for rice porridge. Both my parents burst into tears of relief.

"My father gave the biggest fish from his next catch to the kabiraj who ministered to me. Our neighbors came by to visit with the child who made a miraculous recovery after being struck by an undead demon from the deep seas. Kartik, the shop owner, brought with him the severed stinger of the ray to commemorate the nearly tragic event. This period of celebrity was short-lived. My mother concluded that my father's carelessness had destroyed my future, that now I may as well join the beggar children before the temple who harried the steps of rich men.

"My father did not respond to my mother's haranguing. Rather, he focused on crafting for me an eye-patch made of string and bark from a palm tree. The stinger my mother fashioned into a pendant as a reminder for me to never again be so careless.

"Following my injury, my eye had filmed over, withdrawn into its socket in the manner of a wounded animal slinking back to its cave. But I would come to know that it was far from dead. A miracle was taking place within its ravaged socket, where the ray's venom had taken root, shooting forth enchanted tendrils into my gray matter, bonding to it through unknown alchemy and stoking within me some eldritch magic.

"I first discovered my new powers when I moved my eye-patch over my good eye and tried to look out through the ruined one. I saw only a solid blackness at first, but over time light penetrated and changed into a world of shadows that sharpened over the weeks and months. As the light grew stronger, I began to see twisted shapes—boats that appeared bloated and trembling, tree branches that bloomed like veins, the sea like an inky mass crashing endlessly on platinum shores.

"The greatest change was in people. When their backs were turned to me, I would quickly switch over my eye-patch and peruse them through my ruined eye.

"In most cases I saw only misty contours. But around some people I saw a bright glow, a comforting, warm light. For others— shadows flaring out from behind like the wings of giant ravens.

"I would follow these few strange souls and over time discover a pattern. The slow bovine son of the police daroga who bullied me had black wings. As did the evil old zamindar (thank goodness he has been replaced by Rahim Sahib), who would strut about on his horse. In contrast, the girl I played with, who sat at my door for three straight days while I burned from the stinger's poison, was wrapped in light. As was my mother.

"The ray's blow had taken from my eye sharpness, farsightedness. But it was a trade, not a robbery. Because it gave me the Eye of Judgment in return.

"My father could not look at my face anymore, perhaps because it reminded him that he was to blame for my state. But it made him less likely to beat me. At least for a while.

"One night, months after my injury, he staggered home drunk and roaring, and saw that I had scrawled all over our rattan walls with a piece of chalk I had found outside a schoolhouse. Enraged, he slapped me until my lips bled and I was nearly unconscious. Mother screamed, asking him to stop. Please stop.

"Later, he stumbled off to bed. I stayed in my mother's lap. She tried to console me the best she could, cooing in my ear that my father had not meant it, that he would take me back to the haat the next day and buy me the most colorful kite they sold.

"I only half-listened, switching over my eye-patch to see my father. To really see him as he slept with his back to us. I stared until my good eye ached and my mother's tears mingled with mine, until the lamp's flame died and the moon's silver light replaced its gold.

"But I never saw black wings emerge from my father's back, nor saw an aura of light envelop him. He was just an ordinary man.

"Other than the two of you, I've shared the secret of my eye with only one other—my wife (the same girl who cried at my doorsteps all those years before) on the night of our wedding. Making love for the first time emptied me as I had never imagined. When I climaxed inside her, at most a few minutes following my initial fumbling entrance, it loosened within me a torrent whose undertow pulled everything I had hidden in myself, including the story of my powers. So, as I lay in bed with her, soft and sated, I told her the story of my eye.

"It was a mistake, for even as I spoke, I could see her transform, the expression on her face morphing from surprise to distrust to fear.

"After she drifted off to sleep, I lay awake, convinced that my new bride thought me a madman. But a few days after, when a visitor came to ask permission to borrow my boat for the first time, she asked me if I had looked at the man with 'the Eye.' I gave her a stern look, unsure at first if she were mocking me. No, I told her. I did not see anything wrong in the fellow. But over the years, my eye has taught me that in this world the devils outnumber the angels."

THROUGHOUT GAURANGA'S STORY, JAMIR listens enchanted. As the boat sways gently and the low pinging of the engines subsides, the only sound is that of the water sloshing against the hull, the steady whooshing cadence of the men's breaths.

Gauranga recounts his story with his good eye closed. Upon finishing he turns its bleary regard to Jamir. "But you, my son. When I see you, I don't just see an aura, but wings. Silver wings of light. You are a *farishta*, son. One of God's own angels sent down to rescue us all."

Before Jamir can find words in response, Humayun's booming laughter reverberates in the engine room.

Humayun is not just laughing, but is doubled over and pounding the ground with his fists as tears leak from his eyes.

"If . . . if you bought that, then I have a mermaid's hand to give in marriage," he wheezes. "I hope you don't mind the fish smell."

Gauranga scowls, points to the stinger around Jamir's neck. "You bastard. I carried it for fifty years until I lent it to Jamir."

"He cut it off a ray we caught a few years back," Humayun explains. "As for his eye, he lost it drunk one night falling on a sharpened piece of bamboo. I was there. He was more worried about what his wife would say than the eye."

"Is this true?" Jamir asks, angry at being played a fool.

"Pay him no mind, lad," Gauranga says. "The point of the story is not whether I have the Eye of Judgment, rather that you don't. We can't have the measure of someone just from a look. Truth is a many-sided thing."

He lights a biri. After a few drags, he taps away ash and asks a question of such simplicity that Jamir cannot believe he has not already considered it.

"How do you know the letter is hers?"

"I found it in the hut. She is the only one of us who can read and write."

"That means little. She might have written the letter on behalf of someone else. She might have found it washed up in a bottle. I ask again, how do you know the letter is hers?"

Unable to muster a reply, he sits silently in the gloom of the engine room. But for the first time, immersed in despair, he glimpses a ray of sunlight, a shimmering, wavering shaft a mile above that he can swim to.

The letter is hers because Abbas told me so, he wants to tell the men. *And I believe him, because . . .*

He does not complete the thought. He cannot. "It's possible that I have been too quick to doubt her."

"The senses wander, and when you let your mind follow, you become as a windblown ship," Gauranga says. "According to the Bhagavat Gita anyway."

He queries Humayun, who has leaned back against the wall and closed his eyes. "What does the Koran say?"

"What makes you think I'd know?"

Gauranga claps a hand on Jamir's shoulder. "Wives are a tricky lot, lad. They'll scream at you, make you feel lower than an ant when you come home and shrink your pecker like a turtle if they so wish. But in times of trouble you won't find a faster and truer friend, one who will stand by your side no matter what storms may come. If you doubt your wife, go speak to her before acting rashly."

Humayun stands, stretches and heads for the exit. "For someone who claims to not be a fishwife, you sure talk like one."

After he leaves, Jamir says, "Thank you for your story. Was the part about your father at least true?"

"Aye. I'm sorry to say."

"The memories of my own father are also painful. But in a way different than yours."

"Don't feel obliged to tell your story because I've told you mine," Gauranga says. Sitting on his haunches with his long arms splayed over his knees, he reminds Jamir of a large, benevolent bird. "But I've found in my life that the pain of the past can fester if left inside, poisoning your blood. A way to release it is by speaking of it."

Jamir takes a long sinful sip of the tari before he begins.

"It all started with the woman.

"The first time I saw her, I was helping my father with his boat, a beauty. Big, with a prow that reached for the skies. He said that it would be mine one day. Like yours, my father was a sea fisherman. But that was not enough in those days. So on Sundays he gave boat rides to the English soldiers and their wives that were there because of the war.

"The first time I saw her was during one of those boat rides. She was driving on the beach with her friend. They were doctors or nurses at the British army hospital. I had not seen much of the English before, and I thought the women, with their exotic-colored eyes and hair, were so beautiful. The woman's friend had dark hair, and she had little to say to either my father or me before lying down on the stern to take a nap. But the woman I speak of had red hair. That, combined with her fair skin, made it seem as though she was burning under the sun, a fire being—a djinn who'd stepped out of childhood stories and into my life. She was also much kinder than her friend. She spoke to me and my father as equals, offered me a flat slab of some dark sweet that I would learn later was called chocolate. I took it, of course.

"A week after I met her, my father's boat crew came to see my mother and told her that an extraordinary thing had happened. The Englishwoman came to see them while they were pulling the boats ashore for the coming storm and asked if they would take a Japanese man with them to Burma. A soldier. My father was reluctant, but the money offered was such that he couldn't say no. So he divided half the money among the crew, and went alone to take the Japanese soldier to Burma.

"A storm was forecast that day, and my father's crew was worried for him, but they knew how good a sailor he was. We all had confidence that we would see our Hashim in a day, two at the most.

"And so it was. We spent two fearful and sleepless nights waiting for him. A storm hit the coast while he was away. It spent its fury on our shores. But on the dawn of the second day, when one of my father's crew finally saw his black sails in the distance, from the hills, he ran to our hut to tell us.

"I ran out to the beach. My father was close enough by then that I could see him standing at the prow. We waved at each other. But then I saw for the first time the eyes etched on his boat, eyes that made it come to life. I could see writing there too, a script I'd never seen before. It filled me with fear.

"And then I saw the man.

"I drifted to a stop. He was tall and thin. A *gora*—an Englishman. He stood on the beach facing the sea. He wore a greatcoat. Its tails were dancing in the wind.

"By then my father was very close. He'd jumped off the boat and was dragging it to shore. He had to have seen the man. But it gave him no pause. Perhaps he'd already resigned himself to trouble.

"He stopped when close to the shore. His chest was heaving. The thick boat rope was braced against his shoulder. The three of us formed a triangle—I was on the beach, the man at the edge of the water, and my father in it.

"The man said something to my father. It sounded like a question.

"My father nodded. Then the man shot him.

"He fell slowly, to his knees, then face-first into the waters. Strangely enough, he still held the boat rope in his hand.

"The gora said some words in English that I did not understand and walked away slowly, with a complete lack of guilt or fear. He was in no hurry because he had done nothing wrong.

"I held my father's head. I was small, and it filled most of my lap. He opened his eyes. There was still some light in them. He whispered something to me, but try as I might, I couldn't hear his words over the crashing of the waves. Even though I bent my head so close to his that his lips were caressing my ears, I still could not hear.

"I held him in my lap as the light fled his eyes."

Jamir stops to catch his breath. They fall into a long, contemplative silence that Gauranga eventually ends. "What a hard life you've led, my son. What a thing for a child to have witnessed. All along the coast fishermen have known the story of Hashim, yet all this while I never knew that he was your father. Did you ever find the man who shot him?"

"No. I was too young to understand why my father was taken from me, just that he was taken. We did nothing because we were up against the English, who were more than men back then, more than kings, they were gods. And you did not battle the gods and win.

"But I'd see that woman again. Late one night, a few days after my father's death, there was a knock on our door. My mother was bedridden with grief. So I went out to see.

"Her mouth, nose and red hair were disguised by the tagelmust wrapped around her face, but I recognized her green eyes. She held me to her for a little while, sobbing, whispering a stream of words in my ears. I recognized only my father's name. Her tone was one of apology, remorse.

"She released me, took out from her bag a silver flask that found a way to shine even in the dark, as though drawing the light of the stars to itself. It was heavy in my hands, cold like the night.

"She was offering it to me. I wouldn't know why until later—to relieve her of guilt for having sent my father to his death.

"At home, my mother weighed the flask on a scale. A half pound of pure silver. It was more than my father could earn in a year from the seas.

"That night I lay awake, holding the flask. I was worried that my mother would sell it. I woke very early the next day and while she slept, I walked far up one of the hills, and in an abandoned temple to Kali, hid it under a loose brick.

"When my mother awoke and couldn't find it, she thought we'd been robbed, but one look at my face and she knew what had happened. She beat me, but nothing could make me give up the hiding place. So for the second time in a matter of days, my mother's heart was broken.

"My father was no longer there, but it was as though he'd jumped off the world and entered me. When I would go up to the temple and examine the flask, I felt that it connected us. I would sit in that lightless temple and speak to him for hours, and when I opened the cork-stoppered mouth and set its dark opening against my ear, I could hear him whisper back to me.

"I'd turn it over and over in my hand, run my fingers over the carved design on its face."

Jamir casts about for a drawing implement. Finding a thin wedge of coal, he sketches on the ground, his hands moving assuredly. A shape emerges before the two men.

"What is it?"

"I drew it for years without knowing. My father had a dream, that I would receive schooling, so that I could avoid having my fate tied to the water. But that dream ended with his life. Without a man in the house, without older siblings, my mother could not afford to have me attend school. I'd barely begun learning Bangla letters. But word was spreading around the village that the new zamindar had taken under his wing a gifted young girl—Rakhi Jaladas—and was teaching her to read and write, back when there were few in the village who could.

"One day, a few years after my father's death, I approached the girl in the hopes that she would know the meaning of these letters. We had known of each other, but were not close because she was Hindu and I Muslim. I showed her the flask, told her my story. And she told me hers—how her path had crossed with that of the Japanese soldier whom she found lying half-conscious by the wreckage of his burning plane.

"She and I had seen the same plane that day. It arrived shortly after we said good-bye to the red-haired woman, but where it had frightened me, Rakhi had chased it as it flew over her, scattering leaflets printed in Bangla—meant to get us to support the Japanese against the British. When she found him, she dragged him as far away from the flames as she could. She told me he tried to give her a sash—as a gift or for safekeeping; she was not sure. She soaked it in the pail of water she carried and wrung the drops onto his mouth. Only when she heard the sirens of the British military arriving did she run away, not realizing that she had accidentally taken the strange cloth with her. All those years she wondered about the fate of the soldier, and I had come to her with the answers. The flask was half the story of our lives, the sash the other.

"We'd never be sure, but she thought the letters might have something to do with the woman's name. Rakhi was not confident enough in English letters, you see, and didn't know enough about the woman or the ways of foreigners to know what they would put on their possessions.

"We became friends, very close ones, and although we drifted away from each other for a while, we found each other again years later and married. She took on a new name then, a new identity. For her wedding gift, I gave her the silver flask that first connected us."

"And your father's boat?"

"My mother no longer had the flask to sell. So it had to be the boat. Another fisherman—a prospering one—bought it because he liked the eyes the Japanese soldier had drawn on it, those strange characters. But they were the reason I was glad to see it go. For those eyes, they frightened me. And those characters—even though I did not know their meaning—looked as though they contained a world within themselves. The boat had changed, left us, as though it was given wings rather than eyes. It belonged to the world of spirits and fairies.

"But I'd realize later that my fear went further. It had spread from the boat to the bay. Ever since that day I held my father's head in my lap and his blood ran out to mix with the sand and foam, under the prow of that boat with the all-knowing eyes, I've been afraid of the sea."

"Yet you're a fisherman out in the bay. Why is that?"

Jamir holds his head in his hands for a long time, relives those days for the ten thousandth time. He finally looks up with red eyes.

"A man must provide."

∽

AFTER GAURANGA DEPARTS, HE continues to sit in the engine room, wishing he were on a ship that could sail back in time instead of over water, before all of this.

He has looked at the letter so many times since discovering it, recognizing only the odd letters, his eyes returning to them repeatedly in a gesture of comfort, as one does to familiar faces at a gathering.

It seems a cruel joke that the three letters he is most familiar with, that he can reproduce with the greatest proficiency, are not Bangla but English, letters that spell the name of the woman who killed his father.

The power of the written word, the idea that one could trap sound, thought, names and concepts by inscribing them onto a surface, that was the world of intangible magic his father's death pulled him away from, to one of tangibles: two hands to work with, two legs to take you to your place of work, two eyes full of the blue of the sea, two ears overflowing with the wind; a nose and tongue salted from seawater.

And when he married Honufa, saw how her mind bloomed under Rahim's tutelage, he had to practice weeding the envy from his thoughts as assiduously as a gardener does a flower bed.

But then, since her break with the zamindar, with no books to feed her quicksilver mind, no surfaces on which to practice her penmanship other than rock, stone and sand, he watched her fold into herself, realized the vulnerability of the literate mind—its inability to produce its own sustenance the way his could: by finding patterns in the clouds, faces in the waves; the hints of secret language in the calls of birds and animals.

And he is shamed now to recall the pleasure he allowed himself to see Honufa that way.

He stands to leave and is shocked when a violent lurch of the boat almost returns him to the floor. He balances with a fist on the ground and waits for the ship to right itself. But no other turbulences arrive, and he realizes that it was not the ship that moved, rather his alcohol-addled legs that betrayed him.

With a hand on the wall for support, he makes his way back to his bedroll in the galley. His head heavy from the palm liquor, and with the gentle lapping of the waves to lull him, he sinks into a clammy slumber.

His dreams are steeped in terror. In them, he finds himself running through endless metal corridors while something monstrous pursues him. Hands reach through the walls to snatch at him and impede his progress, slow him down. In panic, he veers too close and is seized by a pair of ethereal limbs that solidify once they capture him, crawling from shoulder to neck to mouth, over which they clamp down with demonic strength to cut off his screams.

"Mmmph!" The chains of nightmare snapped, he tries to sit up but is unable. Something holds him down. A hand. Real this time. Its thick, hard fingers pry his mouth open and shove in a cloth acrid with the scent of diesel. He gags.

Cold sharp metal touches his neck.

"Make a sound and I'll draw this razor across your throat," Abbas says.

The bohoddar looms over him, rummaging through his bedroll and belongings with his free hand. "Where's the letter? Where is it, you fucking illiterate oaf?"

His body slack with terror, his eyes swivel from Abbas to Manik, who sits on his legs, immobilizing them. He flashes Jamir a grin.

"Tie his legs," Abbas instructs his son without taking his eyes off Jamir, and within moments a thick length of nylon rope is wrapped around them, crowned with a tight knot. His hands are secured next, joined at the wrists so tightly that he can barely move his fingers. With his limbs restrained, his eyes run about in their sockets like caged animals, taking in everything, trying to meet Abbas's eyes and plead. *I've harmed no one. Let me go and I'll tell no one*, he wants to scream at them. For the sake of seeing his family again, he is willing to be a coward.

Abbas shoves his hands under Jamir's armpits while Manik takes his legs. Together they lift him up and head to the stairs. He realizes what is about to happen. Shaken out of his terror-induced lethargy, he flails and tries to scream through the rag in his mouth. The sounds emerge as groans.

Dawn has arrived outside, and the world as observed from the deck is painted in topaz shades—the sea a serene but sickly green. The trawler started moving at some point in the night. It now cuts steadily through calm glassy waters.

The boat's railings are the lowest at the aft, and that is where they take him.

"Get ready," Abbas instructs when they are parallel to the railing. Jamir looks down. The sea that has long fed his family has turned on him. It licks the sides of the boat with hunger.

They lower Jamir's body to the ground.

Abbas extracts the rag from his mouth but immediately covers it again with his hand. Jamir gasps for a clean breath.

"I'll move my hand," Abbas says. "You'll get one more chance to tell me where the letter is. If you scream, I'll kill you. If you don't tell me, I'll kill you. Do you understand?"

Jamir nods, but does not speak when Abbas removes his hand, only stares at the man looming over him.

"Fine then. Don't say I didn't give you a chance to live."

While Abbas fumbles for his razor, Manik's grip around his ankles slackens ever so slightly. Jamir uses this opportunity to draw his legs back and kick them out with all his strength.

More shocked than hurt, the bohoddar's son is driven back at least a foot by the blow, his long legs tangling and collapsing under him. Thrashing on the deck like a fish, Jamir wiggles across and under the lower gap in the railing. His body flips in the air. The blue-green sea rushes to his face.

He slams on the water with a slapping cold shock. The belly-first crash drives salt water into his nose. As he opens his mouth to cough, the sea shoves its frigid, salty fists into his throat. He flounders on the surface of the water and quickly begins to sink.

Even as his mind spins and threatens to black out in panic, he hears a voice cut through. Authoritative and wise.

Stop. You know how to do this. Hold your breath. Shimmy up like an eel.

Fathom-lengths below the water by then, Jamir orients himself to the voice so that he stares up at the diffusely lit heavens above. He kicks his feet and wiggles his torso upward. In a way, he is aided by his restrained hands and feet, which streamline his body. Stars explode before his eyes as he desperately squirms, finally bursting out of the water, sucking air in huge grateful gulps.

The trawler has not moved far. Abbas and Manik still stand in the aft. They say nothing to him, only stand and watch as the boat slowly moves away.

Drink the air deep, says the voice. *Fill your lungs and keep your head above the water. Don't worry about those two. They think you're done.*

He spins around. There is nothing but vast stretches of ocean all around.

"I *am* done!" He rebels against this entity, this watery desolation. But again he obeys, takes in a deep lungful of air and lays his head back the way he would as a child in bed, when he was with fever and his mother watered his brows to lower his heat.

"Honufa. My son. I'll never see them again."

You will if you keep your head. What are you forgetting?

"I don't know."

Look in front of you.

He does. The violence of his actions has shaken loose Gauranga's pendant from his shirt, and the stinger now floats in the water before him, still attached to his neck by the string.

He grips it with his teeth, needing several tries before he can get a firm hold. It is the size of a large comb. Hard as ivory. Its feathered edges knife-sharp. He raises his hands to his face. Manik has tied him securely, but it is just one coil to cut through. He brings his wrists to his mouth and rubs the serrated edge of the stinger against the rope. It is difficult work. He stops and fills his lungs with air whenever his head threatens to sink below the water.

Jaws numb from biting so hard, lips bleeding from the sharp edges of the stinger, he persists. After rubbing for what seems a lifetime, he studies the rope and screams with frustration to find it has barely frayed.

You must keep going.

"I can't," he sobs.

You must. Your wife and son, they are still back there on the shore. They will need you before long.

"Are you him? Are you the Boatman?"

This time the voice waits before speaking, and when it does, Jamir knows. He knows.

Weeping, knowing now who has been watching over him for decades, he resumes his efforts.

When the final stubborn bits of rope surrender, he is too drained to exult. He reaches down to undo the knots around his feet and finds that he has no strength left. The world fades and shrinks, a jade marble spinning away from him even as the Boatman tells him that help is on its way. That it is very close.

The last thing he remembers seeing before falling into darkness are eyes approaching him over the water—great, tilted, inhuman—those strange symbols that he saw all those years before inscribed beneath.

The last thing he remembers hearing is the splash of oars.

Shahryar & Anna

Washington, DC
October 2004

A car horn honks downstairs. He looks out the window and sees Anna leaning through the open window of Niten's Range Rover. "Hurry, Baba!"

It is nine in the morning, Thursday. Five days following the fateful call from Niten. His flight is not until one, but they agreed that going to the airport earlier would be preferable. Faisal Ahmed's fate hangs over them like a dark cloud.

His walls bear the ghostly squares where pictures and diplomas used to hang, the closets inhabited only by the odd hanger. His floors are spotless, the cupboards emptied and scrubbed. The sum of his last six years in America are now contained in a medium-sized suitcase and a leather duffle bag. He retrieves them from the hallway closet, locks the door and heads to the elevator.

He sits with Valerie and Anna in the back of the car. Jeremy is in the front passenger seat while Niten drives. The weekend traffic is light on the I-66; they make swift progress, the distance to Dulles unraveling beneath the Rover's smooth, insistent tread.

The morning dawned overcast, battered by wet winds. But the sun breaks free as they drive, painting the cloud edges with gold. He closes his eyes and leans his head against the window's cool glass. A small, warm hand burrows into his. Anna has been somber and distant with him ever since he told her that he has to leave. Certainty, he knows, is what children prize above all else. Certainty was what Rahim and Zahira took from him nearly ten years ago, and in the vicious cycle of life, it is what he is now taking from his daughter.

Val sits on the other side, looking out the window as well. He has orbited her world for a decade now, his life charting an elliptical path around hers. And now instead of finally landing, the matter with Ahmed is threatening to catapult him out.

"I miss him," Val says suddenly, and it takes him several seconds to understand the reference. He thinks back to that day a decade before. Another car. Another drive to the airport to return to Bangladesh. He was not there for Karl's funeral. One of the many things he missed during those years of chasing his past.

"I miss him too," he says and takes her hand in the one that already holds Anna's. They stay that way until they reach Dulles.

ᕙᕗ

"WHAT WILL YOU DO in Bangladesh?" Jeremy asks over breakfast after Shar has checked in.

"I'll spend some time in Dhaka with my parents. Then we'll probably go down to Chittagong. I've fences to mend there."

"When are you coming back?" Anna asks, her tone sullen, challenging.

He looks her in the eyes. "I don't know, but I really hope it won't be more than a few months, six at the most."

He looks to Niten for corroboration, and receives a nearly imperceptible nod in return. Niten has inquired with a friend in the Justice Department, who informed him that Ahmed's arraignment is to be the following Monday. The question of whether he enters into a plea bargain will be settled within the week.

"Don't worry," Niten told him then. "America doesn't have an extradition treaty with Bangladesh. Even if you're snared up in all this, as long as you don't set foot in the States you'll be safe."

At the time, neither man addressed the implications of that scenario—that he may not see Anna again for a very long time.

"I've a small favor to ask," he says to Val and Jeremy.

"Shoot," Jeremy says.

"Do you know where the DC Bangla School is?"

Val smiles. "Anna told us yesterday that she wants to keep going there. I think I still have my old Bangla books. I'll dust them off and do my best to help her practice."

"Thank you."

Anna is still fiddling with her pancakes. Shar thinks of the piece of paper that he carries in a plastic folder in his carry-on, the one bearing Anna's name in Bangla that he plans on framing as soon as he reaches home.

"Thank you," he says again.

HONUFA

Chittagong, East Bengal (Bangladesh)
November 1970

She reaches the hut to find it empty. Rina has taken her son to safety. She has little time to be relieved, as the wind is now strong enough to sweep her off her feet. She scans the surroundings. The choices left to her are few and fraught with risk. With her damaged ankle, outrunning the storm is out of the question. She must seek shelter nearby, but where? Remaining on low ground means drowning when the tidal waves arrive. She has moments to decide, for the storm has arrived and brought the ocean as its dancing partner.

She finds leftover boat rope in the hut. Limping back outside, she looks for a sturdy palm tree, soon deciding on one nearby. It is thick-trunked, tilted at an angle from many years of weathered storms. She crawls along its length, her ankle screaming in agony when she puts weight on it. The rising tide rapidly swallows the shore behind her, seawater engulfing the base of the tree.

The wind strengthens, sending tin roofs cartwheeling across the beach with enough force to cut a man in half. The tree sways and groans. With the birds gone to whatever mysterious sanctuaries they seek out in times like these, the skies hold only the storm's dead fury.

She firmly pushes thoughts of her husband and son aside to focus on the act of living, surviving the storm. Jamir is a man grown, with God to watch over him at sea. He will find a way. Her son is with Rina, protected by the brick and mortar of the zamindar's house. She knows he will be safe there. It is on herself that she must now focus.

She reaches the tree's crown. Even at an angle, she is a comfortable ten feet above the ground as she begins to tie herself to the trunk with the strongest knots she can devise.

How did things become so bad and with such sudden ferocity? Like a rotten tree branch that one day snaps off on its own accord, all her troubles are culminating into this final calamity. Were she to look back, could she pick one decision she might have made differently? One she might have undone in the light of what she now knows?

She finishes tying her legs first. Strong sturdy legs that have carried her all these years, that once carried her to the far west end of the beach, where she met Siraj, who said he was a typist.

There was no reason for her to sit down next to him—with enough of a distance to be demure but still close so she could hear him above the noise of the surf. He was plain. His face held no magic that led her to inquire who he was; why he sat there with the disbelieving awkwardness of a city boy.

She was half her current age, a child in a woman's blooming body. He was four years older, with a thin trim mustache, Brylcreemed hair so black it was as if it never saw the sun. He was from Dhaka, finished with university and dreaming of writing books. He was supporting his elderly parents and a younger brother back north by working as a typist at the local post office.

It was dusk. They spoke for more than an hour, as the sun fled the world. He told her that he thought she had something beyond literacy, education and books—that she was in touch with the infinite. Not in the way the fools prostrating themselves in temples and mosques claim to be, but with the truly unknowable worlds, the radiant beauty and the primitive forms that lay behind the false faces of all things.

With one word, with many, he charmed her. And after they said good-bye that first day, she trawled the beach daily for the next week until she found him again at that same lonely spot, his face brightening when he saw her.

She told him that she had a dream the night before—that the sea, the ocean, all the waters of the world were littered with paper so that every cresting wave was composed of the pages of a great, endless book. Did he know what that meant?

He said he did not, but over the days and weeks he told her of other things. He taught her.

Often, he would bring books—nine times out of ten in English, the authors bearing exotic names that she still remembers: Chaucer, Shakespeare, Blake, Joyce, Wordsworth, Austen, Dickens, Forster, Brontë, Waugh, Owen, Maugham.

He would stand as he read, his strong straight back leaning against a salt cedar, pausing at the end of each paragraph to translate, explain. She would listen, transfixed—a desert sopping up the rain of words. His patience seemed endless; he would answer her innumerable questions, repeat passages and phrases that fascinated her. It seemed impossible to her that one man could contain so much knowledge, be aware of so much and not simply go mad from the wonder and beauty of the world.

Sometimes as he read, she would reach out and trace the curvature of his head, across the widow's peak demarcated by his hairline, disbelieving that the organ inside was the one responsible for reading, interpreting and reciting those beautiful words. It was so easy to give herself to him, completely and utterly.

The following month, her moon blood did not come. Fearful and shamed, she told Siraj. He held her, told her that she had no reason to worry, that they would elope, that his family would embrace her. They went to the forest then, made love once more under the watch of the stars and the surf.

They parted that night with the promise to meet again the next day. In the meanwhile, Siraj would write to his father, inform him of his decision to marry.

But she would never see him again.

Jamir was her childhood friend, and even as she had drifted from him in the early years of her womanhood, he had continued to love her quietly and fiercely. As the village and her family turned on her, it was he who came to her rescue, offering to marry her even before her child was born. To raise it as his own.

⳾

HONUFA GRIMACES AS SAND peppers her skin, the same skin her father once compared to her religion. She could cast neither aside and live.

She was born Rakhi Jaladas, literally—Rakhi the Slave to Water. As for many Hindus, her name was more than a name—it also applied to her the strictures of her caste. A Jaladas could never aspire to be anything other than fisherfolk.

Yet the fisherman's life for Jamir, a Muslim, was not one he had been consigned to. Rather it was one that his family had chosen because of the confluence of skill, circumstance and tradition. She thought the concept just and pure—one could be what one wanted, not what one was fated. Already obligated to him by his offer to marry her, this was the tipping point for her to become a Muslim, even though Jamir had already offered to become Hindu if it should make him more acceptable to her obstinate family, who opposed the marriage. For her love, he was willing to take on the name Jaladas and become a slave to water rather than just a servant.

But Rakhi stopped him, telling him that the beauty of his existence must continue, that she wanted to partake in it as well. She told him that the wives of rich men take on the names of their husbands. But given that he was too poor to possess a last name, she would take on his religion instead. And like one candle giving its flame to another, her immortal soul would glow with the light of his.

Rakhi, pregnant and seventeen, would become a Muslim for her husband. More than nine in ten in the village were Hindu, most had the same last name—Jaladas. By converting she would remain in her community and leave it permanently at the same time.

ᙇᙉᙇ

CLINGING TIGHTLY TO THE tree, she makes the mistake of opening her mouth to gasp for breath, and it fills immediately with dust and dirt. The same mouth that uttered the sacred words of the shahada so many years before, in the sight of Jamir and a cousin who served as the second witness. Three times she uttered that there was no God but God and that Muhammad was his prophet.

She left the faith of her birth to enter another, and took the name of Honufa. Her way back was sealed by the members of her family. She was dead to them, literally. Her mother and father would pass her by and not acknowledge her presence, pretend not to hear her if she spoke to them. When those from outside the village inquired after their daughter Rakhi, they were informed that she had died in a storm.

Any other time, the irony would make her laugh.

Her lowest moment still awaited. The villagers appealed to Rahim—who had offered her quiet support and encouragement in those dark days—issuing him the ultimatum that his patronage of Honufa, the woman once known as Rakhi Jaladas, who had become with child out of wedlock, and was marrying a man outside of her religion who was not even the father of the child, would result in the loss of faith in his leadership.

By then Rahim was showing the first afflictions of age—fear and caution. Too worried about the consequences of maintaining an overt relationship with Honufa, of inviting her to his house as he had over the years to teach her to read and write, he arrived one night at their hut to beg her understanding as he distanced his life from theirs. *Please understand. My love for you and Jamir will not change, but my role requires that I consider the needs of the entire village rather than that of one family, even one so dear to my heart.*

A month later, she gave birth to Siraj's child. Small, gray and stillborn.

Jamir wept with her as they buried him up in the hill, in a small quiet ceremony that beseeched no God and drew no mourners but them.

Her grief quickly gave way to fury, its wider target the village, but with Rahim at its red center. Shattered by what she saw as his abandonment, she sought severance instead. Despite entreaties from both Zahira and Jamir, she refused to meet with her once-mentor, her antipathy for him swelling to such a degree that she returned all the gifts she received from him over the years, selling a cow he helped her buy and returning the money to him in an envelope she left with his chowkidar. Plates, saris, clothes and other gifts were stuffed into cloth bags and left before his gate. In her frenzy of spite, she even wished that she could return the more ineffable of his gifts, and unlearn the letters and numbers he had taught her.

Jamir witnessed these manic acts of physical and emotional divestment with a wary sympathy, and warned her only once. *We are too poor to afford this pride,* he said. *It may kill us one day.*

SHE WRAPS THE ROPE around her belly, which for so many years following her first tragic pregnancy housed a quiescent womb, until that magical event three years before when her son was born, so late in their lives that they had begun to accept that her estranged family had placed a curse upon them.

When he received the news of the birth of Honufa's second child—a son—Rahim sent gifts and favors through a servant: fruits for the mother, pure fatty goat's milk and milled rice for the child, young hatchling chickens and vegetables from his own fields.

It was only her son's small pinched face that stopped Honufa from spurning these gifts as well.

꙳

ANOTHER SWING OF THE rope. This time around her midsection, above her stomach.

Even as her womb blossomed, the bay withered inexplicably the year following her son's birth; the shoals of fish, so thick and abundant in the years past, thinned to vanishing. Jamir's forays into the bay grew longer, the catches smaller. Where before the floor of his leased boat could not be seen because of the hauls of writhing, wriggling silver, now all one saw was wood, flecked here and there with the odd fish. They ate less and less. The milk in her breasts began to dry. He bought time for them by loaning out his boat, working as a sharecropper, receiving little money for a back-breaking amount of labor. Trawlers were more and more common in the bay, and he lobbied their owners for a spot on their boats as a fish-hand. But these captains were loathe to offer these lucrative spots to anyone but family or the most experienced sea fishermen.

They were starving.

꙳

SHE FINISHES TYING THE rope around her chest, her clever sure hands fluent in the language of knots, hands that washed dishes and scrubbed floors when she was forced to take on work as a housemaid in Abbas's house, by then the prosperous owner of several trawlers.

SHE SQUEEZES HER GRAY eyes shut against nature's onslaught. Eyes that can decipher words, that saw the letter when she found it in a bookshelf two months ago, as she dusted in Abbas's house.

Abbas had completed a few years of schooling and fancied himself as an erudite man. Hence the two cases of Bangla (and the odd English) books that had likely never been opened yet graced his sitting room for all to see.

Her first brush with the rooster-feather duster threw up a cloud that left her coughing. So she took the books out individually and wiped them with a damp cloth. She found a copy of *Kapalkundala*, a book she read many times as a child, given to her by (and then returned to) Rahim. It was the force of sentiment that lead her to sit on her haunches and open the pages to read a few lines of Bankim. The prose that she had missed so much over the years.

The letter was tucked between the pages where Kapalkundala—the eponymous heroine—meets the hero—Nabakumar. It slipped to the floor and she picked it up and began to read. It was addressed to Abbas. From a man named Motaleb. It concerned Rahim Choudhury.

She hid the letter on her person, feigned an illness to Abbas's wife and went home. Next day at the docks, she found Abbas alone and confronted him with what she knew. Enraged, he at first denied all, until slowly breaking before her unshakeable conviction.

Why did you do it? she inquired.

Why does anyone do anything? For the money.

That's not what the letter says.

Why ask if you already know everything?

I want to hear it from your mouth.

He considered, then shrugged. *The previous zamindar received word that Rahim was having second thoughts about the house exchange, about relocating here entirely. The old man was desperate to leave here, and he coveted Choudhury Manzil as it was in the heart of Calcutta. As for me, I had my own reasons to want Rahim here. So we had to provide him with incentives to leave India. What better way to make a man sour on his country than to make him feel unwelcome, in constant danger? Motaleb was Rahim's driver, drowning in gambling debt. I traveled to Calcutta in secret to meet with him. We hatched a scheme to have random thugs dress up as a militant Hindu gang and abduct Rahim. It apparently worked because we soon received a telegram from him saying that he would go through with the house exchange after all.*

It nearly killed him.

That was a risk we took. Now tell me how much this will cost me.

I'm no beggar or common thief, she said, the words sticking in her craw because of the hypocrisy of her actions. *I don't want your money.*

What then?

You will take him on your trawler, my Jamir, she said. *He can do the job. The simple justice of eating is all I ask.*

So you do want my money, just with the fig leaf of your husband's work to cover for it. Isn't it enough that you work at my house?

That pays a pittance.

I'll pay you more.

No, give my husband the opportunity to prove himself. Give him a cut of the fish if he meets his worth. He's a good man. He deserves that much. Without work, men die.

Abbas stepped close. She was tall for a woman, but she felt dwarfed by the bohoddar. *If I'm so dangerous that I can arrange for Rahim's abduction from so far away, what's to stop me from eliminating a fisherman's wife who threatens me?*

Because I've given the letter to another, she bluffed. *Should anything happen to me, it will reach the zamindar and he will know of your treachery.*

Abbas appeared disbelieving but was unwilling to take the chance. *Through Rahim's abduction, I was obeying my master, serving him faithfully. But you took from Rahim for years. He raised you like a daughter. You're the traitor. Not I.*

She stood silent as the truth of that statement wormed into her. *Do we have an agreement or not?*

Tell your husband to come see me tomorrow, he said before climbing back into the boat.

Later that day, when she suggested that Jamir ask Abbas a final time for a spot on his trawler he looked at her with suspicion.

Why? What has changed since the last time I spoke to him?

The more fish they catch, the more men they need. Just ask.

So he went to see Abbas, and later returned excited, eager to share the news that he had a place as a fish-hand on the largest trawler on the docks.

Do you realize what this means? After a year of hard work, I might be able to get my boat back. Then, narrowing his eyes, he asked. *How did you know to ask? Did you have something to do with this?*

Call it a woman's hunch, Honufa said, making light of it. And he let the matter rest.

But she could not forget Abbas's comment about her betrayal of Rahim, realizing that by not revealing the existence of the letter to the zamindar, she had become a conspirator to his kidnapping so many years before—a traumatic and life-altering event for him. Abbas's words, burrowed beneath her skin, multiplied like a parasite, poisoned her blood, robbed her of sleep.

Jamir had been working on the trawler no more than a few months when she came to the decision that the letter could not remain with her. But once again, her pride stopped her from approaching Rahim directly. She did not wish to traverse the ashes of all the bridges she had burned over the years.

She decided to put the letter that secured Jamir's employment in the post, send it anonymously to Rahim. What he chose to do after was up to him, but it would at least absolve her of guilt. It would come at the cost of Jamir's new job, and kill whatever sapling of confidence had taken root in his psyche. And would create a powerful enemy in Abbas.

She was coming to the grim realization that they would likely have to flee the village.

But that was before the storm. Before she discovered that the letter was missing.

And knew who had taken it.

⌣⌣

THE STORM ROARS.

For hours it rages. It does not tire. It does not relent. It does not show mercy. Trees standing since before her birth give way, snapping and crashing to the ground with a force that shakes her.

She has seen many storms over the years and knows that this is only a taste of its fury, that there will be a calm when the eye of the storm arrives, which can be a trap for the unwary, the storm's cunning trick. She had an aunt once who had gone out to inspect her livestock as the eye of a storm passed over. But it found her before she could return. As she ran back to her hut, her daughter witnessed her mother get caught in gales of such force that she was swept up into the skies in a flash, just yards from shelter.

Sand is driven into her skin. Her eyes are bloodshot from the spray of salt water—her lips parched and raw. Her palms and chest are bloody from scraping against the tree's bark.

It is only flesh. Protect the part of me that is real, my Lord.

She wonders about her son. Of the kind of life he will have as a man. She wishes now that he were older, that if she is to perish on this tree under the wrath of the skies that he might at least remember her.

AFTER ENDLESS HOURS OF darkness, water and wind, there comes silence and light. She forces her eyes open. The eye of the storm has arrived. But she is in a different land.

She is tied to the tree still, but nothing around her is the same. Seawater spumes beneath her, seething in the storm's leftover rage. Nothing remains of her house but for a few bamboo stumps like the teeth in a crone's mouth. She turns a stiffening neck to the horizon. The sky is a corpse-yellow. The monstrous winds have faded to wisps. They gust desultorily, catching at the wet edges of her sari.

Hours of clutching the tree has turned her muscles to ice. Groaning, she undoes her knots with stiff fingers. It is long and tiring work, and when done, she shrieks with surprise as she slips and finds herself hanging upside down. Lacking the strength to pull herself up and undo the knots around her legs, she swings from the palm tree, her long hair come loose, grazing the waters below.

The wind stills. The sun, cowering in the west, billows out a cloak of wan orange, its component rays tenderly exploring the devastation. Hanging like a strange diurnal bat in this new world, Honufa nonetheless can laugh in astonishment, for being upended has righted her world. The storm's chaos has laid bare the hidden patterns that have ruled her life.

Always a secret fire burned in her—a love of letters, a thirst for learning that was not known to her until that strange, foreign pilot crashed into her life, stoked the flames with his sash marked with the arcane symbols, the leaflets written in Bangla. Rahim had nurtured the fire in her, their serendipitous meeting that day under the palm tree leading her down the path of learning. Siraj threw in faggots of knowledge, showed her a whole new world, made her head spin with the enormity of what she still had left to learn, to master.

Each man had come into her life without warning, and each had left her.

Was that why her rage at Rahim so spiraled out of control? Because he was the last in the series? The last to leave?

Only Jamir remained. Unlettered, unlearned, but no fool. His offerings were for her heart and not her mind.

Did he surmise her secret shame? That despite his betrayal and the passing years a love for Siraj has remained in her like a disease she could not eradicate? Is that who he thinks the letter is from? Is that the reason he has become so glum and withdrawn?

Jamir, my darling. My love for you could fill ten withered oceans.

What was it that he said to her all those years before? That her pride would kill them someday? She scoffed at him then, but has his prediction not come true? Was there a part of her that tarried in the temple not just because the intervening years had eroded her faith in her husband's religion but because of the pride that her heart retained like so many dark remnants, hoping that she would be too late and Rina would take her son to the zamindar's and she would not have to show her face to him, seek shelter from the man she had severed herself from out of spite? Did she really want the answer to this question? This question that is more frightening than a storm could ever be? Was the naked force of its answer even something she could withstand?

MORE THAN ANYTHING, THE storm feels like spun time, accelerating everything around her to their inevitable future states—houses turned to bamboo stubs, boats smashed to kindling, rice paddies drowned and salted; lofty trees made to prostrate into the sand.

Beneath her, the dead begin to drift by, a grim procession of bodies, twisted and unrecognizable. Her hair caresses the bloated face of one, covering it like a momentary, black caul.

Such is her exhaustion that Honufa does not hear the feet splashing against water, rhythmic and slow at first and then taking on a faster cadence as their owner recognizes her. She does not feel the strong hands that release the knots around her legs with practiced assurance. She only opens her eyes when she is gently lowered into arms that have held her every night for eighteen years.

She opens her eyes. Jamir's face is battered and bloody from his journey here, but she does not ask him how he arrived or found her. She simply asks him how long she has been asleep.

"I wouldn't know," he answers.

"How . . . why . . . did you . . ." Suddenly the sun is blinding. Jamir shields her eyes with his hand. About to answer, he pauses. Where will he begin? Where can he? Even after a full day at sea it all seems a dream—being tossed off the boat, the Boatman's voice helping him gather his wits, curb his panic and survive.

Will Honufa believe him if he told her that it was Hashim's boat that found him, the one bearing the eyes and arcane symbols painted on it that his mother was forced to sell years before? Its crew—paddling furiously to flee the storm—fished Jamir out of the water, barely conscious and moments from drowning.

He does not know what happened to Abbas, Manik and the others. The trawler was traveling east, the last he saw, away from the storm's path. As for him, by the time he reached shore the wind had pushed them miles off course, and he had to travel on foot for half a day before taking shelter in a cave a few miles from his home when the storm arrived full force.

She is not ready for this story, so he asks the obvious question. "Where is our son?"

"I've sent him to Rahim's house, with Rina. Along with the sash and your silver flask that I gave to her for safekeeping."

Jamir nods. "That was the right thing to do."

She sits up. Her eyes blaze with conviction as she clutches his hand. "We have to go to him, Jamir. I feel if we don't, we'll never see him again."

But as she speaks, the land dims again. Jamir looks around. "By some miracle we found each other while the eye of the storm was passing, but now the storm is about to return. Let's give it our best try then. Can you walk?"

"Not well. But I can try."

They have minutes at most. He lifts her to her feet. They hobble past the beach, the disintegrated remains of their village, but only manage to reach a cliff-face not far from their hut when the first spatters of the returning rain splash and spit at their feet, and the wind again rises.

They take shelter, for Honufa has no strength left. When she begins to weep, he asks her why.

"I don't think we will see our son again."

"Perhaps. But at least he is safe, breathing and fed."

"How can you know that?"

He takes her hand and places it on his heart. "I feel him here. And I know you do too. Rahim Sahib will take good care of him. He was so kind to you as a child, ever since that day he found you under the palm tree. I know that he will love our son as his own. And that he will have a good life. Grow to greatness."

"There is something you should know." She steels herself to confess, about the letter, about what she has done, her deception, everything. If upon hearing it he chooses to hate her, she will understand. At this, the end of times, she is ready to lay out her sins for the storm to wash away to far-forgotten gyres.

But he places a gentle finger on her lips. "You have nothing to explain."

Jamir and Honufa look south to face what is coming without

fear, her hand slipping into his. The wind strengthens. The sun disappears behind thickets of clouds that rise like colossi, bristling with lightning. A great wave rises in the bay and rushes to shore, giving her only seconds to utter her final words.

"You're my ballast."

Shahryar & Anna

Bangladesh
October 2004

His plane lands at Zia International Airport at eight in the morning. His mother and father await him in the lounge. When they rise to greet him, he notes that their steps are a bit slower, their legs less steady than he remembers. The time he has left with them is not long. He walks over and embraces them without a word.

"No Anna this time, eh?" Rahim deposits his rhetorical questions directly into Shar's ear.

He smiles, hoping the pain does not bleed through. "Not this time. But soon, hopefully. She sends her love by the way."

"When do we see her?" Zahira wants to know. Two years before, they visited her in America for the first time, and they have been waiting for a second meeting ever since.

"As soon as tonight. I brought my laptop. You two should be able to Skype with her if we have a broadband connection at home."

His adoptive parents look at each other, then him.

"I have no idea what any of that means," Rahim says.

⁓

THEY SPEND TWO WEEKS in Dhaka before taking a train to Chittagong, all four of them, as Rahim, Zahira and Rina refuse to let him out of their sights so soon after his return.

Their former seaside mansion has become a government museum, so they arrange temporary accommodations in the city—a flat near the commercial center. It is small but neat, with three bedrooms and a narrow strip of balcony that faces the bay.

Once settled in, Rahim suggests that he visit the TNO's office at the village. The Thana Nirbahi Officer is a village-level administrator, part of the civil service cadre first put in place by the Ershad Regime in the 1980s. Given their power and influence, it is always a good idea to make the TNO the first port of call when new in town, his father explains.

The office is in a small bungalow featuring a trim lawn and a porch. When Shar arrives, he is offered a seat on a rickety wooden bench. He is called into the TNO's room after ten minutes.

Sunil Das is in his late forties. His mustache gives him the appearance of a Bengali Clark Gable. He gestures to the empty chair before him, as Val once did, many years before.

"Can I get you a tea or coffee? Perhaps a cold drink?"

"Just water, thank you," Shar says, taken aback. Government offices do not have the best reputations in Bangladesh, being places where one is either neglected or asked for bribes for the most basic of services.

When he begins to introduce himself, Das raises his hand and smiles. "I know who you are. We all remember Rahim and Zahira Choudhury well, at least, my parents spoke quite fondly of them. Even though it has been many years since they lived here."

"Thank you." The Bangladesh War of Liberation began five months after the storm that killed his parents. Rahim and Zahira were in Chittagong in that time, stretched to their limits with not only helping the community rebuild from the storm, but protecting the populace from the depredations of the invading West Pakistani soldiers. As a new nation emerged in December of that year, in a second bloody birth for East Bengal, Rahim and Zahira were overwhelmed by just how wearying responsibility could be, and how much those shores echoed with memories of all those lost in the storm and the war. So a quarter century following their exodus from India, they prepared for another. They disposed of their assets, set aside a portion from the sales as an emergency fund for the villagers to access in need, and moved to Dhaka, taking Shar and Rina with them.

"So, what can I do for you, Choudhury Sahib?"

"I've come to stay here for some time."

"Why?"

"To um . . . to see what I can do for the community."

"And what would that be?"

Shar stammers. In his head, he pictured himself eloquently explaining why he was needed here, the value of his Western sensibilities and knowledge to the people of the village. Now, before this government officer, those assumptions seem patronizing, uninformed.

Sunil Das smiles kindly. "Sorry, Mr. Choudhury. I didn't mean to . . . how do they say in English? 'Put you in the spotlight.' We can go over those things later. Why don't you tell me a bit about yourself first?"

"Where do you want me to start?"

"How about the very beginning?"

Shar considers. "In that case, maybe I'll have some tea after all."

SIX MONTHS PASS.

One morning, following a knock on the door of his seaside cottage, Shar opens it to find Sunil Das holding up a battered thermos. "I brought tea. Care for a walk?"

They follow the shore, headed vaguely east. The men walk side by side in comfortable silence, passing the thermos of tea back and forth. Since that day in Sunil's office a half year before, they have become friends.

"I was just thinking," Sunil says eventually, "that you've done good work so far."

"Thank you."

Shar allows himself a moment of quiet satisfaction and no more, realizing how much remains to be done. Being far to the south, the village is yet to be visited by the great NGOs that have risen up in Bangladesh and become internationally renowned—understandable, as fishermen see little need for their agriculture-focused offerings of livestock and seeds. Shar has nonetheless shuttled back and forth between Dhaka and the village, writing grant applications for schoolhouses, latrines and communal fisheries to potential donors. One proposal he made for a sustainable shrimp hatchery is nearing approval; a forward detachment of experts from Australia is scheduled to touch down in Chittagong in a week. In addition, he has persuaded a large NGO to open a brace of primary schools, and another to build cement latrines in a number of homes. His parents are looking into reviving the emergency fund they set up years before. He sighs. This may mean another grant application to apply for seed money.

"Something the matter?"

"Just that there's a lot left to do."

"There's a union council election coming up for the village," Sunil says. "The outgoing chairman's already declared that he's not seeking reelection; he's got a Parliament seat in mind."

"And why are you telling me this?"

"You should run."

"I think I'm doing what I'm best at."

Sunil shakes his head. "We need good people. We face big problems, Shar. The Burmese are running pogroms against the Rohingyas, pushing them across the border, and our government's pushing them back saying that these refugees are not our problem, all the while they wallow in neglect at best, or face abuse in camps. On our side of the border, the Hindus are increasingly frightened of the militant Islamists, so there's a steady flight of them leaving for India just like during the war. All this is happening while we're plucking the bay empty of fish and coring out the hills to build homes. These issues won't be solved by a few schoolhouses or cement toilets, as welcome as they are."

He stops and puts a hand on Shar's shoulder. "As council chairman you'll report directly to me. You'll have the power and resources to make a real difference. That day you walked into my office all those months ago, I didn't yet have the measure of you. I do now. The people of the village look up to you. You can make this a better place, as Rahim and Zahira Choudhury once did."

"What I'm doing right now gives me options. Being chairman will tie my hands."

"Well, you haven't won the election yet, but I think it's not your hands being tied you're worried about, it's your feet. You're afraid that you won't be able to leave."

"You doubt my commitment to the community?"

"No, rather I respect the one you made to your daughter. I know you wish to see Anna again."

"I do," Shar says.

"She'll always be your little girl, and you'll always be her father. You carry your love for her in you. I can see it. It lights you from within, like a lantern in a hut. Ten years, twenty, however many pass, you won't lose her. I know this in my heart. But the people here, they're fragile. If you leave again, you might not be able to find a way back."

Shar looks down at the ground. The prerogative of orphans is to be able to amortize their grief—dole out the pain of loss across the years and make it bearable. He was never allowed that.

This, perhaps, is a way.

"I have to think about this."

"I'll do you one better," Sunil says, looking at his wristwatch. "Go to the village haat and see who you might be running against. If that doesn't give you enough incentive, nothing will."

"Who?" Shar's heart beats faster.

The wind strengthens, whips Sunil's hair around his grim face. "Go see for yourself. I'll stay behind. If you're running, it's best we're not seen together."

SHAR FOLLOWS THE SHORE east to the village, to the haat from which his mother was excluded once she left her religion, the haat to which his father brought his catches. There is a crowd gathered there today, facing a makeshift dais of canvas and bamboo. Shar freezes as he recognizes the man atop it.

The last Shar heard of Manik, he was running a cement business in Dhaka, having moved away from trawlers following his father's death. But now he has returned to the village of his birth, and his ambitions have grown. Old, but possessing a leonine grace, he paces the length of the stage, shouting into a mike, promising to return prosperity to the village through the tourist trade, build more mosques for the devout Muslims who are too often ignored in favor of minorities, and, of course, drive back across the border the Rohingya refugees who are taking food from the mouths of hardworking people. All they have to do, he exhorts the crowd, is to elect him.

A smile breaks out across his face as he notices Shar. "Look who has decided to join us, brothers and sisters," Manik says. "A great salaam to you, Shahryar Choudhury—most educated and honored benefactor."

The crowd's attention turns to Shar, the expressions ranging from friendly to serious to guarded.

"I hear that you may run for council chairman this year, against me."

Without a mike, Shar must shout to be heard above the rising winds. "You hear wrong."

He walks away, already sick of the man. The crowd parts to let him pass.

Manik tosses a parting sally his way. "Good. It's best for you to leave. It seems you take after your father, Rahim, the zamindar. Fancy foreign degrees and being the son of a rich man won't get you the votes of the people here. You have to be one of us."

Shar stops, turns back. He climbs onto the stage. Manik's body-guards crowd around him, glowering. But Manik laughs. "That's alright. Let's see what the young man has to say."

The men make space, forming a semi-circle around the two. Shar stands no more than an arm's length away from Manik, and when he speaks, only those closest to them can hear what is said.

"You're right that the zamindar raised me, Manik," Shar says. "And he taught me a thing or two about honesty, hard work and being just, but that's not the only man I learned from. Do you re-member an illiterate fisherman, whose wife was born a Hindu? You and your father tried to kill him on a boat thirty-four years ago."

Abbas's son blanches, jaw hanging open on his pockmarked face. "You, how . . . how did you . . . "

"A group of fishermen rescued him. He told them everything. And they told me."

Manik recovers quickly, turning to his security contingent, he says, "Lies. Nothing but lies. All of it."

"See you at the polling booth," Shar says.

༄

HE WALKS TO THE zamindar's mansion. A few months before, at Sunil Das's behest, the government set aside a section of the building for Rahim, Zahira and Rina to use as their living quarters. The three moved in with mixed feelings, but quickly reacclimatized to their former home. Shar declined to join them, worrying, among other reasons, about the optics of a community organizer living in grand accommodations.

His parents greet their son warmly and usher him to the dining room, where Zahira and Rina have prepared lunch. Over crisp fried fish, daal and braised greens, Shar tells them of his decision to contest the election against Manik.

They are supportive but concerned, all too aware of his opponent's reputation.

"Are you sure this is wise, my son?" Zahira asks.

"Evil wins when good men do nothing," Shar replies. "And until they find a good man, I'm the closest thing to it."

"Then we will do everything we can to help you."

FOLLOWING DINNER, HE OPENS his laptop and logs on to Skype. In a few minutes he would call Anna. He sits and watches the gray circle next to her name on his list of contacts, waiting for it to blink and turn green.

Beside his desk, through an open window that looks out to a bay swarmed by rain clouds, a gust of cold wind bursts into the room and sprays the papers on his desk to the floor. Walking over to close the shutters, he stops. A storm gathers strength outside. There are flashes over rain-swept waves. The soft thrum of thunder.

He does not flinch when the first cold drops strike his face, his hands. He has shelter once again. He is safe.

He closes the window. From a cloth bag stored in the wardrobe, he removes and places on his desk the objects that at once broke apart and rebuilt his past all those years ago, that brought together his mother and father.

"Hi, Baba," Anna says when she calls, her voice warbling from the weight of the distance now between them.

"Hi, Anna."

She sees the flask and the sash. "What're those?"

"I'm going to tell you," Shar says. "Got time for a story?"

"I do, Baba."

He smiles.

EPILOGUE

RAHIM & ZAHIRA

Chittagong, East Pakistan (Bangladesh)
November 1970

Sometime during the night, as the storm showed no signs of abating, Rahim fell asleep on the large leather chair in his study, exhausted. Zahira, who draped a shawl over her husband to keep him warm, shakes him awake at dawn.

He blinks—his eyes bloodshot—looking older than his fifty-one years. "Is it over?"

"Just about," she says, her voice barely above a whisper.

"How is it?"

"Come and see."

They walk out to the balcony, the same one they first sat in years ago, eating chicken curry and rice and watching the sunset.

"My god," he gasps as he surveys the damage. Little of the beach can be seen under the pile of debris now swept onto it—bamboo, palm trees, kelp and kindling from boats and homes smashed to pieces. The land is flooded for miles around, the water opaque and turgid under gray skies.

He sees the bodies.

They are everywhere—entwined around trees, floating in shallow water, buried under detritus so that only the odd limb shows. Broken, bloated, twisted and crushed. Every age, shape and gender. Often lying side by side with the animals. Evidence of the storm's cruel equity.

Zahira holds his hand, closes her eyes. They weep in wordless despair. Calcutta, and now Chittagong. Death on a grand scale has followed and found them again after so many years.

"Where's the boy?" he asks.

"In the spare room, with Rina. They're resting. But he was asking for his mother throughout the night."

"Let him be. We have to find his parents."

They walk out to the hellscape. The families that sought shelter in their home follow, stunned. They cry when they find their dead livestock, wail when they find friends or family. But many appear stoic—the scale of the devastation carrying them to a place beyond emotion.

Rahim and Zahira walk on, two figures leaning on each other, against the backdrop of the ocean, the lone specks of life and movement on the scarred shores. Their progress slow, they do not arrive at the remains of Honufa and Jamir's hut until midday.

⚬⚬

THEY RETURN HOME AT sunset, exhausted from a day of fruitless and heartbreaking search, their minds seared by the images they have witnessed. Standing before the door of the room where Rina rests with the boy, there are tears in Rahim's eyes, his face wracked with doubts.

"What will I tell him?"

"For now we must comfort him. His mother and father might be found yet. We can't give up hope."

"This is my fault. They might have been here if I hadn't abandoned her all those years ago."

Zahira takes his hand. "We can't take back what has been done. But by the grace of God, we have a lifetime to make amends."

"Right," Rahim says, wiping his eyes. "You're right."

They open the door. The boy sits on the bed, attended to by

Rina, who is cooing words of comfort in his ear. He turns to them when they enter together. There is no recognition in his eyes, nor is there fear or mistrust.

Rahim squeezes his wife's hand, a gesture of reassurance, of promise—*No matter what happens, we will keep him safe. No matter what happens, we will love him.*

"Hello, Shahryar," they say.

Acknowledgments

Sultana Nahar is my mother and an author herself, who for years demonstrated to me the art and craft of writing.

Shalon (Asha) Anwar is my daughter, an inspiration for the book and so, so excited about it!

Ayesha Pande is my wonderful agent, a relentless champion who believed in this book so much for so long.

Anjali Singh is my indefatigable co-agent, who whipped a promising but unwieldy manuscript into incredible shape.

Iris Tupholme, my Canadian publisher and editor, gave me indescribably good editorial advice, midwifed this novel into the world and is a tireless advocate on its behalf.

Rakesh Satyal, an accomplished author and my American editor, saw something in this novel from the very beginning.

Shuofu Lian and Jens Laurson provided keen eyes, respectively with Mandarin and German translations.

Members of the First Page Writing Group in Toronto read more versions of this novel than they will admit. They are Michelle Alfano, Michelle Boone, Justine Mazin, Josée Sigouin, Elizabeth Torlée and Tina Tzatzanis.

Many others read early versions of the book and offered valuable feedback. They include David Booth, Cresencia Fong, Michelle Josette, Ranya Khan, Shelly Nixon, Aaron Paul, Greta Perris, Carmen Ruf and Mike Tissenbaum.

Emiko Ohnuki-Tierney's *Kamikaze Diaries: Reflections of Japanese Student Soldiers* was an invaluable resource while writing this book, as was Louis Allen's *Burma: The Longest War, 1941–1945*.

Si (Sandra) Lian is the love of my life, the woman who helped make this book happen and the wind beneath my wings.